Madam St. Clair, Queen of Harlem

Raphaël Confiant

Translated by

Patricia Hartland

and

Hodna Bentali Gharsallah Nuernberg

DIÁLOGOS BOOKS
DIALOGOSBOOKS.COM

Madam St. Clair, Queen of Harlem
Raphaël Confiant.
Translated by Patricia Hartland and Hodna Bentali Gharsallah Nuernberg

Copyright © 2020 by Raphael Confiant, Patricia Hartland, Hodna Bentali
Gharsallah Nuernberg, and Diálogos Books.
Original Publication: Raphaël Confiant, *Madame St-Clair, reine de Harlem* ©
Editions Mercure de France, 2015.

Printed in the U.S.A.
First Printing
10 9 8 7 6 5 4 3 2 1   20 21 22 23 24 25

Book design: Bill Lavender
Front cover painting by Hodna Bentali Gharsallah Nuernberg

Library of Congress Control Number: 2018962682
Confiant, Raphael
with Patricia Hartland and Hodna Bentali Gharsallah Nuernberg (translators)
Madam St. Clair, Queen of Harlem / Raphaël Confiant;
p. cm.
ISBN: 978-1-944884-56-7 (pbk.)
978-1-944884-57-4 (ebook)

DIÁLOGOS BOOKS
DIALOGOSBOOKS.COM

Also by Raphaël Confiant

In English

Eloge de la créolité / In Praise of Creoleness. (bilingual edition) (with Jean Bernabé
and Patrick Chamoiseau). M.B. Taleb-Khyar, trans. Paris: Gallimard, 1993.
(translation appeared in *Callaloo* 13.4 [Fall 1990]: 886-909.)

Eau de Café. James Ferguson, trans. London / New York: Faber and Faber, 1999.

Mamzelle Dragonfly. Linda Coverdale, trans. New York: Farrar, Straus, Giroux, 2000.

Selected Works in French

Le nègre et l'amiral. Grasset, 1988 (Prix Antigone-Ville de Montpellier).

Eau de café. Grasset, 1991 (Prix Novembre-France).

Aimé Césaire: Une traversée paradoxale du siècle. Stock, 1993; Écriture, 2006.

Ravines du devant-jour. Gallimard, 1993 (Prix Casa de las Americas-Cuba).

L'allée des soupirs. Grasset, 1994 (Prix Carbet de la Caraïbe / Prix Shibusawa-
Claudel, Japon).

Le meurtre du Samedi-Gloria. Mercure de France, 1997 (Prix RFO-France).

Le galion: canne, douleur séculaire, ô tendresse! Ibis Rouge, 2000 (Prix du Salon du
livre insulaire d'Ouessant).

La panse du chacal. Mercure de France (Prix des Amériques insulaires et de la
Guyane), 2004.

L'Hôtel du Bon Plaisir. Mercure de France, 2009, (Prix de l'Agence française de
développement).

Citoyens au-dessus de tout soupçon. Caraïbéditions (Prix du roman policier du Salon
du livre insulaire d'Ouessant), 2010.

Le bataillon créole: guerre de 1914-1918. Mercure de France, 2013.

Selected Works in Creole

Jik dèyè do Bondyé. Grif An Tè, 1979 (French translation by the author, *La Lessive du
diable*, Le Serpent à Plumes, 2000; Écriture, 2003).

Kod yanm. K.D.P., 1986 (French translation by Gerry L'Étang, *Le gouverneur des dés*,
Stock, 1995).

Marisosé. Presses universitaires créoles, 1987 (French translation by the author,
Mamzelle Libellule, Le Serpent à Plumes, 1995).

Dictionnaire des titim et des sirandanes. Ibis Rouge, 1998.

Le grand livre des proverbs créoles: Ti-pawol. Presses du Châtelet, 2004.

Un voleur dans le village, by James Berry, trans. from the English (Jamaican),
Gallimard Jeunesse, 1993, (Prix de l'International Books for Young People),
1993.

Les voix du tambour, by Earl Long, trans. from the English (Sainte-Lucie), with Carine
Gendrey, Dapper, 1999.

Moun-andéwô a, by Albert Camus, trans. from the French, Caraïbéditions, 2012.

Contents

Madam St. Clair, Queen of Harlem

To Mérine, Maguy, Suzy, Joëlle and Louise:
sister Martinicans, comrades in spirit

First Note

E'er since Miss Susan Johnson
lost her Jockey, Lee
There has been much excitement,
more to be

You can hear her moanin'
night and morn
She's wonderin' where her
Easy Rider's gone?

—W.C. Handy, "Yellow Dog Blues"

Chapter One

I always knew that one day Madam Queen (Queenie to her friends) would vanish, that Stéphanie St. Clair would recede from the world's view. It would not be a sudden disappearance, nor a frenzied flight. Nor, even, would it be a sinking into dementia's dark abyss (the sort attributed to manioc ants back in my native Martinique). No.

Rather, Stéphanie St. Clair would succumb to a steady erasure. Like a smear wiped clean by a window washer, paid no mind by those strolling past, in an almost automatic gesture.

I was Queen, but am no more, alas! From the very first days of that century, called the most brilliant in all of humanity's history, I had all of Harlem at my feet. Oh, yes, and Sugar Hill, too—the neighborhood of refuge for the Negro elite, far from the endless gunfights and the destitute, miserous Lowblacks. Sugar Hill, but also, yes, Edgecombe Avenue, where I kept a suite in one of New York's tallest buildings—fourteen-stories high. For a long time, I harbored a fear of that diabolic invention that is the elevator—a fact that never failed to get a rise out of Duke, my bodyguard and occasional man-of-the-moment. He used to tease me, "Queenie, if you keep dragging yourself up those stairs like that, one of these days you'll slip right through the floorboard cracks!"

The brute was right. Though no weed, I'd never been a very voluptuous woman, and I've always had a chip on my shoulder about it. As a young girl, my mother (though *mother* might be too strong a word) made me eat heaps of breadfruit, Chinese cabbage and yam, all of it copiously drenched in oil. According to her, it was my only hope of catching a man's eye. Not to mention the spoonsful of cod-liver oil that she made me gulp down well beyond my days as a little marmy-scamp. But it never amounted to anything because, gorger though I was, my body never seemed to hold on to any of these foods, so I stayed stubbornly zoklet-lanky and unplumped.

"A mongoose!" my mother cackled.

"A weasel!" Roberto would laugh, much later. Roberto would sometimes introduce himself as a Corsican, sometimes as a Neapolitan, and his sonorous tones enchanted me all along the Marseille harbor; he compelled me, guileless as he was, to open the door of my intimacy to him with no further ado.

And so, I'd climb step after step, floor after floor, alone in the half-dark of that endless staircase, all the way up to the ninth. At each landing I'd look out over the quadrangle of streets teeming with harried crowds scuffling against the current of ever-more abundant automobiles, spitting thick clouds of smoke in their wake.

This little mountaineering feat of mine often recurred two or three times in a single day, and yet Madam Queen never lost heart. On one such occasion, my closest neighbor—a jazz musician and, since 1923, celebrated star of the Savoy Ballroom—stepped out of the elevator, calling for his maid. Breathless, I made my way to my apartment, where a certain resigned Duke awaited. As my neighbor and I crossed paths, he gently ventured, "I quite understand you, Ma'am! Back on those islands of yours, everyone lives close to nature, isn't that so? Ah, how you must long for the open air...."

For a long while, I simmered with rage. Stupidly.

"I am *French*, understand?" I shot back, the veins of my neck throbbing. "Je suis française, monsieur!"

"Oui, madame," he responded in French, making use of what were undoubtedly the only two words he knew in my language, before hurrying toward the safety of his apartment.

But memory fails me, the way everything surfaces in spits and spurts. See, I'm an old lady now, and the century—the twentieth, to call it by its name—is more than half over. Two world wars have come and gone, and in this Queens nursing home where I'll finish my days, the way these white nurses care for me—with deference and without the least regard to my epidermal color— astounds me, still. My dear nephew, I see your hand lurching across your notebook. I hope you've scrupulously taken note of everything you asked me to recall... even if my words are a bit disjointed.

Of course, I didn't always live in this handsome building. Like all those dreaming of America, their pulses quickening at their first glimpse of Lady Liberty, I was dealt my share of vexations. Not to mention, *my* glimpse of that great statue didn't come till much later, because on the day I arrived, the fog was so thick that she was invisible to the *Virginie*, the vessel I boarded in Marseille on a whim, or more precisely, with a broken heart. When we finally made land, the customs officials scrutinized and re-scrutinized my passport, some of them dubious, others incredulous. ("A *Black* Frenchwoman, how about that! Since when did Paris start taking in *niggerbastards?*") So they confined me in a storage room while the port authorities verified my claims, and I watched the dregs of humanity file by: filthy, rag-swathed Sicilians, their faces drawn blade-thin by hunger; the people of Eastern Europe, Polish for the most part, bawling at the slightest provocation and baritoning their joy at finally setting foot upon the New World; sickly Jews from all-over, searching for the Promised Land with eyes always lowered and hordes of young children trailing at their heels; blond, slim-waisted Irish oozing dignity from deadened eyes as they clutched their battered suitcases. Ah, those rotten Irish.... I regret ever feeling compassion for them! You see, we'd been quarantined in a vast building that occupied three quarters of what we would learn was Ellis Island—we, the third-class passengers. Meanwhile, the first and second classes entered American territory with absolutely no difficulty. We were waiting for our turn to undergo a medical examination. Passengers from the ship that had arrived two days before ours wandered aimlessly, gripped by despair and clothed in rough canvas tunics that had been tagged with a hastily scrawled letter: 'H' or 'E.' We came to discover that these unfortunates suffered from a diseased *H*eart or infected *E*yes. And they were left to drift in this state as they awaited deportation back to their countries, southern Italy for most of them. Their American Dream was shattered before it could even take shape! To tell the truth, I never fed myself on such illusions. I only left Marseille on an impulse. I could have just as easily boarded a ship bound for Valparaiso or Saigon. As far as I can remember, for the first twenty-six years of my life, all spent in Martinique, I never heard a single soul—neither Black nor Mulatto nor even White Creole—glorify those United States of America, and certainly none of them hoped to *live* there. No. France was our sole compass.

When my passport was returned at last (and on this point, the customs officials were reluctant, as I could see their suspicions had not totally dissipated), I took it upon myself to come to the aid of a suffering Irish mother and her family. She was a good deal younger than I and already had three children, including a baby she was practically wrestling to keep in her arms. Instinctively, I offered her my help, and her husband kept silent. He continued down the dock like an automaton, mumbling something I couldn't make any sense of (at the time I could only stammer out one or two English words). Had he lost his mind? I had no idea and, in any case, didn't care. For the first time, a little being was squirming against my chest. Me! I, who, in my own country, had rejected in horror the idea of becoming a *Da* for some big rich family of White Creoles or Mulattos. It was my mother who'd clung to the idea and, for a long time, that nag wouldn't let it go. She adorned the profession with pretty names: *Nounou*, *Governess* and on and on. So, I screamed in her face, "Not never! Pas jamais! You understand me? Not never! Pas jamais!" She was always ready with her defense. Clearly, I couldn't speak *du bon français* and, if I'd just accept a position with the Beauchamps of Malmaison or the Dupins of Fromillac, I'd be speaking as well as the Larousse dictionary in no time at all. Not to mention the *excellent* wages. Hah! Idiotics!

Out on the street, there was no one to greet the immigrants. Except for a row of taxis, whose drivers hailed their clients in their native languages. One of them, turning up his nose, agreed to take us, but never bothered to ask our destination. Throwing his weight against the horn while crossing what I considered to be impressively broad avenues, he began crooning a melancholy song. It was rhythmic, though its meaning was lost on me. The Irish family didn't make a peep. As if they'd decided to abandon themselves to destiny, as if resigned and ready to endure every peril; I, on the other hand, had to contain my enthusiasm. I was in America! I wanted to whoop with joy, to jump out of that rickety taxi and embrace each passerby whose path I crossed. Every fiber of my being, every pore of my skin felt electrified. But, all of a sudden, we were in the midst of a half-dilapidated neighborhood whose streets were teeming with grubby-faced throngs of people. Mostly men, some of whom brandished bottles full of what I figured was alcohol. What a shock! Those creatures, who seemed to revel in their degradation, were of every race: Blacks, Whites and, above all, undefinables.

"You're at Five Points. That'll be forty dollars!"

Angus, as I heard his wife call him, stiffened. Setting the boys on his knees aside, he ventured in a timid voice that contradicted his imposing figure, "That's too much, sir...."

The taxi driver didn't spare a second on useless bickering. Yelling, he got out of the car and called on bystanders to bear witness, shouting that we were a bunch of Irishit who should've stayed put on our shitty island instead of infesting America with our lice and our mange. I couldn't quite make out the details of his ragery, but for some reason, each of his strange words etched themselves into my mind, even though I didn't know the language yet. And later, much later, they'd resurface, especially at night, in the moments before drifting off to sleep when I'd retrace my life after Martinique—because I must admit, my dear Frédéric, that memory was fading, overtaken by Harlem and my handsome Edgecombe Avenue apartment. My old habit—or obsession, to be totally honest—sent me plummeting into revelry and irritated Bumpy Johnson to no end. Bumpy was my employee, bodyguard, my middleman in mafia dealings and, above all, my man… that is, once Duke was fired. But I'll tell you about that later.

But see, Bumpy had an old habit of his own. As soon as we got into bed, no matter the hour—maybe nine or ten in the winter, midnight or later during the other seasons—he would pounce on my person and wordlessly remove my nightgown before impaling me, after which he would straddle me savagely, all while heaving and moaning grotesquely. I'd watch the massive bump that adorned the back of his skull—that's what had earned him his nickname—as it wobbled ridiculously from right to left. During our first meeting—back when I'd just reinvented myself as a banker in the clandestine lottery (oh, the audacity!), putting up the ten thousand dollars I'd managed to save during my stint with the gang of Forty Thieves and with my earnings from the Jamaican Ginger trade—which I'll tell you about later—that anomaly (or infirmity, I don't know how to describe it) disgusted me. But, provided you could look past it, Ellsworth Johnson was a strapping man, and above all, he had completely mastered the art of persuasion, which was made all the more exceptional thanks to his ever-so-slight southern accent; it was a point of pride for him, being born as he was in Charleston, South Carolina.

But I digress: That taximan was a fool. A real loon! A nut gone fou an mitan tet, as they say in Martinique. There he was, unbaggaging his vehicle, opening our suitcases and, when the clasps wouldn't unclasp, gutting them with a knife, all while calling upon the world as witness, "Citizens of the United States, let's not let these bands of savages strip us of all we're worth! These shitsoaked Irish hicks! Look, I'm confiscating this! And this, too! Get the hell outta here before I call the police!"

He didn't even notice I was black, I told myself at first. I was wrong: He didn't notice me at all. I was an invisible creature, an insignificant being or, better yet, some domesticated animal that merited no more than a distracted glance. Or maybe he'd taken me for the Mulryans' servant. There we were, in a state of shock, on the sidewalk of that fleabag skid row, Five Points, incapable of gathering our few possessions, which a brutal wind threatened to scatter, Angus limply holding the hands of his two boys, who were wearing funny little hats, Daireen, the wife, draping her shawl around the bawling baby, and I, Stéphanie the Martinican Negress, suddenly naturalized Irish by some thick lout. Before leaving Marseille, I'd managed to learn a few American expressions and didn't need to beg strangers for help to take my first steps (and being needy gets you nowhere!). The man who'd taught them to me, an old man who'd been an English teacher at some religious institution, had intrigued me because, every morning when the weather was fine, he'd stroll down the Vieux Port dressed as a sailor, a cap stuck to his head, melancholic. I finally approached him, shyly, because I was worried that he'd be afraid of Blacks, as were many of the inhabitants of that nonetheless joyous city whose cloudless blue sky left me stupefied. Back home in Martinique, miraculous good weather like that only graces us a couple days a year, normally in the very beginning of September, a lull before the season of storms, and in any case, our pale blue has none of the brilliance of that Mediterranean indigo.

"Sor… sorry to… to bother you, sir," I stammered, attempting an inviting smile.

The man stopped short, inspected me from head to toe, warily removed his pince-nez, then took my hands. His were soft and old with prominent veins. I wasn't surprised: When I was a child, the Sainte Thérèse priests would come greet us like that during catechism. Back then, it was unthinkable that a man of the church could be black. Later, much later (after I'd come to America) I let my very first bodyguard, Duke, bring me down to the Baptist church on 135th Street, and I was shocked to discover a pastor of my race before a modest altar. He wore a violet gown and was jerking about, his arms flailing toward the heavens, as he sermonized with a vengeance before ending up rolling onto the floor. I narrowly avoided bursting into laughter, and Duke stared daggers at me.

"Are you an African Negro or an island girl?" the old sailor from Marseille asked me in a kindly tone.

"I'm from... Martinique."

"Ah, what a shame! Martinique? But I visited that island, and several times. A magical land if ever there were one!"

And he cited an et cetera of place names: Morne Rouge, Pelée, the Cul de Sac Bay, Rivière Salée, Coulée d'Or, Caravelle. Then he gestured for me to sit down alongside him on the dock. As our feet dangled a couple meters above the dirty water crowded with ships flying a multitude of flags, he revealed the truth. He had never in all his life, *never* traveled anywhere at all. His knowledge of the world, of *the universe*, as he so pompously called it, had been gleaned from geography books, atlases, novels and, above all, from contact with the sailors returning to Marseille from South America, Vietnam or the African coast. The ones he ended up befriending would, at his request, bring back exotic souvenirs—parchment from India, bows and arrows from Guinea, caftans from Muslim territories—that offered him a better sense of those lands he himself would never see. He laughed, but not unkindly, at my desire to settle down somewhere in the vast expanse of the world. He suggested America and spent a whole month gleefully recounting the battles between the cowboys and Indians, the Civil War, the mass extermination of bison and the general impossibility of losing one's way amid the gridlike structure of those immense American cities whose streets had the benefit of being numbered and not named like those of the Old World.

"Everything here is old, mademoiselle! There's the Old Port, Old Europe, Old World. Ha ha ha! Try your luck over there! I can't understand why you didn't go there straightaway—Martinique is so close to the United States...."

I didn't dare admit that I'd wanted first and foremost to explore the France we'd learned to revere like a second mother. The fact remains that he taught me the rudiments of English, which, my dear nephew, were of almost no use at all when I landed in New York, a city where thirty-six different accents rubbed shoulders. But it did help me decipher a sign in that filthy Five Points neighborhood where the taximan had abandoned us: *For Rent.* You see, I hadn't realized that my Irish companions didn't know how to read! I was dumbfounded because, in my little native Martinican mind, it was inconceivable that Whites wouldn't go to school. I was ringing the doorbell of what seemed to be a vacant building when a middle-aged lady leaned out a first-floor window and hollered, "Get lost! Dirty niggerwoman!"

Then, noticing I was accompanied by a white family and that I held their white-colored baby in my arms, she softened her tone. "Thirty dollars a week, due up front! No charge for the black girl. She'll help with the housework and can sleep in the kitchen. Well?"

The Mulryans had come to America without one red cent! Unless they'd been robbed clean on the ship.... In third class, that kind of villainy was standard order, seeing as most of the passengers were ex-convicts or other criminal types fleeing their country in hopes of building a brand-new, stain-free life for themselves. Few women voyaged alone, and those who did all turned out to be whores, plying their trade on the high seas in exchange for a couple dollar bills or a bottle of Italian wine (for the less attractive). A maniac Sardinian, who boasted before god about being a bootlegger of great renown and who was sauced from morning to night, gagging and heaving every second step, tried to proposition me in his own rather unusual way. In a show of high hoggery, he accosted me, "Hey, you! Come let me fuck you, whore! I want to see if your blackness rubs off on my skin. Ha ha ha!"

Seeing that I hadn't reacted in the slightest (I tended to withdraw myself in such situations, catatonic-like), he was emboldened, groping my breast, which was, admittedly, not well endowed. My black blood boiled, boiled like the blood of yesteryear's slaves who'd been lashed by some diabolic master's rigoise whip. My temples throbbed hot. My pupils contracted. I clenched my teeth, then... BAM! I rammed the toe of my shoe right into his testicular soft spot. The Sardinian collapsed without a word as the other passengers looked on in stupefaction, thrilled at the prospect of a little distraction. He lay curled in fetal position on the bone cold third-class floor, whining like a colicky babe. Silence set in, and it was a good hour before everyone returned to their own activities, quite a feat for the anchovy tin we'd found ourselves packed into with no other diversion than a couple foul-smelling toilets and a dining hall that seated thirty and served two meager meals a day. I was the only black woman aboard and, also, the only Frenchwoman—a real oddity, in short. But once I walloped that Sardinian bootlegger, they began to size me up, some amusedly, others with anxious deference.

Angus and his wife kept silent, at a complete loss for what to do. I had no choice but to come to the aide of those penniless Irish once again. I had felt moved by the sight of them when we debarked at Ellis Island, but here all I felt was pity. It was such a strange sentiment for someone who'd grown up on an island where Whites were always on the top and Blacks, necessarily, on the bottom, that I flushed with embarrassment, a profound embarrassment, to tell the truth, as I pulled sixty dollars out of my wallet (the landlady required a deposit and rent upfront). But enough about me, tell me something about you, my darling nephew! You know, when I first got your letter, I didn't open it right away. To be honest, if you hadn't written your name and address on the back of the envelope, I most certainly would've left it on my desk to languish. Frédéric Sainte-Claire, 26 Boulevard de la Levée, Fort-de-France, Martinique (French West Indies). Ha! See there? I still have a few crumbs of memory, despite my seventy-six years. So, you say you'd like to know all about my life, but you say you're not a writer. That's all right, then, just jot down what I say and try to fix it up later as best you can.

Thank you, in any case, for coming to see me....

Chapter Two

The Verneuils lived in nostalgia for what they referred to as—always in hushed voices—*the Paris of the Caribbean*, in other words, the city of Saint-Pierre, Martinique, which had been destroyed, despite its stately stone manses, one fine morning in May of 1902 by Mount Pelée. Gone was the theater where visiting lyric troupes from In-France performed; gone was the Chamber of Commerce; gone was the coastguard tower; gone was the tramway with its impressively muscled horse conveyance. A handful of fortunates escaped. Some had sailed to Fort-de-France just days earlier aboard vessels captained by the Girard Company. A few others from the surrounding countryside had panicked at the fumaroles spewing up from the volcano and followed the mass exodus of animals—both domestic and wild—to safe ground. But the other thirty thousand inhabitants of the archipelago's second-most-beautiful city (after Havana) perished in a handful of minutes. Faster than a flea's leap, as Stéphanie's mother's man comically put it. He was a good-for-nothing who spent his time pulling part-time djobs and, one can only assume, running the occasional racket at the port. He'd toss a quick shoulder-shrug Félicienne's way whenever she started in on him about finding what she called *real work*. For her daughter, Félicienne envisaged no more or no less than the life of a person upright behind a chair, another colorful expression. This enviable existence was reserved for poor young girls who'd been placed in rich households and who, during meals, hovered within ear's reach, ready to respond to the former's commands. In effect, after Félicienne had burned through a slew of menial jobs—laundress, coal picker, plate lunch seller, municipal sweeper and even psychic medium (yes, she claimed herself capable of seeing the future for a hundred-franc bill!)—and worked herself to the bone, worked enough to send her daughter to school for five years, she felt her strength starting to give out. In her neighborhood down Breadfruit Alley, she'd always been the first to rise and the first, coco-broom in hand, to sweep her minuscule dirt yard clear of dead leaves and the over-ripe fruit that had fallen in the night. The neighbors valued her sense of cleanliness, especially when her over-exuberance led her to clean their yards, too. As long as little Stéphanie's rump remained seated behind a school desk, her mother forbade the girl from lending a hand. See, she harbored a wild dream: for her daughter to rise above it all and get hold of a diploma, the golden ticket to a job as an attendant at the colonial hospital. Or even something with the wholesalers on the coast as a clerk for one of the Békés.

"Ay résité lison'w olié ou rété la ka gadé mwen!" she'd crow if the young girl seemed poised to pick up a broom, encouraging her early-rising child to go off and study her books instead of standing there gaping.

It was hard for Félicienne Sainte-Claire, a robust and quick-tongued Blackwoman, to believe she was the one who'd brought this girl into the world, a child as taciturn as she was spindly. She often wondered who her father could've possibly been. See, she'd long courted an array of men from whom she'd expected nothing more than a good kou-de-koko romp in the sack every now and again, as she put it, which always shocked the sensitive souls— though, to be honest, they numbered very few down Breadfruit Alley. And Félicienne wouldn't pause a beat before insisting, "The only thing good about a man is what hangs between his legs—to hell with the rest of it!" Whatever name she bequeathed to that nether realm (koko, lolo, lapen, pork dagger, screwdriver), everyone understood she appreciated the thing, she a devout Good-Godder who went rushing off to nine a.m. mass at the Lord's house every Sunday. She'd always dress Stéphanie in white: white shoes, a white dress, white ribbons in her hair. For herself, she preferred a soberer tone: gray. And even when she placed herself, as she was scrupulous to do, in a back-row pew, the bourgeois Mulattos turned their noses up at her. Félicienne had only very rarely attended mass at Fort-de-France's two other churches, in Terres-Sainville and Sainte-Thérèse: those were reserved for the Lowblacks.

"Man sé an moun kon tout moun. Man pa piti pasé pèsonn!" she'd exclaim to her neighbors' horror, shocked as they were by the sheer recklessness of claiming herself not inferior to anyone else.

Her closest friend among them, her real kokote-dear, Louisiane, was a Câpress who did the whole neighborhood's seamstressing and who loved being shocked by the escapades of Stéphanie's mother. She was a one-man woman herself and completely conquered by her thick rustic brute (a soubarou, as they say in Creole), who tended to tjuiyi mango anba lè kot, or to gather mangoes under her ribs, which is to say that he beat her hard and often, even just for blinking wrong. He came and went as he pleased, and they nicknamed him *viper* because he'd strike in an instant and always left a mark. He'd saunter in with bravado, expecting the seamstress to drop everything and make him a meal of two slices of breadfruit and a piece of dried cod. Then he'd demand a bottle of 55-proof rum and slump himself at the bamboo table he'd constructed for his use and his use alone. Then, in the shade of the lime tree that grew behind her shack, the man would proceed to wordlessly gorge himself. Well, without a gentle word, at least. There were plenty of grunts to fill the air, the surreptitious *mph!*'s of satisfaction that escaped from his overflowing mouth now and again. Then he'd grant himself an intermission on Louisiane's bed and sleep off the side effects of his gluttony before waking up two or three hours later, rolling over and bellowing in his crude Creole for his bitch to come spread her legs, "Vini isiya wouvè dé fant katjé'w bam wen, madigwàn-la!"

The seamstress obliged without a second's hesitation, be it eleven in the morning or five in the afternoon, because *monsieur* never spent the night down Breadfruit Alley. And the entire neighborhood would be subjected to the grotesquery of that windbag's panting and moaning and belching whenever he decided to buck the girl he'd promised to marry, provided she be good, in other words, so long as she didn't let any other sod sugar her ears. Stéphanie's mother was the only one scandalized by such conduct; the neighbors managed to derive great pleasure from it all, especially as they were otherwise bored stiff with life down the alley, with the lone exceptions of Christmas and carnival season. More often than not, Félicienne would start in on her daughter, "Stéphanie, there's no way in hell you're staying in this godforsaken country, no, no, no! It's impossible to live here as a woman. When you grow up, go to Panama or Venezuela. But whatever you do, get out!"

The little girl set to dreaming of those countries that she envisioned as fantastic other-worlds as different as could be from her sordid Martinique where Blacks were treated with less respect than an earthworm. She felt it in the scornful glances of her schoolteacher, a spinster Béké with an aristocratic surname, *Delacroix* or *Delaroche* or something of the kind. At the slightest grammar mistake or miscalculation uttered by a student whose complexion was too dark for her liking, she'd launch into a tirade against that "Alsatian imbecile Victor Schoelcher who wanted to free the slaves and let them go to school at any cost." In these moments, Stéphanie would close up like the leaves of a touch-me-not flower, wondering about that man who, according to her teacher, had enabled her to end up in that place. One day, she dared to bring it up with her mother, who immediately swatted her away because children should listen to grown-ups and keep their mouths stitched. Well-raised kids, in any case.

"Just because we don't know where our next meal is coming

from and we wear the same rags every day and we don't have two francs to our name doesn't mean we forget how to behave, Stéphanie."

The little girl's mother was up on her high horse about two things: housekeeping and education. She required Stéphanie to introduce herself clearly to everyone who passed down Breadfruit Alley, even complete strangers. Before she left for school, Félicienne checked her daughter's teeth, ears and fingernails as if her life depended on it. She turned out to be a good student who brought home good grades to prove it, despite the ostracism her teachers subjected her to, sometimes going so far as to refuse her entry to the classroom when Félicienne, desperate to finish her plate lunch preparations, had only enough time to whisk Stéphanie's hair into tight bantu knots. Scatty hair in sheep caca lumps like that was banned in respectable places, which was why Félicienne held an iron over hot coals every Saturday before dragging it through her and her daughter's hair. The smell of singed hair sickened Stéphanie, but she never complained because whenever she gave her mother any lip, Félicienne would gesture for the mahault-rope whip hanging over the kitchen door and then she'd lay into her daughter's legs with its raspy woven banana leaf fibers.

Stéphanie learned to read in no time, but at home the closest thing to a book she could get her hands on were a few old magazines from Over There, which her mother brought back from the port once or twice a month. They were probably given as gifts by some white sailor who was hoping that Félicienne might eventually succumb to his advances. Despite her youth, Stéphanie knew all about the business of sex. Their shack was too cramped to muffle the rhythmic pounding on the wall whenever her mother's what's-his-name lover stayed the night and, as for the poundings of their neighbor Louisiane and her boor of a man.... Well, there's nothing more to say about those two! In any case, Stéphanie was accustomed to seeing naked or nearly-naked men bathing with the gutter water they'd collected in metal barrels here and there down Breadfruit Alley. Venereal relations, to speak in euphemistic terms, held no mystery for the girl, nor were they of any interest to her. Which explains why she didn't make any trouble about it when, shortly after the Verneuil family took her on as a maid, their eldest, a boy named Eugène who was finishing his baccalaureate degree, came into her unlocked room one night, slid into her bed, unveiled his ugly hard-on and impaled her without uttering a single word. Well, to be sure there was a word, whispered the next morning while she served his breakfast and he prepared to set off for Schoelcher High School. Instead of the words of love she stupidly hoped for, he hissed, "Don't say anything to anybody! Got it, *madame*?"

The young man had addressed her formally, as he did with his parents. He was formal with everyone, save his two younger brothers and the baby of the family, an adorable little girl with a pretty name, Heloise. Unmoved, Stéphanie gave him a quick nod of her head before hurrying off to begin the morning chores she'd been assigned by M'man Ida, the chieftain of all the servants and the nanny of the Verneuils' children, who affectionately called her *Da*. Stéphanie didn't know whether it was the Creole word for nanny or just an abbreviation of her first name. Eugène would carry on in the coming nights, and not once did Stéphanie attempt to resist his brutal embrace. She had Sunday afternoons off, and she happily returned home to Breadfruit Alley, where she handed over all her earnings to her mother.

Félicienne was eaten up with remorse. "My girl, it's not my fault I couldn't send you away to school.... Life's getting harder and harder for Blacks in this country. You're intelligent. You know how to read and write. I have absolutely no fear for your future."

Félicienne would bring up Stéphanie's imminent departure

again and again. She'd be twenty-one before she knew it. In a flash. Then she'd lovingly describe Paris—she'd seen some photos in an old issue of *L'Illustration*, one of those magazines her lovestruck sailor brought her. The only thing was not to let some n'er-do-well stick her with a polichinelle, a bun-in-the-oven that would decimate every effort Félicienne had undertaken all those years to raise up Stéphanie. It was not without apprehension that the young lady returned to the Verneuils' villa on Avenue Victor Hugo on Sunday evenings. The villa had a courtyard, which was shaded by a grand old bassignac mango tree and a pond with running water—it was unrivaled by any home in all of En-Ville. The night of her return, Eugène, the future graduate and inheritor of all that Mulatto family's riches, would climb up onto her stomach, which would inevitably end up swelling. By then, she'd already witnessed one too many cases of barely-nubile girls flaunting their rounded bellies all along Breadfruit Alley, without even being quite sure which ant had bitten them when they'd stepped into one anthill or another.

To quell the wave of terror rising inside her day after day—or more precisely, night after night—Stéphanie took advantage of her rare moments of freedom to cast an eye upon the wealth of encyclopedias and atlases decorating the Verneuils' parlor. Afraid of getting caught by M'man Ida, the nanny, she contented herself with the maps of countries and continents—oceans, too. She exalted in their names: Burma, Argentina, Turkey, the Indian Ocean. Her eyes bugged at the sight of all those different peoples and their glimmering outfits—she was sure that one day she'd set sail on a journey of no return. It's not that she didn't love her mother, Félicienne, but she'd been haunted by a somber presentiment since her earliest childhood: Her mother would board the ship to Galilee before reaching old age. Her death would be quick, abrupt even, but painless and without suffering. It was an unfounded feeling, even more so given Félicienne's unflagging good health—she almost never had cause to see a doctor—but there it was, rooted deep inside the profoundest depths of the young girl. And although it had, for a time, filled her with sorrow, she'd eventually gotten used to the idea. Without her mother, what family would she have left in Martinique? A father she'd never known and who'd never tried to know her? A couple of aunts she saw once a year on Easter, who lived on the southern tip of the island, way down in Vauclin? Ah, if only she'd had the fortune of siblings!

But inexplicably, even though all her neighbors on Breadfruit Alley produced broods five, six, even seven kids strong, Félicienne Sainte-Claire had only one and one alone: Stéphanie. Some wondered at this oddity, others accused her of evildoing. Like Gratienne, for instance, who seemed to have it out for everyone in creation and for Stéphanie's mother in particular—and this notwithstanding the fact that everyone strove to keep a fair distance between themselves and her majestic figure. Despite the elephantiasis afflicting her left leg, she was still quite the coquette, winding brilliant madras cloth around her hair and, a clay pipe dangling from her lips, she'd drag her heavy carcass from doorstep to doorstep of the shacks she rented out, admonishing her tenants for their truant payments. Popular ill-feeling had it that in her youth, Gratienne had been a splendid creature who peddled her charms to white Admiralty officers, which had garnered her enough capital to construct the shacks she rented out down Breadfruit Alley. If Gratienne came across as unsympathetic toward her defaulting lessees (she had a ferocious Major from over in Bord de Canal who provided eviction services as necessary), she really went in on those over whom she had no sway: her fellow homeowners. Félicienne Sainte-Claire was at the top of that list. Gratienne jumped at the chance to rage over even their slightest faults, and she took an intense pleasure in letting loose her infamous barrage of nastiness.

And she reserved a particular genre of derision for Félicienne. "Either your womb is dryer than sugar cane pulp or else you get a kick out of murdering the babies in your belly with your evil sorceress potions! They say unripened pineapple rinds are especially effective... eh!? In the first case, you're pitiable, in the second, you're a real vagabond-whore...."

Stéphanie's mother refused to react to such villainy. Whatever the reason for her sudden incapacity to bring more children into the world after her daughter was born, she kept it to herself. But Stéphanie would have liked to know the how-and-why of it; she, too, seemed to be barren. The Verneuil boy had already impregnated no fewer than two little servant girls before she'd been taken on by that family, where even the mother, a piano teacher, seemed to encourage her noble heir down his path. At least implicitly: One night she'd brusquely entered the closet-like room at the very moment her son began braying, and she'd closed the door on them without a word. Nor did she utter a word about it the following day. Stéphanie had heard from old M'man Ida, the nanny, that as soon as a servant's pregnancy was brought to light, the girl would be kicked to the curb without so much as a thank-you-very-much. With no more than two months' worth of wages to soften the blow. "I've worked for the Verneuils for thirty-six years," she added. "I knew Monsieur Verneuil's papa, an upstanding Mulatto who treated us with respect. But his son and that grandson, Eugène, in particular, are two bally pig-boys!"

One day when the house was empty, the Verneuils having gone off to Morne-Rouge for a change of air and the governess having taken advantage of their absence by heading off to visit her sister, who lived up in some distant North Atlantic village, Stéphanie took out the atlases and seized the opportunity to give them a more careful study. The pictures of wild animals native to Africa fascinated her, as did the Indians of the Amazon basin. The Great Wall of China stopped her short. But it was one unremarkable New

York City street shot that truly captivated her. In it, a gregarious-looking black man of about fifty with a debonair smile loitered outside a store which—although Stéphanie didn't understand English—seemed to sell sweets, given the window display, which read *THE MIRROR CANDIES*.

But the funniest thing was that the man, elegant in his top hat, wasn't promoting the candy establishment, but the dentist's office next door. Written on the apron draped around his waist were the words *DENTAL PARLOR*.

And to his left, inscribed on a glass display filled with dentures of all kinds were the words *THE WORLD DENTAL ASSOCIATION*.

The atlas included a magnificent array of photos from all over New York City—from Washington Bridge and the avenue that ran alongside the Harlem River to a Greenwich Village hot dog festival—but it was that smooth-peddling Negro that really held her attention. Maybe because he reminded her of the Syrian hawkers who'd started establishing themselves down in Fort-de-France. At first, fresh off the boat, they'd been a bunch of sorry wretches; they'd landed on the island clutching ragged suitcases and incapable of producing a single word of French, much less of Creole. They got started pushing carts laden with bric-a-brac, but by the turn of the new century, some of those Levantines had begun to prosper and had opened up boutiques of their own. Before long, the Lowblacks preferred buying from them—they could haggle and pay on credit—than frequenting the high-class businesses along Schoelcher, Lamartine and Victor-Hugo streets.

"I'll go to New York!" Stéphanie declared in her heart of hearts, shocked by her own audacity. From that day on, she made the most of each moment of aloneness to dig through the Verneuils' library in search of more extensive information about that city of dreams. Unfortunately, beyond the atlas, the Verneuils had scant material on America. On the other hand, their shelves were lined with complete collections of Balzac, Zola, Stendhal and Maupassant, which the young servant forced herself to read but never quite managed to finish... except for *The Skin of Sorrow*, written by the above-named Balzac, which actually stirred something in her and haunted her for several weeks on end. She figured out that the eldest boy, Eugène of the violent nightly ravages, had a particular taste for Zola and for *Nana* in particular, which he'd filled with underlines and annotations. She recognized his handwriting because he often left notes for her in her tiny room, always under her pillow, always asking the same thing: *Do you have your period?* She'd respond with a simple *yes* or *no* and deposit the note in the young man's room after making his bed in the morning, after he'd left for school. For curiosity's sake, she plunged into the book in question and others by the same author, but just as quickly gave it up because the vocabulary was too complicated. Once, she stumbled upon another book that she managed to finish. Its author had a beautiful name: Francois René de Chateaubriand. A White Creole name, she thought to herself, imagining him as a great plantation owner somewhere in France before she realized that such a fantasy was a crock of nonsense; they didn't have sugar cane or coffee or cacao or bananas over there. Either way, Stéphanie liked the title of his book, *Atala*. For the first time in her life, she read a book twice in a row, then once again the following week and again after that until she almost knew it by heart. She became brazen, too, stealing it without fear of being fired as the Verneuil family's library, which had been inherited from the famous grandfather who'd always been so gentlemanly with old M'man Ida, was inexhaustible. In fact, hardly a week went by without Monsieur Verneuil, his wife or son Eugène replenishing it with a new book. As a result, a pile of them had started up in an alcove up by the rafters, a place visited only when some screeching bat needed to be chased away.

At night, as the bell tolled six, when the sun fell like a rock over En-Ville, especially during the winter season, the mistresses of the bourgeois homes allowed their servants to sit by the front door of their kitchen, or even of the laundry room, if it commanded a good view of the street. There, lovers would come to whisper sweet nothings to their girls, right up until the dinner hour, when these little madams were obliged to return to their posts. Florise, the servant charged with the Verneuils' laundry and floor-scrubbing (Stéphanie busied herself with the meals) would gussy herself up in a burst of frenetic energy, dousing herself with cheap perfume in hopes that her man would come. That gourgandine-flirt's hopes were only fulfilled one time out of two (three might be more honest), but his waywardness never seemed to bother that strumpet. She was always on the watch, straddling the threshold with one foot inside the house and the other on the sidewalk, powerless to quiet the agitation coursing through her body. She'd start humming love songs in French, a language she barely knew, to fortify herself with courage. As for her workmate, the scrawny-zoklet girl from Breadfruit Alley, she refused to surrender any amount of energy to such foolhardy evening exploits. It's not because Stéphanie was the most goody-goody in the world, but that she found these standing public displays grotesque, the couple pressed against a doorframe, their barely muffled grunts seemed to sail from house to house, provoking great hilarity among the boss-families. No. She preferred to sit by herself in her tiny room where Florise would find her lost in thought. Ever since the day she discovered Chateaubriand's book, nothing could keep her from reading and re-reading the adventures of Chactas and Atala, crying hot tears every time she came to the part where the young Indian girl decides to end her own life, preferring poison over falling to the temptation of desire because her mother declared chastity to god on her behalf before she was born.

"Pa di mwen sé an liv ka fè dlo koulé nan zié'w kon sa?"

Florise scoffed, totally incredulous that a book could make so many tears fall from anyone's eyes.

As time went on, Stéphanie began to see herself in Chateaubriand's heroine, even to the point of using some of her phrases, which stupefied Madame Verneuil, who nonetheless never managed to identify the source of what she considered to be the stupid affectation of a Blackgirl obviously attempting to raise herself beyond her own station. The first America that Stéphanie dreamed of was a land as bucolic as it was tragic, a vast forest populated by Indians and Christian missionaries, fur-trappers and bootleggers. Meanwhile, and utterly inexplicably, Eugène's venereal appetite had finally quelled, which gave her the chance to have a decent night's sleep. But soon another worry, much more serious, consumed her: Her mother's health had taken a sudden turn for the worse. One afternoon while scaling fish by the fountain in the courtyard, Louisiane—their even-tempered seamstress neighbor who accepted her man's mischief without batting an eye—arrived at the villa's iron gate, cowering in intimidation.

"Stéphanie, hey! Hey, come over here, please!" she hissed, frantically looking right and left with worried eyes.

It was Madame Verneuil's siesta hour, a stroke of luck because servants of the bourgeois houses in the center of Foyal (another name for Fort-de-France, affectionately coined by the well-to-doers) were strictly prohibited from gossiping with passersby, Levantine hawkers, street venders and, obviously, sweet-talkers bearing flowers. At risk of immediate dismissal! Stéphanie approached the gate with caution. Louisiane looked completely shaken.

"Sa ka fè pasé twa jou I pa ka doubou.... Fok ou vini wè'y!" she whispered, fearful that the mother's three-day sickbed lay-in required Stéphanie's immediate presence.

A deep chill crawled up Stéphanie's spine, but not one tear

blossomed from her eyes. She nodded to the seamstress and turned her back. The young woman went to sit in the kitchen, incapable of working. She remained in that position until noon, when she was supposed to set the turned mahogany table in the living room, the pride of the Verneuils because it had been passed down for three generations. An exclamation made her jump from her seat, "Estéfani, s aka rivé'w? Ou vini dekdek oben ki sa?"

What had happened to her, indeed? Had she lost her mind as accused? It took her a moment to recognize the voice because her mistress rarely spoke in Creole. In fact, she only used it with the pacoteeyers—those wandering knickknack salesmen that roamed across most of the Caribbean—or to scare away an imprudent kid who was trying to knock mangoes from the gorgeous tree in her courtyard whose branches stretched out over the sidewalk. Stéphanie turned slowly. As if seized by something, she was incapable of moving her lips, her gaze frozen.

"I will *not* tolerate love affairs in this house, young lady!" Madame Verneuil barked. "If a man's caught your eye, well, that's your business. But it is out of the question that I should tolerate such behavior! Go collect your things from your room! I'll settle your payment, in any case.... Oh la la, what a time we're living in! Not even the help can be counted on anymore!"

Stéphanie made no attempt to protest. Nor did she try to explain herself. She followed Madame Verneuil's orders like a robot. The other servant, Florise, was immediately moved to oven duty because Monsieur Verneuil was due back any minute, and he tolerated absolutely no slip-ups as far as household operations were concerned. Stéphanie didn't get a chance to say good-bye to her workmate. As for the rest—all in all, she owned no more than three dresses and a few underthings, which she quickly stuffed into her woven basket—she was ready in five minutes. Madame Verneuil, without deigning to offer the girl the slightest sign of sympathy or gratitude, pushed an envelope into her hands and muttered, "Go. Live your life, mamzelle! *Everyone* knows what you're worth now."

Stéphanie easily deciphered the threat veiled in this statement from the woman she'd considered a sort of second mother: There was no chance that another bourgeois house would hire her, at least not in En-Ville. This thought affected the young woman no more than the realization that she would soon become an orphan. It was as if she had turned to wood. Or better yet, marble. A strange heaviness weighed down every step, every movement, even blinking was an exhausting chore. Paradoxically, a sense of well-being began to spring up inside her. She walked toward Levée Boulevard, which divided Foyal into two distinct parts. On one side, tidy avenues lined up neatly to frame the cathedral, on the other, the flea-ridden Terres-Sainville neighborhood spread out toward the yellow-fever-ravaged swamplands. A putrid canal littered with trash flowed along the boulevard, a canal where sows grunted at all hours of the day as they foraged through the debris. Likewise, unruly packs of children played along the banks, at times fighting over some discovered left-over with the pigs-gone-wild. Stéphanie thought of Monsieur Verneuil's refrain, "What rotten luck that we're forced to live in this nothing cul-de-sac we call Fort-de-France! The streets of our beautiful Saint-Pierre of old flowed with fresh water straight from the slopes of Mount Pelée... the clearest, bluest water, yes...."

A crowd of people had gathered in the middle of Breadfruit Alley, talking loudly and bursting into laughter here and there. When they saw Stéphanie, everyone went quiet. Their voices softened, their faces fell and their bodies tensed. The girl understood immediately that some awful disaster had come to pass... the biggest disaster that could befall a child with no father, no brother, no sister. So, there she was, completely alone in the world! She hesitated outside her mother's shack, afraid to enter where the mourners had already begun to stir up a racket. And then she vowed in her heart of hearts, "I'm not spending another minute in this country…. I'm going to leave it in the dust! New York is waiting for me, I know it…."

Chapter Three

I, Stéphanie St. Clair, a Black Frenchwoman disembarked smack-dab in the American frenzy, had the good luck of arriving in Harlem just as its first inhabitants began emptying out—first the Irish, then the Italians—and day after day, apartment after apartment, giving way to crowds of deep South Negroes with their drawling Mississippi accents and their ridiculous outfits spun from Alabama cotton. They weren't necessarily welcomed by their Northern brothers, either, who often looked down at them as country bumpkins and kept their distance. Sugar Hill, the stronghold of the black bourgeoisie, overlooked the Valley, which was the term given to the heart of Harlem where all manner of villainous sods, minstrels and street musicians, heroin traffickers, vagrants and women of dubious virtue, and every shade of humanity were heaped together in their miserousness. And no one batted an eye at a knife or a Colt .45... not even the New York Police Department. For ten years, I commingled with that world, a stranger in everything, especially the language. I never got the hang of pronouncing that terrible *th*, and everybody mocked me for it, teasing me for the *ze* I used instead. A stranger to the Negroes who pretended not to understand me and to the Whites, or let's say to the police, who arrested me ten times—twenty times, even—for vagrancy. And those swine refused to release me until they'd been paid what they referred to as a deposit, and which was, in fact, nothing but a bribe. A stranger to the Spanish Harlem Latinos who'd just begun to establish themselves—what a bunch of yammerers—though I certainly felt closest to them. Ten long years during which I stood fast, squatting in abandoned houses, selling drugs both soft and hard... on occasion even selling myself, but not to the highest bidder like the syphilis-scarred sluts on 47th Street. No, I reserved myself for the types who treated me like a lady, a requirement that surprised the gallivanting Whities. Because from the very first day I stepped foot in America—which wasn't so far from my native island, after all—I swore I wouldn't let anyone walk all over me anymore or treat me like a little Negress. No one! And that fat slob, O'Reilly, he knew full well what I was about. O'Reilly was the leader of one of the most formidable gangs of New York, the Forty Thieves, and he hired me because I convinced him that I could jabber in all kinds of foreign tongues, most importantly in Italian and Yiddish. My work consisted of haunting bars and brothels to keep tabs on the ones that were on the up-and-up, information I'd report back to that grump of a spit-sputtering Irish who couldn't string two words together without slicking you with phlegm. Individuals dressed in trench coats and fedoras would then turn up at the aforementioned establishments, asking to speak with the boss and then sticking him with a tax whose sum was not open to negotiation. The recalcitrant ones—and these were rare, mind you—came to their senses thanks to a round or two of bullets through their front windows or, for the real bull-headed, a bomb; but the latter were never really dangerous, since they were delivered in the morning when such places were near empty. Nonetheless, everyone understood it as the Crime Syndicate's first warning.

That job didn't bring in as much money as I had hoped, but I certainly made a good deal more than my flatmates. Angus Mulryan had been hired as a road mender or railway worker; I can't remember now. It was somewhere in upstate New York, so he'd get up at three in the morning just to make it up there on time. As for his wife, who had inexplicably lost her air of frail helplessness and grew more and more confident every day, she offered her services in a public launderette. Daireen had wanted to ensnare me in that wretched profession—standing around in the wind and cold, hoping some bourgeois family might see fit to dump their dirty laundry at your feet. I didn't last past a dozen days doing that because Stéphanie St. Clair did *not* come to America to clean the raggedy underwear of folks who bathe but once a week. I kept up with that old Martinican habit of washing myself every day, morning and night, which most certainly enraged our landlady at Five Points—she felt I was wasting water. Naturally, the water fee was included in our rent.... I paid her on time at the end of every week, but she didn't go a day without threatening to kick us to the curb. She never spoke to me directly, but always through Angus.

"Tell that girl of yours that, in this country, water costs money! I guess she's used to sharing with the crocodiles and hippopotamuses in that swamp she comes from, but things are different around here!"

Angus made a show of scolding me, but he knew he needed me, not only because I contributed to the rent and bought groceries, but because it fell on me to take care of their baby whenever they had some Irish festival or other to attend. In those moments, I got overwhelmingly sad thinking about how I was the only one without a community to take me under its wing. The Yiddish celebrated Hanukkah, the Irish had St. Patrick, the Italians had a mass of Catholic saints and the American Blacks (all of whom were Baptists or Evangelists) had their own ceremonies, which I was a complete stranger to. If their gospel songs moved me, I found the get-ups of their faithful to be completely ridiculous and their writhings to be grotesque. I always found myself alone when the festivities started up, and the day a white neighbor invited me to Thanksgiving dinner, all I could do was stand there in front of her, unable to make the slightest response.

"I've seen you around here for months now, miss," she said to me one morning as I was rushing off to a meeting with O'Reilly, the boss of the gang of Forty Thieves.

A burglary had gone bad—the target was the strongbox of the uncooperative proprietor of a nightclub that, despite its shabby appearance, had a plum location along the Harlem River and, thus, a regular supply of heroin rolling in. I'd managed to get hired as a cleaning lady there and worked for two good months. I took note of all the comings and goings, all the mutterings and the constant flux of unmarked crates and boxes that got moved in the club's back alley. Most of my fellow cleaning ladies— all black, predictably enough—were hardly much for cleaning, what with their hordes of marmy-scamps trailing them wherever they went... and there was always a run-away in the bunch or one stuck in bed with the flu. More or less dressed in tatters, faces blank, mouths shut tight, these women scrubbed and swept the floors as if inwardly gnawed by rage, like they were doing battle with some personal enemy. Every now and again, one of these ladies would break into a fit of hysteria, without a stitch of warning. She'd untie her headscarf, tear off her apron, give a hard kick to the bucket of soapy water and brandish her broom in the air like some kind of assegai spear. We'd watch them vehementing, "I'm fed up with this motherfucking life! God, you don't listen to my prayers... you forgot my kids and me, but I've been prayin' to you every night, for years and years. To hell with this job! I don't give a shit about it!"

Signore Silvio Mancini, a short-legged Neapolitan, would rush from his second-floor office and, in broken English (his was much worse than mine, even though he bragged about being in America for ages), would hurl insults at the woman in question till he was blue in the face and she was reduced to tears, then he'd chuck her out the door for good. What really shocked me, though, was that not one of the other employees so much as attempted to take a stand for the lady who'd be out on the streets by the next morning, begging to fill her children's mouths. It was ruthless, each to her own. After the big to-do they'd all go about their business, dusting the window curtains or mopping the hallway without a dime of protest. There was only me, hard-headed female that I was, an angry Martinican Blackwoman, who seemed choked with rage. But forget about it! I'd been entrusted with a mission: first of all, to identify the exact location of Signore Mancini's hidden safe-box, then to tally up the number of Mafiosi standing guard. It wasn't such a difficult task because, like I was saying, I was the hardest working employee he had, and thanks to my French accent, I was treated differently than the others. The thirty-seven dollars given to me every Saturday at noon was exactly the same amount given to the other cleaning ladies. But Signore Mancini, who personally attended to this dispersal, treated me with a hint of deference. And I can say not one of my misery-comrades nor of the three arm-bearing Mafiosi who followed the signore wherever he went, calling him *il capo* or *the boss*, appreciated the attention.

"Come stai, mia piccolo Francese nera? Ha ha ha! Ho viaggiato nel tuo paese prima di venire qui," he'd chuckle, unable to refrain from reminding me, his black French darling, that he'd seen my country before landing in America.

By force of immersion, being surrounded by Italian conversations all day, I got used to their language and picked it up pretty well. It seemed I had a gift for languages, and it was certainly the only gift that famous Lord God (whom everyone— Blacks and Whites alike—except me believed in) had deigned to give me. As a child in Martinique, I'd tried plenty hard to make myself believe in Bible school, but I couldn't bring myself to believe that there was some white-skinned, bearded and blue-eyed being up in the sky, keeping watch over all his creatures of creation. But I was always very careful to keep my miscreant thoughts to myself. Especially here, in America, where he seemed to be held in such esteem. All the Mafiosi, including Signore Mancini, wore gold crosses around their necks, and at every round of gunfire, they'd furtively make the sign of the cross as they grabbed their guns. As it happened, the Vesuvio Club wasn't a particularly peaceful spot, even if the thugs were sometimes placated by the long legs of the charming French cancan dancers who'd taken the stage.

I quickly became Signore Mancini's favorite. I won him over once and for all when I got it in mind to babble out a few words in his language, and then, in no time, was speaking in complete sentences. I was charged with cleaning his office—other than his guards, I was the only one allowed into this sanctum. When he'd host another *capo*, he'd lead them into a room up on the third floor whose curtains were always closed tight against the terrace and fire escape. It was, in some sense, the holy of holies and only Signore Mancini's mother was allowed in. She told me she aired out the room at nightfall—we'd become fast pals—and was careful to clean up all the Cuban cigar stubs and the empty bottles from the whisky and gin that her son and his gang consumed religiously. The mamma, as everybody called her, came off as a modest woman without much to say. At any rate, she was indifferent to people's skin color. She jargoned not one traitor word in English and it seemed unlikely that she had ever ventured past the two-block radius around the Vesuvio Club. I became, in a way, her confidante.

"Stéphanie, if you knew the number of assassinated souls weighing on my Silvio's conscience, you'd run for your life! Ah, Dio mio, proteggi mi! I beg our Father for forgiveness all the time, I plead for my son, but does he have any chance of getting in to Purgatory? I just don't know...."

Twice, when I'd come in to work early, seeing as I was starting to have it up to here with my Irish family and their wailing little ankle-biters (since reaching the Promised Land, Daireen had brought two more into the world, one right after the other), I'd seen a couple odd-looking bundles coming down the stairs from that precious third floor. Bodies, evidently, wrapped up in dirty sheets and tied with rope. A couple of the Mafiosi transported them by car to a secluded edge of the Harlem River not far from

42

the club and tossed them into the murky waters. It didn't take me long to realize that the Neapolitan was working to extend his territory and that, inevitably, he'd gone to war with his fellow countrymen, or perhaps with the Yiddish and Irish gangsters. O'Reilly, my boss and the leader of the Forty Thieves, went about his business in a different way. Rather than developing a kingdom (which was the pipe dream of any gangster worth his salt in New York), he preferred to carry out raids here and there. Besides, that nutjob Irish didn't abide by the mob's golden rule: Only kill your own and never, but *never*, lay a finger on any policeman, judge or politician. Never! The latter needed only a little pocket greasing to turn them into harmless little lambs. Some could even be blinded to the worst of our trafficking by such a maneuver. And all the trafficking, cheating, scheming and so forth was especially present at the races, where tens of thousands of dollars were bet legally and three or four times that bet behind closed doors.

"Don't ever mistake me for that pansy Lucky Luciano!" O'Reilly would bellow whenever a member of our gang tried to soothe his anger after he had gunned down an overly curious cop or sent orders to that effect or demanded a bomb be rigged up in some politician's car.

O'Reilly was a terror. A perfectly uncontrollable being. Paradoxically, even though he saw women as no more or less than pawns in his business or as pieces of ass for the taking, he really liked me. In his eyes, I was a dancing dog, or maybe just a pet. Go figure! A Black Frenchwoman who wouldn't be taken for a fool and who looked at him square in the eyes; it made him laugh. He was enraged because Signore Mancini refused the protection he'd offered him; I'm not sure at what price, but certainly no less than what we charged less popular places. It was a kind of state secret. O'Reilly alone knew, and the other thirty-nine thieves kept their lips locked tight — including me, the high-and-mighty. Because he paid us our due without batting an eye, a bandit but on the level. Dishonest with the outside world, but honest as can be with his gang members.

Upon gaining access to Signore Mancini's office on the second floor, I quickly discovered a wall draped with a heavy red curtain whose function couldn't possibly have been strictly decorative. It took me a while, but I found the strongbox, which was hidden so well it seemed to be actually embedded in the wall behind this curtain. O'Reilly rejoiced when I told him, kissed both my cheeks with an enthusiasm that he quickly put in check, but not soon enough to stop the men who'd witnessed it from mocking him for it.

"Just fuck her and get it over with!" one of the old-timers, a wrinkly-faced and freckled but high-ranking thug, bellowed. Salvatore—that was his name—specialized in burglarizing rich people's homes in Manhattan, where his plumbing expertise fooled the necessary parties. He was especially good at nabbing jewelry and, almost every week, would bring back pearl necklaces, rings inlayed with precious gems, silver bracelets, a whole ornament factory's worth of knickknacks (that's all they were, in my eyes, at least.... I never did like being hindered by the junk womankind willingly abide in order to appeal to men). The booty would be distributed among us to resell. O'Reilly was clever: He never unloaded all his spoils in bulk, and that's how he avoided suspicion. Every member of the Forty Thieves was entrusted with a piece of jewelry or two and ordered to sell it for a decent price within the week—otherwise, it'd be reclaimed and entrusted to someone else. And then it was bye-bye bonus! Farewell to the 20 percent that crazy Irishman would ever so regally bestow upon us. Oh, it was easy for me because my prospecting grounds included all of Harlem and everybody knows how crazy those Negresses go over such baubles. Back then, Five Points really suited me, and I was not inclined to go live in a neighborhood filled with miserable Negroes with whom I'd never identified, anyway. That shocks you, huh, nephew? I'd go up to the first female individual who came my way, provided she didn't seem completely broke, and I'd discreetly flash her the jewelry. In general, they'd be dumbstruck, but once the greed started to shine in their eyes, they'd invite me up to their places. Some ladies kept wads of bills under their mattress or a loose floorboard in their apartment, the fruit of their decades-long toil, but that never stopped them from decimating it in one slapdash purchase, enthralled as they were by the ring set with a big Colombian emerald or the gold-trimmed cameo. Sometimes I'd refuse to make the transaction if the woman couldn't come up with the full sum, and when I'd take the goods back, a look of profound distress would fall over the unfortunate at hand. In these cases, I'd get to work drawing the men in, but would apply myself to this angle with extreme prudence, because, in Harlem, it only took one false step to get dragged by the hair down a deserted alley by one of those brutes, where they'd pin you to the wall and smash your pussy-chagatte to a pulp. The Whites' sweet-talking, sik-sosé-an-miel kind of love was nowhere to be found in that notoriously godforsaken neighborhood! Whoever simpered after a woman would immediately be taken for a pussy or a limp wrist, which inevitably led to humiliation. So much that I'd approach the male sex abruptly and keep it real cool.

"Hey, man, you want to see something nice? Don't look at me like that, baby! I'm no devilwoman...."

Lucky for me, the combination of my shabby clothes and tomboyishness paid off, because they didn't take me for a streetwalker and, more often than not, the men would stop to look at whichever mysterious object I had on offer. Some of them handled the jewelry with a carefulness I found pretty comical. Others would whistle in genuine admiration. But without fail, all of them would try low-balling me.

"Two cents?"

"Fuck off, man!"

"Ok, ok, how 'bout six cents?" the guy would try, surprised that a person as scrawny as myself could be so bold when toe-to-toe with a representative of the stronger sex.

"Is that how much your mamma's pussy's worth? C'mon, my man, figure this: That little gem-of-a-piece you've got in your hands belonged to the Queen of England's niece herself!"

"Alright, how much, then?"

Without a moment's hesitation, I'd quadruple his second offer and half the time he'd go for it, positive he'd be able to hawk the bauble for more than my asking price. Back then, I must admit, I was a real tomboy. Though I never abandoned myself to total charognery-filth, I had no taste for the finer things, beautiful clothes or makeup. Much less for perfume. I was a fully-fledged member of the Forty Thieves, the terror of all New York, not some kapistrel-strumpet that had to be chaperoned home at night with a kiss on the hand and a tap on the ass. Most nights I left the Vesuvio Club at the stroke of midnight or maybe even one a.m. because, when all was said and done, I'd been promoted; Signore Mancini had made me responsible for cleaning the upstairs, and I even had under my command three old big-bellied ladies (they'd gotten that way from spawning so many kids) who had no more hope for their lives. I ordered them to clean the third floor and the terrace and left the second floor for myself, where the strongbox was hidden. I'd never seen the boss open it and wondered when he'd deposit the rather generous earnings from his heroin business. His bookkeeper, a tall, dark Sicilian without a penny's worth of good looks, was a real walking tomb. He presided over his numbers in a back room perpetually plunged in darkness, situated behind the stage where all the dancers strutted out. I'd been back there two or three times to bring him something to eat—the club had a restaurant in it, too. When I caught his eyes, he looked pretty nervous because mountains of precariously stacked bills were piled up in front of him, and by the looks of it, most of them weren't singles, either. I reported all the information I'd managed to gather to O'Reilly, and he concluded that the prime time for attack would be a Monday, late at night, because by then the dancers would be on break and the restaurant would've slowed down. But clearly something hadn't gone right because that crazy Irishman had summoned for me straightaway to tear me a new one, "You got it all wrong, Stéphanie! The thing you thought was that old fossil's strongbox was just a boxful of personal papers and nothing else! It seems he's had some trouble with the law in Sicily and with immigration services here...."

So that rageful hot-blooded Irishman blew up the nightclub. It was the day after Christmas in 1915, or maybe it was the year after, it's hard to keep track. Luckily, no one got caught up, but it really pissed the New York Police Department off, and we had to keep a low profile for a few months. The cleaning ladies, myself included, were all unceremoniously arrested and interrogated, but we played dumb the way every Negro knows how to do when faced with a White. And I, who was really the only one implicated in the business, managed to slip through the net without a fuss. That's when I began seriously considering quitting the gang of Forty Thieves. I was, both figuratively and also quite literally, a dark stain on that gang, being as I was the only woman *and* the only Black. I wasn't skilled with a blade or gun like my colleagues, and I had certain scruples when it came to laying in on the down-and-out. Sure, I'd *play* the man, but I wasn't one and, sooner or later, it was going to come back and bite me in the ass.

And then, the Irish Mob, as they were called, the Celtic mafia that had ruled over New York since the middle of the nineteenth century, was starting to lose a serious amount of its territory to the Yiddish and to the Italians, in particular. Those kilt-paraders (especially on St. Patrick's Day) had managed to establish a sort of aid organization, the White Hand Gang, but they hadn't managed to contain the newcomers to only practicing their pathetic portside trafficking. Day after day, the wops moved in on New York and started to meddle in bootlegging, contraband, horse racing, and—as they grew ever bolder—drugs. O'Reilly railed against his compatriots with the thunder of god, "Now they're turning bourgeois! Strutting around like they're a bunch of damned limeys and look what's come of it!"

Our gang of Forty Thieves, who'd profited greatly from the omnipotence of the Irish Mob, refused to affiliate with anyone at all. Which meant risking that they might be phased out at any minute. And not sometime in the distant or near future, but overnight! We'd had some desertions, and it was getting harder and harder to recruit. Aside from the Vesuvio Club flop, I had managed to carry off the missions I'd been assigned. Period. But that damned O'Reilly was always asking for more. He even tried getting me to turn tricks in one of the verminous-looking underground bars that he suspected was raking in the dough since it was known for having the most sublime and leggy New Orleans Quadroons. He didn't want to hear it when I tried to make him see that nature hadn't endowed me with the voluptuousness that made men drool and that no manager in their right mind was going to hire me for the job. Brimming with rage, that ruddy-faced and befreckled Irishman, whose cosmically blue eyes made you avert your gaze when speaking with him, thought that he could strong-arm me. He took me by the throat with one hand and started slapping me with the other as he hollered, "Stupid. Black. French. Bitch!"

My Creole blood went hot. I grabbed him by his grenn-balls and crushed them so hard he couldn't breathe. He swooned onto the sidewalk and soon passersby were making a show of skirting around his limp body. It was almost six o'clock at night on that autumn day. A nasty wind had been blowing since morning, and the streetlights had not yet been lit. I threw myself on top of O'Reilly, beating him till he was senseless, kicking him in the face till he was out for good. Then I opened the fly of his pants, pulled out his brakmarr-dick and his cobblers and razored them right off. No, my dear Frédéric, I kid you not! An inhuman howl drowned out whatever hubbub might've lingered in the near deserted street, quickly followed by cathedralesque silence. I was suddenly as if statuefied; if a cop had happened to pass by on patrol right then and there, I would've been a goner. A Negress castrating a White; that's a death sentence for sure! By some miracle, I had time to get a grip on myself and hightail it back to Five Points without a word to my Irish family. The very next morning, the Forty Thieves had put a bounty on my head, so I had to seek refuge with a toothless old lady from South Carolina whom I'd given a helping hand on a couple previous occasions. I stayed locked in her house for three weeks, long enough for the gang to say farewell to O'Reilly and to forget all about my humble self.

"So, you French Negresses are a lot worse than us, huh?" Miss Coolidge murmured, half-grinning, half-concerned.

I offered no objection. At that time, I was not yet cultivated enough to relate to her that during the time of the whip and chains—as I would later learn straight from the mouth of the famous black scholar W.E.B. Du Bois—White American plantation owners would threaten to sell their slaves to their counterparts in Martinique should they show even the slightest sign of resistance or revolt. I didn't learn about any of that (or any number of other important things) until I became the queen of the underground lottery—Madam Queen, alias Queenie— and started rubbing elbows with the Edgecombe Avenue elite: Negro poets, historians, philosophers and musicians. Yes, when I committed my first murder (there would be one or two more thereupon… or maybe three or four, I don't remember anymore), I was still wrapped up in a reclusive shyness. My only friend and sole protector was that old razor I'd been given by the barber when I set sail from Martinique. He was the best on Levée Boulevard and, like his peers, he'd tried hard to sugar my ears those mornings when I found myself down at the Levassor canal, emptying out the Verneuils' chamber pots, just like the dozens of other servants who'd come to do the same. In general, we all got up before early dawn to avoid running into the bourgeois ladies on their way to the six o'clock mass at the cathedral. But we tried to stay off that street any earlier than we had to because of the lawless, faithless chumps roamrunning around every which where, looking for action: those larsonners, snake oil charmers, black vagabonds, unthirsty drunkards, your-money-or-your-life-ers, winos and other scoundrels. Florise, the Verneuil's laundry girl, had been assaulted by one of those filthy creatures well before the blood started flowing from between her thighs. Out of the blue, she'd been brought back from some faraway field by Monsieur Verneuil, who simply offered to anyone who'd listen that "Stéphanie has a little too much work. Ginette, the new girl, will take care of the meals…. She's been recently orphaned."

No one peeped a word, nor asked for further explanation. Certainly not Madame Verneuil, who saw her husband as a kind of embodied demi-god. Ginette was a puny child with perpetually sad eyes. She'd never been in charge of emptying the chamber pots (there were three in the house, which multiplied my roundtrips to the canal), but one day when I was obliged to stay in bed because of the terrible pains plaguing my stomach (in no relation to my period), she took my place. When she returned to the house, her nightgown was torn and dirty. She was haggard, stuttering incomprehensibly, and her body was wracked with unnamed tremblings. In a dark side street on the way to the canal, two hairless-dog scums had thrown themselves onto her and had ruthlessly cocked her one after the other, then beat her to the ground before decamping; her cries had alerted the neighbors. How old was she? Fourteen or fifteen, maybe. No older than that. From then on, I equipped myself with a swordfish snout that I bought from a fisherman. My boss got angry when he saw it, "Stéphanie, I know full well you're an evil-tempered girl, it's written all over your face, but if you hurt or kill someone with that, I'm taking NO responsibility. As for you, you'll go straight to the guillotine!"

Yes, I had my temper. Good or bad, I didn't know which. By the age of sixteen I was ready to stand up to the whole universe if it came to it and, my word, I was certainly proud of it, which annoyed my mother to no end. She'd serenade me with her favorite adage: "Hardheaded Blackwomen never make it far in life." But even if I was in a position to stand up to those vagabonds and skirt-miners who haunted the streets of En-Ville at dawn, I was—at least initially—completely powerless in the face of that diabolical creature we called a dorlis and that my boss referred to in his prim-and-proper French as an incubus. Word got around in En-Ville that an invisible dorlis (invisible except, o inexplicable!, for its blue eyes) had started haunting the maids' rooms and that a number of these girls had been found by their mistresses in the early hours with haggard eyes, torn nightgowns and welts all over their bodies. I knew perfectly well that to chase away a dorlis, you had either to wear a pair of inside-out black underpants or to set a half-calabash filled with sand or grains of rice at your threshold or jab a pair of spread-open scissors into the floorboards... but I imagined myself strong enough to do battle with the aggressors and rapists of the world, even those who were in league with the devil. I was never afraid of anything, and down Breadfruit Alley, I'd been deemed a terror in the Creole sense of the term, which is to say brazen—cocky, in fact. No walloping from my mother's horsewhip nor anyone's threats could make me lower my head, which occasionally provoked the laughter of those who'd underestimated me on account of my weakling appearance. So, I didn't take any special precautions after eight o'clock, the curfew time enforced by our mistress. It must be said that I was never a restful sleeper, even though my mother was the type to drop into a deep slumber soon as her head hit the pillow. And after the Verneuil family had hired me, my insomnia got only worse. I never really slept for more than three or four hours a night in their house, but somehow wasn't the least bit tired come morning. I kept this secret to myself, and only Eugène ended up figuring it out. See, when he'd snaked into my room that first night and started pulling up my nightgown, I propped myself up on my elbows. That really threw him for a loop! He jumped to his feet, unsure whether to carry on or to make a break for it. I took my own clothes off, turned down my blanket and spread my legs, offering myself in silence and stillness, hoping only that he'd get it over with and get out! Overexcited, the boy orgasmed in less than a dozen seconds, then tiptoed out of the room as if ashamed. I had only two fears: getting pregnant (as I mentioned earlier, dear nephew) and getting fired. While I wasn't a believer, or I was at least indifferent to the Good Lord and all the airs and graces his followers put on, I started believing that an occult power, a divinity of some kind, protected me.

Being too sure of yourself comes with a price, and I ended up paying it. The incubus finally broke through the flimsy reclaimed wood walls of the little shack the Verneuils had constructed beside their villa. Florise, Ginette and I shared the shack, our little rooms separated only by a thin sheet. The diabolic creature started whirling about my body, without making the slightest sound as it morphed from a kind of transparent veil into a monstrous half-man, half-animal. It floated there menacingly, and I could feel it trying to blind or hypnotize me. In any case, my eyes were searing with pain, and I struggled mightily to keep them open. Then, suddenly, I felt light, so light I seemed to be floating above my bed. In a rush, the creature started pulling off my nightclothes, and I was transfixed, unable to resist. Just as it was about to penetrate me, I gathered all my strength and managed to shake myself free with a shout. It must have been ear-splitting because the entire household came running into my room. First Florise, followed by the Verneuils, then my boss lighting the way with a gas lamp. The incubus disappeared with a sucking sound so ghastly it froze everyone to their spot. For the very first time since living with that family, I felt treated like a fellow human being. Madame Verneuil brought me a glass of Carmelite water and dabbed my face with camphor; Monsieur Verneuil examined me to ensure I hadn't been wounded. They didn't have to ask anything, so obvious was it that I'd endured the attack of a dorlis. From that day on, they insisted that I wear a pair of black underwear inside-out to bed. After that night, whenever I served my boss's visitors punch out on the veranda, he'd brag, "You see this kapistrel before you, friends? Don't be fooled by her appearance! She escaped an incubus attack!"

Excuse me, my dear Frédéric, for rambling on, you can fix everything up when the time comes! No doubt it's because of (or thanks to) my rebel nature that, soon after castrating O'Reilly, I ended up with a soft spot for a Black Jamaican, despite his baboonesque features. He'd go harangue the crowds in Central Park, at least in the part of the park that had been reserved for the Negroes over in Harlem. On the other hand, he had a good-sounding name: Marcus Garvey. At first, I took him for a fool. Him and his followers. They called him Black Moses, for crying out loud! While I never fell in as a fervent Christian, it sounded blasphemous, to say the least. He'd get really stirred up as he spoke, his eyes would gleam flashes of lightning, his voice fury-bound, and when summer hit, he'd conjure up an infinite number of handkerchiefs to sponge off his forehead. During this time his troops (I call them that because they all wore multicolored military-like outfits) would plunge into curious crowds of onlookers and shout, "Read *The Negro World*, the only newspaper telling the truth about the horrors inflicted upon the black race in this abomination of a country we call America!"

I ended up buying a copy and read it attentively, even though my man of that era, Duke, shrugged his shoulders and jeered, "Bullshit, man! Let them go back to Africa if they think they'll like all those crocodiles and giraffes! I say our place is here, where my ancestors worked as slaves on the cotton fields down south. Black sweat made this country into what it is today. To hell if we're supposed to leave it all to the Whites!"

It was, indeed, a strange idea, and one that had never crossed my mind. Yet, back at the port of Marseille when I decided to leave for New York, I'd had the chance. I could've boarded any number of ships setting sail for Tangier, Saigon, Dakar, Cotonou, Libreville, Valparaiso, Tahiti, Pondicherry and plenty other places I've surely forgotten by now. Ah, yes, there were plenty of South American destinations, too, and now that I think about it, I did hesitate between Rio de Janeiro and New York. But Africa! No, I wasn't tempted, not for one split second! As a young girl, I'd accompanied my mother to the pier in Fort-de-France one fine afternoon in April or May of 1880-something. Hundreds of people had come out of the woodwork from all corners of En-Ville, especially the plebeians: idlers, drunkards, sinister-looking vagrants with switchblades hidden in the pockets of their khaki canvas shorts, shitpan collectors and street sweepers, for the most part Indian-coolies. And women, too: laundry maids from Rivière Madame, coal haulers who emptied the bellies of the big transatlantic ships, vegetable sellers, day servants, so on and so forth. It was all for a big to-do that had been spread by bush telephone—supposedly, an African king and his court were being escorted to Martinique because he had revolted against France in a country named Danhomey or Dahomey. Something like that. They were touting him as a sorcerer, adept in voodoo and other odditying, which brought all the crowds out eager to see him. People were already joking about it. "A black king, that's some beautiful business! So, maybe they got carriages and palaces in the jungle? Ha ha ha!"

Others succumbed to a frothy enragering that gathered spittle foam at the corners of their lips, "My skin is black, sure, I know it, but you're trying to tell me that some bugger blacker than last night is glorying with the title *king*? It's nothing but bunch of bullshit!"

"Blacker than sin, you mean!" one man interjected as he looked my mother up and down with hunger in his eyes.

She took me into her arms as the dinghy approached shore, so I wouldn't be smothered by the dense crowd. I saw with my very own eyes a strapping man, dressed in an animal hide and a strange conical hat, coming down off the boat. He was surrounded by a dozen young Blackwomen all baring their naked chests, and he looked out over the universe as haughty as could be. A long pipe dangled from his mouth and a plume of white smoke curled up from his parted lips every now and again. A wave of *oooohs* rose up from the mass of spectators, and the police guards had the worst trouble attempting to contain them on that tiny dock of La Française, where—I'd hear this from my mother's mouth much later—the governor of the colony and his right-hand-men had come to collect that notorious black king who went by the name of Behanzin (the funeral storytellers would later ridicule him as Berzin-d'An-Neuf). The king and his court were locked up at Fort Tartenson, under guard by white soldiers and, little by little, the population began to lose interest in those African oddities. As for me, I remember being struck by how they held themselves with exceeding dignity, especially Behanzin, although I didn't have the words to describe it back then. Well, you see, I discovered that same look of steadfast resolve in Marcus Garvey, the man who hoped to unify all the Blacks of the world from his perch on a Central Park bench there smack-dab in the middle of New York. He preached, not without conviction, a return to the motherland, to Africa, for the descendants of American slaves. The only difference between those two men were their clothes: traditional African garb for the Dahomey revolter and a farcical generalissimo suit for the Jamaican descendant of slaves.

None of this means that I aligned myself with Garvey's enflamed pleas. I hadn't left my Martinique just to become the third or fourth wife of some African despot. I came to America to *conquer* that type. To become somebody, even more than somebody. And, my word, things took a turn for the better after a few years of infamy, since, voila, I'd become the worst nightmare of the most ferocious gangsters in Harlem and even in parts of the Bronx. I succeeded in subduing those two-faced Sicilians, the drunkard Irishmen, the hypocrite Yiddish and, above all, those Anglo-Saxon cops (who all thought they were above the rest of the world just because they were fluent in English and had a Colt .45 at their hip), one after the other. Well, my dear, now I'm starting to get ahead of myself again. Before I rose to the top of the food chain, though, I certainly came across my share of hard knocks....

[DECLARATION OF THE RIGHTS OF THE NEGRO
PEOPLES OF THE WORLD (1920)

Preamble:

Be It Resolved, That the Negro people of the world, through their chosen representatives in convention assembled in Liberty Hall, in the City of New York and United States of America, from August 1 to August 31, in the year of Our Lord one thousand nine hundred and twenty, protest against the wrongs and injustices they are suffering at the hands of their white brethren, and state what they deem their fair and just rights, as well as the treatment they propose to demand of all men in the future.

We complain:

1. That nowhere in the world, with few exceptions, are black men accorded equal treatment with white men, although in the same situation and circumstances, but on the contrary, are discriminated against and denied the common rights due to human beings for no other reason than their race and color.

We are not willingly accepted as guests in the public hotels and inns of the world for no other reason than our race and color.

2. In certain parts of the United States of America, our race is denied the right of public trial accorded to other races when accused of crime, but are lynched and burned by mobs, and such brutal and inhuman treatment is even practiced upon our women.

3. That European nations have parceled out among them and taken possession of nearly all of the continent of Africa, and the natives are compelled to surrender their lands to aliens and are treated in most instances like slaves.

4. In the southern portion of the United States of America, although citizens under the Federal Constitution, and in some States almost equal to the whites in population and are qualified land owners and taxpayers, we are, nevertheless, denied all voice in the making and administration of the laws and are taxed without representation by the State governments, and at the same time compelled to do military service in defense of the country.

Declaration memorized by heart and in its entirety, and in no time at all, in order to soak it up, but also to improve her English, by Stéphanie St. Clair, having been gifted by Mother Nature with an elephant's memory.]

My apologies, my dearest and dearly beloved nephew, if my mind unravels like an old worn out dress. Yes, it's true that I came to see Harlem as the most beautiful place in New York and, therefore, in the whole world. I savored that old saying popular among the most ancient of the Harlemites, "I'd rather be a lamppost in Harlem than governor of Georgia."

Well, speaking of lampposts! Duke, the man I called mine during my first forays into the numbers racket business, (that cheeky old bastard who'd never put all ten of his fingers to work a day in his life), wanted to parade me out on the street just like that Irish moron from the Forty Thieves. That was just my kind of luck with those damned pimps! To hear them talk, you'd think there were mobs of slobbering hounds with a taste for tomboyish women such as myself, and, seeing as there weren't any like me strutting the streets, they figured I'd make a killing if I tried it out. They promised to guard me while I worked to keep back any nutjobs who'd dare knife me after getting what they came for, just in order to get away without having to pay. That actually happened to two young ones on 145th Street, elegant creatures newly arrived from Louisiana with the most deliciously lilting accents. I'd seen them around and occasionally knocked back a couple of scotches with them at the Cotton Club in the depths of the night, which is to say when the rich Whites came to mix with the riffraff and the black mafia boys went home with their arms around a young chick after having sweetened their ears with the sound of the Charleston, the lindy hop and other music I never got a taste for.

I answered Duke with a resounding "NO!" and he took the liberty of slapping me across both cheeks like he did with the whores he controlled and who'd bring him back tidy sums of money. I looked the other way when it came to his operation because my philosophy has always been clear: Men's business is men's business and women's is women's. And anyway, he knew that I'd castrated a man and not just any old man—a white one. A white mafioso. O'Reilly, the most feared leader of the no less feared Irish gang of Forty Thieves from Five Points.

Duke should have been a little more careful around that

scrawny island lady with her French accent. I certainly didn't look like much, but for a man to impose any kind of control over my life was out of the question. I didn't react to those slaps of his right away. I played docile. We went back to our place and on the way there, he began with his sweet talking, calling me honey and taking me by the waist to land kisses all up my neck. *Wait and see, you sonofabitch!* I thought to myself as we walked. "You're going to get it, and sooner than you can imagine." No sooner thought than done. I went to the kitchen, took a fork out of the drawer and plunged it into his right eye. He fell to his knees, trumpeting so loudly in pain that I had to run out of the place before our neighbors came yelling, "Wha'ss goin' on?"

As it was, I didn't know when I left the nightclub that I was going to mess the guy up, so I hadn't planned out an escape. I was still wearing my evening gown, which appeared mighty suspicious to the manager of the grubby motel where I found refuge. Luckily, I had enough money on me to spend a few days there, time enough to be forgotten, especially as scraps between Negroes only vaguely interested the New York police. Why should they bother themselves to open a case when two traffickers in Harlem try to kill each other when they're already turning blind eyes to the white mafia? That's why Lucky Luciano and his associates could sleep so soundly at night. Nevertheless, Duke's henchmen would be hot on my heels, so I had no choice but to leave town as fast as possible to find safety. But where? I had no family in this country, no real friends, no one I could tell about my situation. So, a crazy idea took seed in my head: make it down to New Orleans. I knew it would be a long haul, but it was the only place in the U.S. where I figured I could go unnoticed. Where my accent, French or Creole (the Americans were completely incapable of differentiating), wouldn't betray me. Early in the morning, after a night of tossing and turning, anguished as I was by the slightest creak on the staircase, I dashed to the bus stop and jumped into the first one out: It didn't matter to me where its south-bound route would take me since each minute I spent in Harlem only increased the likelihood that they'd manage to get their hands on me! I knew the price I'd have to pay for lifting a hand against a gangster boss. They'd tie me up and drive me to an empty warehouse in East Harlem, where they'd take turns raping me before putting a bullet in my head, rolling me up in a sheet and tossing me into the East River under the cover of darkness. And it wouldn't make more than three lines in the newspaper the next day or the day after—"The body of a young colored woman was fished out of the river yesterday morning," etc.

Aside from a hoary-faced old bum busy murmuring a blues song under his breath, I was the only colored person on board, but no one paid us any attention. The man didn't even toss me a glance, but then I understood when I saw his white cane. The journey started out smooth, which reassured me. But I jumped when the blind man raised his voice and I recognized Duke's favorite song: *Yellow Dog Blues*. He'd serenade me with it morning till night, and it had started to get on my nerves, but nonetheless, I remembered all the words—even though my English was far from perfect. The man's rough voice drowned out the sound of the motor:

> *E'er since Miss Susan Johnson lost her Jockey, Lee*
> *There has been much excitement, more to be*
> *You can hear her moaning night and morn*
> *She's wonderin' where her Easy Rider's gone?*

Suddenly, to my immense surprise, the other passengers joined in on the next verse, swaying in their seats, their eyes half-closed:

> *Cablegram goes off in inquiry*
> *Telegram goes off in sympathy*
> *Letters came from down in "Bam"*

And everywhere that Uncle Sam
Has even a rural delivery

I was used to the Whites who turned up in the Harlem cabarets on Friday and Saturday nights, Mafiosi with bulging pockets for the most part, but artists and writers, too, or simply admirers of fresh black female skin. The Charleston, the black bottom, the lindy hop or the breakaway no longer held any secret for them. They'd lose control on the dance floors with partners of their race, whom they'd abandon in the middle of the night, or maybe send home in a chauffeured car before seeking out the black or less-black whores on the second floor of these establishments. Nothing out of the norm: Just like in Martinique, hasn't the Whiteman sought out women of color to satisfy his carnal desires for centuries? But there, on the bus, to my astonishment, the passengers were separated by leaps and bounds from those types. They were workers with worn faces and callused hands, women with empty eyes carrying shapeless baskets, some of them saddled with two or three runty kids. The other America! The one no one hears about abroad, and if I had, I would've surely been dissuaded from embarking on that ship from Marseille to New York! Even the driver started humming the blind man's song, and everyone soon forgot about the enormous potholes dotting the road that the bus would hit with a grinding sound that should've worried us. The bus made stops along the way and more passengers boarded, including more than a few colored folk. I'd rarely had the chance to travel by car, and if I feared that modern invention rather less than I did the elevator, I was still far from reassured. I held tight to the seat in front of me and tried to look at ease, then realized that all the other passengers were preoccupied by the same worries. They'd sung *Yellow Dog Blues* in an attempt at rallying up some courage. In effect, the few who hadn't joined in (it quickly became a real hullabaloo) were old ladies in extravagant hats, feverishly rubbing their rosaries.

Seizing my courage with both hands, I asked my closest neighbor, a redneck with rosacea-covered cheeks, the final destination of the bus.

"Are you joking, niggerwoman?" he grumbled rudely. Then, calming down, he laughed, "We're going down South, milady! Toward my father's cotton plantations. Ha ha ha!"

The pleasantry loosened up the other passengers. The sun started to set, and we kept rolling straight on. No stop seemed to be planned and a terrible thirst overcame me. At least I was putting distance between me and Duke's henchmen, but I still sat with one fear: Would I never be able to return to Harlem? Newly blinded in one eye, my old companion and bodyguard would surely be living only to see the day I'd be held to account, and I could only hope for one thing. One single thing: that he might come to an end beneath a rain of some mob boss's bullets, as was often the case in our neighborhood. I said *our* as if I'd been born and raised there, even though I was twenty-nine when I landed there. I had actually, let me remind you, Frédéric—pardon me if my speech has gone unstitched in my old age—spent the first three years of my life in America in Five Points, first with that Irish family, the Mulryans, with whom I got saddled on Ellis Island, then as a part of the Forty Thieves, also Irish. Deep down, I'd practically become a Black Celt, and I liked the sound of their bagpipes parading down the streets in celebration. For a long time after leaving Five Points for Harlem, I'd hear that sound in my head during my bouts with insomnia. Being around that community so much, I managed to pick up quite a few morsels of their language, which sounded so good to my ear, but looked (in my humble opinion) so ugly on paper. Especially *conàs a tà tu?*—a salutation that came in handy a number of times after I'd moved to Harlem and the police started harassing and arresting me under all kinds of flimsy pretexts. A number of their men were Irish or of Irish origin, and invoking this little phrase saved me more than a few times, music as it was to their nostalgic ears.

My seatmate in that rickety south-bound bus had no kind of charitable soul, and I would figure that out quick. Before night fell, the driver stopped at some kind of inn a little way off our track, and everybody, including me, descended from the bus. Except for the Blacks. I was so thirsty that I didn't notice the establishment labeled *Colored* was closed. I called out to the man who had called me "milady," handed him a ten-dollar bill and asked him to buy me a bottle of water. Suddenly he was engulfed in a twenty-devil rage.

"You taking me for your boy, or something, you filthy Negress!? Where'd you steal that money from anyway, bitch?"

The white passengers who were waiting their turn to be served burst out laughing, but not at me; instead, they were mocking the guy that I had the misfortune to solicit. My god, the horror! I had publicly humiliated a White. I got back on the bus, abashed, and the black passengers all started cursing me out with a thunderousness that knocked the wind from my lungs. The blind man, no doubt informed of my blunder, came at me with the most poison.

"You think you're in Boston or Philadelphia or something? These Northern Negresses are stark raving mad... if you'd lived down in Georgia like me, you wouldn't be flaunting that arrogance of yours in front of the Whites. Even after abolition, slavery lives on, and at the plantation where my father toiled to the bone, the overseers still whip any fool who doesn't fall into line."

"Don't bother explaining all that to her!" groaned a surly looking woman in a ridiculous candy-pink dress. "She must be working for a liberal white family. That's it, eh? Those airheaded Whites that are convinced that one day the Negroes will be their equals in this land."

"You're right," another woman weighed in, clenching a Bible to her chest. "We'll get our equality in the next world. Our

Lord Father promises us that. For now, we must endure the pain inflicted on us by God in the name of our ancestor, Ham. The Curse of Ham. Pray, my dear brothers and sisters, for this young lady who's got nothing but a bird's brain in her head!"

As the white passengers filed back into the bus, laden down with provisions of all kinds, the miserous Lowblacks started swaying in their seats again, shouting "Hallelujah!" and "Oh, Lord!" A few whiskey bottles, guzzled down in quick succession, worked to appease the ire of my neighbor and his compeers. The bus turned back onto the road just as night fell. Soon, some among us were completely asleep, snoring and grunting like pigs being led to a slaughterhouse. As for me, sleep had flown the coop so long ago that I can't recall the last time I managed to keep my eyes closed for a full night. Maybe I had back when I first started working for the Verneuils, in Fort-de-France, when the chores I'd been given weighed so heavily on my shoulders, young as I was back then. Or maybe because, for the first time in my life, I was sleeping in a real bed and not on a pallet, even though my tiny room couldn't be called more than a shack. Lost in my reverie, I hadn't noticed that the bus driver had turned down a road that snaked into the countryside. The darkness was cut only by a few distant lights, probably from the neighboring farms. A wordless anxiety descended on me. It was completely unfounded since I had no idea which way we were supposed to be heading, but still, I could feel my throat going dry. My redneck neighbor had been reveling in the lap of Morpheus for a good hour by then, so I pilfered the bottle nested in his huge canvas shirt pocket. That was a truly insane thing to do. All it would've taken was one person to catch me in the act for me to get thrown unceremoniously out on my ass. Alone, black, female, barely able to speak English and on an isolated country road—there'd be nothing left for me to do but hand my soul over to the devil since god surely would've turned his back on me. But all the same, I didn't put any stock in that fable about the Curse of Ham, even clearly written as it was in the Bible. Or rather, I had my doubts that Ham himself had been black. How could he have been when his supposed father, Noah, and his two supposed brothers, Japheth and Shem, were immaculately white-skinned? And not only that, but I couldn't understand why no one had condemned Noah's drunkenness when he took to gamboling naked through the streets before his kind-hearted eldest and youngest managed to catch up to him and drape a sheet around his nudity. The Bible has it in for Ham because he was ridiculed by his father, who chased him from his house, condemning him and his descendants to all kinds of evil, starting with slavery. And until the end of time! The whole thing sounded pretty far-fetched, a hoax, but truth be told, I've never been any kind of Good-Godder. I'd been forced to put up with the First Communions my very Catholic mother had inflicted on me, even though she barely had the means to receive our ceremonial guests with any dignity! Afterwards, once I reached the U.S., I had to get used to the deafening noise of the Adventist, Black Baptist and Evangelist churches, which I found even more maddening.

Suddenly, the bus was surrounded by a throng of hooded men on horseback. They were all dressed in white and brandished torches. Our driver ground to a halt, rousing the passengers from their slumber. Thinking there'd been an accident, two or three old black ladies started praying to the Holy Father, but they snapped back to reality fast. The riders' faces were obscured by their white hoods, their heads topped with long pointy hats, also white. They shouted incomprehensibly and continued their frenzied circling around the bus.

"The Klan! It's the Klan!"

The exclamation of a black passenger who was seated near the front of the bus made our blood freeze. That word alone (no need to say Ku Klux Klan!) was enough to terrorize any man or woman of color, even those who, like me, had never been subjected to their abuses. We'd read in the papers that they burnt down black folks' homes, kidnapped and lynched them, burned them alive tied to stakes. But all of that happened in the *Deep South*, where (I'd learn about this later from the mouth of W.E.B. Du Bois himself) they hadn't yet come to terms with their defeat during the Civil War. But we were no further than maybe 40 miles from New York, definitely heading *toward* the South, but we wouldn't really reach it for another three or four days. I'd have to change buses a few times first. I hardly had a second to plunge myself into speculation. The one that seemed to be the leader of the band—he was wearing a chain around his neck with a huge cross dangling from it—ordered all the black passengers to descend from the bus. His growling voice has stayed with me all these years, having literally liquefied me.

"Get the hell out of that bus, niggerbastards!"

I was sure my final hour had arrived. The Klansmen dismounted and encircled us before lighting a huge bonfire. Their leader separated the men from the women. No one among us protested, nor even opened their mouth. We all knew it would do no good. I still recall the perplexed (and, in some cases, vaguely frightened) expressions on the faces of the white passengers on board the bus. Our aggressors erected a huge post—hacked from the trunk of a tree that had clearly been freshly felled, given its surplus of live branches. They seized upon the old blind man, grabbing him by the collar of his shirt, and violently dragged him over to the post, to which they trussed him. The bluesman remained impervious to this treatment, taking up his favorite song in an even, unwobbling voice:

> *Ever since Miss Susan Johnson lost her Jockey, Lee*
> *There has been much excitement, more to be…*

His voice was so captivating, so profound, that the Klansmen seemed surprised and looked to each other for a cue. But, too quickly, they returned to their senses and two among them rushed the blind man. Sending his hat and white cane flying, they tied his hands behind his back and their leader, completely bent over with laughter, shouted, "Hey, you niggerbastards, what'll it be? Should we hang him to a tree or grill him like a... huh, well, like a what?"

"Like a pig!" one of the Klansmen guffawed.

"Or more like a rack of lamb, seein's how he's got that white wool covering over his head," another goaded.

The night became suddenly cold and I shivered. Curious as it sounds, I was indifferent to the situation back then. I'd fled New York to escape the rage of my lover and in the hope of making a life for myself in New Orleans, but if it was my destiny to succumb in the most dreadful of ways, on an isolated road in the middle of the night, all because of a band of thick brutes who made Negro-hating their reason for living, then what could I do about it? In fact, dear nephew, I'll tell you right now, my fate (if such a thing really exists) was to return to New York! Everything unrolled as in a bad dream: The Klansmen, without waiting for our response (of course, their questions were just a way to mock us further), trussed the old blues singer to the pole and lit it on fire. The white passengers, still seated in the bus, looked like ghosts, like frightened ghosts. The gleam of the flames, already burning bright, flickered against their incredulous and somehow apprehensive faces; in other circumstances, they would've looked rather comical. To my great amazement, the bluesman did not cry out or struggle in any way. It was as if he'd accepted his lot, a kind of Jesus on the Cross. Some of the black passengers must have had the same thought as me because they all began to chant a deeply sad song that I couldn't understand because the words to it seemed to be in some kind of old English. Visibly unnerved, the Klansmen commanded them to shut their traps, striking the bravest singers across their faces with the whips they'd used to spur their horses into the road to encircle our bus not so long before. It must've been quite a spectacle, skilled riders as they surely were.

"These damned niggerbastards are the devil's sons, I tell you!" the leader of the hoods shouted again, pretty shaken up by the unflappability of the old bluesman all throughout his ordeal.

That poor man must've lasted for thirty minutes. Maybe longer, I don't know. I was as if in a trance. As if I was hovering above my body, above the scene. I was indifferent to everything, and it felt like I was in the audience of some dull play being performed by a bunch of shitty actors and everyone already knew what was going to happen. One by one, the black men were hung or burned alive. None of the rest had the same courage as the bluesman, and the thick country silence was transformed into a concert of supplication and howling. Then the Klansmen, who seemed to be wearing out, turned on us, the women. At least, to all the young or young-enough. I had just entered my twenty-ninth year, I had only been in that damned country, the so-called land of dreams, for three short years and voila, I'd already found myself confronted by the worst fate imaginable for a descendant of Ham. The old ladies urged us to hold strong, promising it would only last for a few brief, terrible minutes. That it was a way of atoning for our sins. That Jesus on his Cross and God in Heaven were looking over us and, above all, our souls, because true happiness awaited our race in the afterlife. They psalmodized all this nonsense while swaying and clapping their hands. Never had I felt more distanced from the American Negro as I did in that moment. It hit me, definitively, that I could never become a real member of their community. Never. I had tried, and I would keep right on trying to become a true Negro woman if, by some miracle, I managed to escape my present nightmare, but each night, during those rare moments when sleep actually deigned to take me in its arms, I dreamed of one thing and only one: my native Martinique. Not that I considered returning one day, dear Frédéric, because way back in 1912, the year I left, I already knew it was for good, but because she stayed in me, buried deep inside my being. She was something I could rely on, a secret weapon that helped me overcome the pitfalls of an existence that I could only hope would be the least painful possible. That's why, or perhaps it was thanks to that piece of Martinique—certainly more and more evanescent as time went on—that I managed to grit my teeth when two Klansmen leapt on me and dragged me into the brush. Unlike my sisters in misfortune, I didn't resist or hurl insults at my torturers. I'd turned to ice. As cold and as rigid as that snow that transformed Five Points into a sort of ice floe come February. At first it had enchanted the islander I was, even if my Irish family never ceased to calumny what they called *shitty weather*. I even enjoyed running across the ice, laughing out loud when I fell flat on my stomach, venturing out onto the completely frozen Harlem River with a couple of other risk-takers. That first enchantment never disappeared, even when I stopped appreciating those fleeting and timid rays of sun, which disappeared as soon as they showed themselves, and the deep cold that froze my bones.

The Klansmen didn't bother to undress me. Instead, they tore my dress and underthings and took turns plunging themselves into me with a rage that made their eyes gleam bright behind their hoods. To rally up my courage, I reminded myself that they were hardly any different from the incubus that had attempted nightly to assault me in my shack at the Verneuils', and I wasn't even sixteen yet back then. And I thought about Eugène, their eldest son, and his furtive visits to my bed and how, thanks to some miracle, I never got pregnant. But this time I was fouled, truly fouled. The ejaculate of the hoodeds ran all down my thighs and stank enough to make me gag. I heard the other black passengers lamenting, and the elderly women, whose decrepitude had rescued them from this depravity, continue to plead for the Lord's mercy, the Christian god they so faithfully believed in. Hadn't they realized by now, those poor idiots, that the Klansmen were in no way human beings, but ghosts? Confederate soldiers back from the dead to take out their revenge on the Negro! The first glimmers of day surprised us all—especially our aggressors, who hurried to mount their horses as their leader scolded the stragglers. The spectacle the sun illuminated for us as the clouds parted was one of nameless desolation: The charred body of the bluesman dangled from its post, curled up from the flames; ropes gently swayed in the breeze from the branches of imposing trees that we hadn't been able to make out in the darkness and, swinging from ropes, black men whose pink tongues lolled exaggeratedly from their mouths in a giant *fuck you* to the universe; dazed and disoriented young women, the light in their eyes probably extinguished forever; the white passengers bundled up in their seats, having not succeeded in getting any sleep, some of them furious, others vaguely shamed.

The driver started the bus up again without a word. I noticed that he was half-drunk because he was dangerously zigzagging all over the road. Fortunately, the dirt road was less trafficked than the southbound highway onto which we eventually turned. The bus was almost empty at that point. In any case, he was no longer transporting a single black man. My neighbor, the redneck, the one who'd mocked me with his *milady* address, simply ignored me. He stared out at the road ahead and the houses that whizzed past at an increasing frequency. We were approaching a city, but I wasn't sure which. No way was I going to ask him anything. I was much more preoccupied with the state of my clothes. I clutched the top of my torn dress closed with two hands, but still couldn't quite manage to completely cover my breasts which, fortunately, were not prominent. Finally, we arrived in a dilapidated neighborhood populated by Blacks, many of whom seemed to be at loose ends. The driver ordered us, the Negresses, to get off immediately without even turning the engine off.

"Good luck, milady!" The redneck murmured enigmatically. "You're a brave soul, you know."

Passersby approached us and, noticing our distress, directed us to a tidy looking house. In its window a big sign read *NAACP*— the abbreviation of the National Association for the Advancement of Colored People. I'd had the occasion to hear men from this organization speak, intent on improving the lives of Blacks but, busy as I'd been with the Forty Thieves, I'd deemed it of no use for me to learn more about them. In any case, they welcomed us with unequalled compassion, we who had crossed through a night of hell, pillaged and devastated by those barbarians in white hoods. The city was called Ramsey and wasn't at all on the road to the South, but the Northwest. I'd boarded the wrong bus in my haste to flee New York!

Either way, thanks to those good souls, my darling Frédéric, I would make it back some months later, to New York, never to leave it again....

Chapter Four

From that point on, I rented a room in north Harlem, a fairly vast room equipped with its own bathroom, on the upper floor of a deceptively nice-looking house, at least on the outside. It was pretty dilapidated inside. My landlord, respectfully addressed as *Sergeant Fitzroy* by everybody, had come back from the battlefields of Europe with a jacket decorated with medals. But he never showed them off since, to his mind, all his sacrifices had amounted to nothing. His parents ended their days in miserous filth, and all that remained of them was one damaged photo of his mother seated in a rocking chair, his father on the stairsteps that led up to the narrow stoop of a tiny cottage. As for the young woman he'd left back in Cherokee County, a near-empty town in South Carolina, she hadn't waited for him and had, instead, gotten married. The pension he received as a disabled veteran (he'd lost an eye and limped on his left leg) was just enough to keep the Harlem house, which he'd acquired for next to nothing and had spruced up as best he could, from falling into complete ruin. Although something of a loner, he'd decided to rent out part of the house, and it had apparently been my French accent that sold him on me, seeing as it was out of the question that he'd shelter a *harlot*, a word I'd never heard before and by which he meant a prostitute.

"My combat unit fought in the Battle of the Somme," he declared in a revelry. "And in Belgium, too." Apparently, Sergeant Fitzroy had fond memories of the French, specifically the French women. When he got drunk, which happened at least once a day, he'd brag about conquering the hearts and bodies of French ladies by the dozen. He'd also acquired a fondness for wine there, a topic he loved to bring up with me and that terrorized me: I'd only lived in France a few months and couldn't for the life of me tell the difference between a Burgundy and a Cabernet. I'd try to be vague with my responses, deepening my French accent at these times to seem more credible. See, I'd told everybody that I was born in Marseille. I lived in constant fear that Sergeant Fitzroy would discover my fraudulence, which is why I paid my rent on the thirtieth of every month without fail, even if it meant I'd barely have enough left to keep myself fed. At first, no one could believe that a woman (and a foreigner to boot!) could establish herself as a banker in the numbers game business, which was referred to with various official-sounding terms like *numbers* and *policy*. That last one, *policy*, never sat well with me; it sounded too much like *police* to my ear, maybe because English wasn't my first language. In truth, though, the NYPD never took a real interest in the activity of *niggers*, so long as such activity was confined within the borders of Harlem, completely absorbed as they were with hunting down bootleggers in the white neighborhoods. Turns out I landed in a country of lunatics! It seemed like all anyone could talk about was Prohibition. Based on what I learned from my landlord, who'd figured out—I never knew by what means— how to get his own supply, the law against producing, transporting or selling alcohol had been contrived by a league of women fed up with the way their husbands squandered their salaries in saloons and came back home so drunk they'd end up beating their wives and children at the drop of a hat. A country without alcohol is a daily torture when you're from Martinique. Thanks to centuries of rum commerce, there was always a surplus on the streets, and I was used to swimming in the constant smell of alcohol from my earliest childhood. Whenever I was sick, my mother would rub me with camphor rum or bay rum from the island of Sainte-Lucie. But over here, in the U.S., bootlegging was a white venture, and an extremely lucrative commerce compared to our modest underground lottery business. The Chicago bootleg circuit was run by the infamous Al Capone, and here in New York, one of his fellow countrymen, the Italian Lucky Luciano, ran the show.

Harlem's thirsty! everyone had been hollering since my first day back in the ghetto. *Very thirsty!* At first, I thought they were complaining about a water shortage and hadn't understood they were talking about the obliteration of whisky, gin and beer. That is, until I paid my respects to the only Catholic church in the neighborhood, where the priest thundered on—clearly nearing the end of his rope—about how he could no longer facilitate Mass seeing as there was no more wine. He seized the opportunity to badmouth *those damned protestants* who, according to him, all looked favorably upon Prohibition. "Same goes for the Ku Klux Klan!" he added, his voice lowered.

In truth, I had hardly paid attention to the new Prohibition movement, completely occupied as I was with the prospect of starting all over again in New York City, where the golden rule was to show no mercy, not even to your own race. When the people at the NAACP had graciously repatriated me after providing me with accommodations for four months back in Ramsey, I spent some time roving around the no man's land between the Bronx and Harlem, until the day I heard that Duke, my darling Duke, my bodyguard and lover, had taken a bullet right to the head, caught in a gunfight between the Irish and Italian mafias. The imbecile thought it was a good idea to offer his services to the Crime Syndicate and, thanks to his reputation for ferocity, was recruited on the spot. He landed, in other words, right in the midst of a raging war over control of bootlegging operations, he who'd been lucky enough not to be called for service in the war against the Germans that was just ending! Without a doubt, that bastard had been tramping around with a false name, I bet he even lied to me, the woman he called his *beloved Frenchy* in his moments of tenderness (or, to be more precise, whenever he loosened up a little). Later on, I brought the subject up with Marcus Garvey, who reprimanded me, "But Stéphanie St. Clair isn't your name either! No descendant of slaves has been able to keep their true name. Mine too, Marcus Garvey, is just a combination of Latin and Anglo-Saxon words. Nothin' to write home about! Once we're on the other side of the Atlantic, gods willing, we'll reclaim our beautiful African surnames."

Although I was reasonably intimidated by the vastitude of that man's connections—he who was, back then, trying to raise funds to set up the Black Star Line, the navigation company that would carry out the return to the motherland that was his life's ambition—I was proud to be a St. Clair. Actually, back in Martinique, it was spelled *Sainte-Claire*, and it was only upon reaching Ellis Island that it was peremptorily shortened by the immigration officials. Either way, Sainte-Claire or St. Clair was a pretty name compared to all those Prudents, Petits, Bellérophons, Théophrastas—or worse, Coucounes—with which most of Martinique's people of color had been saddled. I never dared ask my mother about the origin of our name, but she'd sometimes let it slip—in conversations with neighbors down Breadfruit Alley—that she had a white ancestor on her father's side. Not a Béké, but a white villager, a *manant* as they're called. One of those adventurers or tortured souls who'd decided one fine day to set sail from France for the islands of America, hoping to turn a page in their lives. It was a hope as futile as waiting for a male papaya tree to bear fruit. Most of those fortune-seekers ended up ruined by alcohol abuse and the syphilitic thighs of strumpet Blacks or Mulattos, who they'd ultimately end up marrying in an attempt to salvage some semblance of respectability. As for their children, any trace of infamy was erased, mostly thanks to their skin color, which turned out lighter than the *vulgum pecus* and which allowed them to pass as Mulattos or, at least, climb out of the ranks of the Blacks with their pockets full of air. But why didn't we, despite our name, achieve that same feat? I never did find out, since my mother kept her lips shut tight against all matters of her past and person.

So, exit Duke, and with him my fear of returning Harlem and suffering his reprisals. My landlord, the sergeant, had an ear to the goings-on of every nook and cranny of his neighborhood, and he took great pleasure in filling me in whenever the rain kept me inside, since the gambling market never rolled in a storm. He never knew Duke personally, but his reputation of brutality was something of a cause célèbre. His notoriety explained why the Italian mafia had recruited him to do their dirty work—shaking down restaurants (if not quite chic, they were at least slightly so) or nightclubs and casinos, some high-class pimping (which was carried out in underground brothels), rigging the races, overseeing the trafficking of heroin and all sorts of small-time illicit activities. But by the end of the Great War, the juiciest little morsel to get your hands on was the bootlegging scheme, thanks again to that asinine Prohibition story. Even before the end of hostilities in 1917, protests started sprouting up in front of all the bars.

"Because, my dear Stéphanie, those establishments were, for the most part, owned by the German-Americans," Sergeant Fitzroy explained. "These were people who'd called America home for two or three generations, who'd never even set foot in Europe!"

These Americans of Teutonic origins were absolutely the only immigrants with which I'd never had even the slightest acquaintance. It's true that, for the most part, they had done much better than the rest of us, and many of them continued to use the language of their grandparents, especially in their superb Lutheran churches. According to my landlord, they were the scapegoats of a coalition comprised of everyone from Wasps, Italians, the Yiddish and Irish and even the Polish! Down with the Teutons! Bootlegging was on the up-and-up, and clandestine distilleries were sprouting up everywhere, along with equally clandestine bars, the infamous speakeasies that would flourish all throughout Harlem.

"Your Duke worked in high places, my little Stéphanie. As black as he was, they still thought of him as a first-rate gangster, and it was Lucky Luciano himself who entrusted him with eliminating the Irish from the business."

I learned that, during my stay in the town of Ramsey, my ex-lover had spread terror throughout Five Points, the first neighborhood I had called home upon my arrival in America, where my Celtic family probably still lives, unless Angus Mulryan managed to find more interesting work in Manhattan, which had always been his dream. Duke, the big man in his band of pistoleros who pissed on order and shat on law, turned up unexpectedly one night in one of the Irish-operated speakeasies and rained bullets down on anything that moved. With a Tommy gun. Occasionally, he and his men would use an even more expeditious method: bombs. In the blink of an eye, the wops absolutely toppled the green-eyed gingers and, from that moment on, the business was on a whole other level. The quantities of alcohol that the market demanded became too substantial to produce in their small-scale factories, especially as they had to keep their activities under cover. So, Lucky Luciano set his eyes on a scheme that would stretch to America's two neighbors.

"Canada is gorgeous in the summer, dear Stéphanie, though sadly it doesn't last very long. Otherwise I would've moved up there ages ago.... Over on the European battlefront, I rubbed elbows with Canadians. They aren't racist like our Whites here, though they look just like 'em. And they've got a nice little accent, to boot. Ah, and some of them even speak French like you. But I couldn't hold a conversation with them since I don't know your language...."

Duke, my own Duke, who I'd thought of as just another small-time crook, an unrepented ex-convict, just the guy to serve as my protector and stallion, had become a boss bootleg traffic organizer, overseeing exports between the Canadian border and the city of New York. His gang and he were in charge of protecting the convoys that infiltrated American territory on well-forested and seldom-traveled routes. As Sergeant Fitzroy described it, my Duke had become a true boss, respected not only by his Italian employers, but all the other Mafiosi, too. With his name on everyone's lips, even Al Capone himself got wind of his prowess and asked him to come to Chicago, but he refused. And I know why! He was resentful grudge-keeper and didn't want to leave New York until he got his hands on me and made me pay for what I'd done. Half-blind as he was, he certainly never forgave me, and he must've been chomping at the bit—choking on rage, even—as he waited for his vengeance. Without a doubt, he scoured the streets with his one good eye, watching out for any woman who looked anything like me. It couldn't have given him too much work, since nearly every American Negress back then was fat-bottomed and curvy by her thirties. But I knew you by heart, my Duke! And surely he put all his henchmen on the hunt, too, to sink their hooks into a scrawny café-au-lait gal, all spruced up and rambling in a thick French accent. Yes, Duke wanted me dead. No doubt about it! But some unknown divinity protected me, a divinity I nonetheless never worshipped. And surely it was that divinity that pushed Duke to higher ranks, to become a real mob boss, a Sicilian *capo*. To reap his spoils right under the New York Crime Syndicate's nose, all left none-the-wiser. To unload said spoils in the only place where he reckoned they wouldn't catch a grip on his goings-on: the black ghetto.

"They started opening speakeasies all over Harlem," Sergeant Fitzroy continued in a melancholic tone. "Even I became a regular at the one hidden behind the Savoy Ballroom, though I've really only got a taste for wine. Incidentally, the Whites who showed up for the jazz ended up getting their thirst quenched, too! Ha ha ha!"

Duke started stealing whole barrels of the liquid gold for his own profit and playing the nabob, rolling in a show-offy Ford with a white chauffeur, a messenger-boy type from some Eastern European country—maybe Hungary or the Ukraine—who'd failed to make more of himself in America for some obscure reason. I'd seen him a couple times in Harlem, roaming around with a thick book in his hands, stopping the passersby to spread the Good Word. Thinking he meant the Bible, these latter would willingly stop, amused by the idea that a White dared to venture into our black fiefdom (and with a mind to converting them!), but when the nutcase revealed the cover of his book—*Capital*—and started spewing a torrent of incomprehensible sentences, they'd turn their heels and run chop-chop. His slogan still rings in my ears: *Proletariats of the world, unite!* He called for unity between Whites and Blacks exploited by the odious capitalist system, in hopes of creating a society where all were equal. We'd die laughing, because we knew with absolute certainty that we Negroes were at war and every day was a battle. We also knew that our war would never end, and we had only one way out: as winners or as losers. Why on earth had Duke hired that crackpot as his chauffeur? Why didn't he choose one of our own, which would've been much more discreet? I saw it as proof of a frustrated man's inborn arrogance, he who could barely read or write and who had revenge to take on life itself. The fact remains that by dint of his pilfering, his double-crossed wop bosses were forced to cut short the life of that man for whom it wasn't enough to openly defy the unwritten rules of the mafia—the first of which was absolute honesty and devotion to one's superiors—no, he was only satisfied with reaching for the ultimate luxury of humiliating the white race. In addition to the bullet that shattered his skull, his chauffeur, the *Capital* preacher, took two in each of his temples. At least, that's how the newspapers reported it the day after that execution.

So, I was finally free again to roam around my New York City, where they'd started constructing huge, vertiginous buildings of fifteen, twenty, even thirty floors high... even in the colored part of town, or at least in Sugar Hill, where the rich *Coloreds* found refuge. For a long time, I had harbored a fear of walking through that way, since at every building front there'd be a baton-equipped guard ready to chase off any ne'er-do-well who passed by too close. Let's be honest! I'd turned into a scaredy-cat, easily frightened and ready to jump out of my skin at the slightest provocation ever since that frightful episode on the bus with the Ku Klux Klan. The NAACP had generously granted me eight hundred dollars to help me get resettled in New York, but that money melted fast, and if it hadn't been for the generosity of Sergeant Fitzroy (he didn't expect too much in the way of rent monies), I would've found myself on the street like a common beggar. I had to absolutely remake myself. And the faster the better! Prohibition posed some difficulty, even though there were rumors of its eminent abolition. Everyone knew that the city's mayor frequented the 21 Club—in the back rooms of which they served an excellent alcohol imported by the mafia from Europe, after transiting it through a French island off the coast of Canada called Saint-Pierre-et-Miquelon. If the name of that island meant nothing to anyone, and especially not to the natives of Harlem, I could perfectly remember the horseshoe shape of its miniscule archipelago, surely battered by the Atlantic winds, thanks to the afternoons I'd spent leafing through the colored atlases in the Verneuils' library when I was an adolescent servant in their employ.

It was no easy task to worm into the bootlegging game and, especially, to assert myself in it, but it was out of the question that I let myself rot away as a mere small-timer. I came to America to find success in life, get a nice house, have maids under *my* command, hire employees for a company of my own founding and have loving men at beck and call, adorning me with flowers and jewels. It wasn't just a dream, but a certainty that had taken hold of me the instant I left my native Martinique. An old quimbois-sorceress' prophecy had a lot to do with it, too. But a woman in the mafia? That was like a dog aboard a yole (as my mother's favorite Creole proverb went) or an elephant in a china shop, as they say in that *bon français* that I only know from books. To work as a lackey, sure, any gangster, white or black, would willingly take me on. Messenger, pillow talk confidante, odd-hour meal deliverer to messieurs that met in secret, or even—less insignificantly—spy... those were the kinds of tasks reserved for womankind. But as far as I was concerned, I absolutely refused to submit to the subaltern condition they forced on us. A man is a man, a woman is a woman, sure, but I don't see anything that makes us inferior to those pants-wearing, fedora-bedecked fools. I thought all those temperance leagues were ridiculous, for the most part led by white ladies who hunted down moonshine all because they claimed a sober husband would return home at a decent hour and abstain from striking his conjoint. Yes, ridiculous! As far as I'm concerned, I couldn't understand how a man could claim control over my life and even less so how he could dare to raise a hand against me! Oh, sure, I've always been labeled a rebel, a tomboy, a real bullhead since day one! But I've gone on all the same without treatment or cure, living for no one but me, and I'll keep it that way.

If getting a foot in on Harlem's Midwest-made, corn- or tree-bark-based alcohol racket wasn't easy, there was always the *Jake* (we called it Jamaican Ginger) trade, which promised real opportunities. To tell the truth, that stuff got me out of one hell of a mess that had threatened to drag on forever and plunge me into some deep despair. One day I'd gotten sick, which rarely happened, so I reluctantly brought myself to the sergeant's doctor. At least he came highly recommended; the sergeant told me this doctor was the only one who'd managed to heal his war wounds, specifically the knee that had been shot when his regiment was attacked in the Ardennes and nearly made him a martyr. All in all, Dr. Johnson seemed to be a good practitioner… nothing like those charlatans who order you to pull off your blouse and in one-two seconds drag their stethoscope across your back before taking your pulse, mumbling, "I see, I see!" with real gravitas. Then, all slapdash, they hit you with an exorbitant bill as they pretend to be distracted by their superior thoughts. Just another racket, if you ask me.

"Do you smoke?" Dr. Johnson asked me, his voice tinged with paternal concern, though he was clearly younger than me.

"Cigarettes, yes… Chesterfields. Every now and again, I allow myself a nice Cuban cigar."

"You must curb that habit immediately. Your respiration is too weak for your age. I fear for your lungs. How many per day, young lady?"

"Ten, twelve… sometimes twenty, it depends…."

He was starting to get on my nerves, that know-it-all doc with his butterflied bowtie and his accent, which reeked of affectation. The good Uncle Tom that all the liberal Whites (who flattered themselves by claiming to be broad-minded) loved so much. Undoubtedly, he was married to one of those Caucasians, low-born and ugly as sin, who'd been passed over by those of her own color. Here as in Martinique, everyone's trying to lighten the race, but hypocritically, without really admitting it. Oh, those Protestants! Dr. Johnson prescribed a medicine I'd never heard of, Jamaican Ginger. I'm not crazy about ginger, but the minute I heard its Antillean-island name, not far from mine, I ran straight off to the pharmacy. And unlike in the past, those very rare times I'd visited a doctor's office, I immediately tore open the prescription. And after all, despite being a bit too bitter for my taste, wasn't ginger reputed to possess certain aphrodisiac virtues? Maybe this Jamaican thing would reawaken my too-quickly anesthetized sensuality. I'd felt nothing when Eugène, the Verneuil boy, forced himself on me. In that shady hotel in Marseille, I faked it with Roberto, my Neapolitan intrigue, in the hope that he'd take me with him. I'd closed my eyes every time that grumpy beast Duke climbed up onto my stomach. I'd even managed to remain impervious, colder than marble, during my run-in with the demoniac Ku Klux Klan, who had raped me nearly all night long. But when I really look it in the face, the absence of orgasm in my life was never something I was upset about. I never saw it as a flaw, even when my friends, like Shortie or Annabelle for example, recounted their tales of the ecstatic states they'd reached with such or such companion. On the contrary, every man had the same effect on me. Exactly the same. Only their smells differed.

Stupefaction! That famous medicine, so prettily named Jamaican Ginger (and nicknamed Jake), contained alcohol even while Prohibition remained fully in vigor, though admittedly voices were crying out louder and louder for its abolition. Even as cop squads carried out raids on trucks suspected of carting barrels in from Canada or on the speakeasies that they'd ransack at the drop of a dime, tearing apart distillery operations piece by piece. I noticed it right when the first drop touched my lips. Although I'd never been a real drinker, I definitely enjoyed my little glass, usually away from prying eyes. Martinican rum, wine in Marseille and, once I got to America, gin and whisky. Alcohol. The taste was good. Not only did this medicine dissipate my desire to smoke (though I still carried around a cigarette holder), but it also put me in a suspiciously euphoric state. I hadn't sung one note for such a long time, but once I swallowed the dose prescribed by the doctor, I started belting out an old beguine of Saint-Pierre's that evoked a certain Marie-Clemence:

> *Marie-Clemence maudit! Tout baggage li maudit!*
> *Patates bouillies'lles maudit! Madadanm li maudit!*

Roïï, larguez moin! Larguez moin! Moin ké néyê cô moin
Dèriè gros pile roches la dans grand lanmè blé a…

Catching the sonority of my Creole, my closest neighbor got all riled up with an unknown glee. She was a middle-aged, crotchety sort of woman who only spoke to Sergeant Fitzroy once in a blue moon, and most certainly never gave *me* the time of day, surely casting me in her mind as an imported frog. I caught her one day talking dirty about me in front of my landlord, and when she thought I was out of earshot, she tossed a *foreign bitch* out in my direction. That insult left me completely indifferent; I didn't come to America for anybody else's jollies and definitely not for those of the American Negro. I was me, and to hell with the rest, even if I'll always feel gratitude for the NAACP for all they did after that episode with the Ku Klux Klan. Stéphanie St. Clair didn't owe anything to anyone and certainly had never asked for anyone's charity. I'd accepted the helping hand of those defenders of the Black cause, but I never asked for it. In any case, even if it took time, I'd get back on my own feet once and for all. I've never been the self-pitying type, even as a girl in the grips of that eldest son Eugène…. I wonder whatever became of him. Is he a lawyer like his Papa? Or maybe a doctor or pharmacist? Worst case, he became a teacher at his old school, Schoelcher. I've caught a smile on your face, my dear Frédéric! You'll tell me what that maniac has made of himself later, eh? In my time, all the bourgeois Foyalais kids had their lives already set out for them, while we the reject-plebes, had to invent something for ourselves. Well, I'm exaggerating. We *tried* to invent lives for ourselves. Failing that, our destinies were all laid out for us too, although quite differently: The boys would end up working in the port of Fort-de-France as porters for some shopkeeper or some Big White Creole, or maybe they'd become masons, carpenters or municipal trashmen. The girls were bound to become servants, street sweepers, coal haulers, or mothers to marmy-broods of turbulent little brats a dozen-heads strong. Has all that changed now, dear nephew? For my part, I'd shunned that gloomy fate and wasn't about to let myself be intimidated by a shrew whose companion had probably abandoned her years ago and who still hadn't managed to find herself a replacement. But she was seized by a mad laughing fit when she heard the Creole jubilating out of my mouth, a deep hearty laughter, that jostled up the nearby folks (mostly idlers who got by on odd jobs in the trafficking market).

"Listen dat girl! Ha ha ha! She speakin' African! Ha ha ha." Then, all of a sudden sobered, she said in a solemn voice, "If you've got that kinda joy in your heart, honey, instead of flayin' our ears with that catscratch from the jungle, I'll teach you a real gem. Wanna hear it?"

I nodded, half-drunk thanks to that madcap medicine meant to squelch my tobacco addiction, that Jamaican Ginger blessed with the power to turn your head into a spinning top even before it reached your throat. Sergeant Fitzroy regarded me with newfound astonishment. He allowed me to rent one of his rooms because he had a good impression of me from our first meeting. He proved to be a very obliging man when it came to my late rent, because he could sense I was an honest type of gal. Then voila! Without warning, there I was, drunk like any old wino!

"Alright, repeat after me, young lady!" our neighbor continued, merrier and merrier. With difficulty, impeded by my inebriated state and imperfect grasp of English, I obeyed.

> *Oh, dere's lots o' keer an' trouble*
> *And ol Sorrer's purty lively*
> *In her way o' gittin' roun*
> *Yet dere's times*
> *When I furgit 'em*

As the Jamaican Ginger's effect began to wear off, I began to understand the meaning of the song, which I caught myself humming with a mixture of scorn and superstition. After all, why shouldn't it have had a soothing effect on me? Except for the fact that the man in question forgot his troubles with the banjo in his hands, whereas I had no means of escaping from the dead-end my life had turned into. Sure, I'd been able to come back to live in Harlem, and Duke's menace was no longer a sword of Damocles, but I was only getting by. I was still far from being able to realize even a crumble of a dream in this country, which seemed to offer them more generously than any other country in the whole vast world. Lucky for me, Prohibition and Jamaican Ginger would, at least temporarily, save my hide. Sergeant Fitzroy, after tasting it, declared that it contained more alcohol than medicine. This fortuitous discovery got me thinking hard for days and nights on end, right until I decided to open up to a small-time gangster, a rigged race specialist who'd been hanging around me for a few weeks. His name was Ed, and he lived just four doors down from mine. The animal had my comings and goings on surveillance, drenching me in compliments and little gifts that I systematically refused: contraband perfumes, stolen jewelry, things like that.

"It's the Good Lord that's sent you, Stéphanie!" he jubilantly exclaimed when I alluded to the Jamaican Ginger. "I'd always believed that he only favored the Whites, but there you have it, without doubt, he really did think of us after all, we po' Blackfolk."

I let some time go by to think about what he really was driving at. When he unveiled his plans to me, I played the skeptic, because to make booze out of corn or tree bark in a hidden distillery was one thing, but I couldn't see how we were supposed to procure that plant, the ginger, from an island so far away as Jamaica. Not to mention, we'd have to find a chemist who'd agree to prepare the recipe and make it look, to the eyes of the law, like it was just medicine and nothing more. Inconceivable! Ed gave my remarks serious consideration and, thus, escalated what would become our business, fantastic as it seemed at first blush. But it became a reality, step by step. Primo: Exert some pressure on the docs in Harlem and the Bronx so that they dole out prescriptions for Jamaican Ginger to anyone we suggest, but not without some small retribution for their efforts. For anyone proving to be too stubborn or else too scrupulous: a back alley, where we'd help them to see reason. In general, the cold barrel of a pistol against the temple was enough to bring around the most fervent admirers of the U.S. Constitution, who'd in no time at all manage to dispose of their loftiest principles without even the raise of an eyebrow. As for the malingerers, we'd win them over, too. A few dollars never did any harm to those types festering out on the street, living off scraps salvaged from restaurant dumpsters. In Harlem at that time, there were whole regiments-worth of them! My job was to drum up these poor souls, the ones who appeared be suffering enough to be credible when they presented their prescriptions to the pharmacists. In effect, circumventing those whitecoats would've been way too risky, since their dispensaries were under constant watch by the formidable brigades of the NYPD. Medicine delivery was strictly controlled, and all suspicious packages were immediately seized and their addressees escorted to the closest police station for an interrogation that could lead directly to prison. And not just any, but the one with the most sinister reputation: Rikers Island.

"We'll start off modestly," Ed laid out the scheme. "We'll see how things go and if everything's OK, then we'll take it up a notch. How's that sound, Stephie?"

Not only did this ass call me "Stephie," a childish name I hated, but he went so far as to promise me marriage once our enterprise saw a profit. I went along with it all, interested in none of it except for the Jamaican Ginger. I needed to get my head above water as fast as possible. To hell with getting nowhere! I couldn't conceive of marinating in my own juices with no prospects for even one more second. To my great surprise, our operation was up and spinning like a wheel. Flattered that I'd take an interest in them, passing like I did as one of those good Sisters, intrigued by my accent, or taking me in as a piece of eye candy (as I know some of them did), not one hunger-dying man refused the deal I offered in my feigned-compassionate voice. By the month's end, Ed and I had the satisfaction of splitting six thousand dollars. Later, much later, when I'd become Madam St. Clair, Queenie, the queen of Harlem's illegal lottery and all those other flattering names they bestowed upon me, that sum would come to seem pathetic! Ridiculous even. But at the moment, I was bounding with joy. My first act as a woman with pocket change was to pay Sergeant Fitzroy all that I owed in back rent.

"Is everything working out as you hoped, my girl?" he asked me, perplexed.

"Well, yes, it's all happening.... Why?"

"Good, then.... Take care of yourself! Harlem's getting more and more unlivable."

The Great War veteran was in no way duped. He knew perfectly well that the sudden boost in my financial condition couldn't have been a product of *legal* activity. I had no skills to speak of, nothing that could turn me into a nurse, ballet dancer, blues singer, mailwoman or rail worker overnight. The only luck I'd had was five good years of primary school on my native island and, of course, the Verneuils' library, which I'd pillaged on occasion. I could read and write better than most Harlemites, even in English, thanks to my excellent visual memory. The only worry in that department was pronouncing that damned *th* sound, which I ended up giving up on, anyway. Eventually, I realized that those little faults in my English only added to my charm, and I learned fast how to exaggerate my French accent (or rather my Creole accent, but as I think I mentioned earlier, my dear Frédéric, it was all the same to the Americans) when I had to start something with those chumps who underestimated me on account of my scrawniness.

I figured out a lot more quickly than my associate that our little business wasn't going to last forever. As it was, pressure against Prohibition was on the rise everywhere and not only from alcohol-lovers. The fact was that the intended effect never came to pass: Husbands continued to batter their wives for the slightest reproach from the latter, the thirst-stricken turned to heroin and—worse still—the mafia had figured out how to evade the traps set by the police brigades and were getting away with most of their exploits. Clearly, Prohibition was a total failure. A *HUGE MISTAKE!*, as the prestigious *New York Times* dared print on page one. Unlike my business associate, Ed, who seized the day and spent his money without even counting it, I started to turn things over in my head. Particularly because I couldn't ignore the debilitating effects that Jamaican Ginger had on our heavy-using clients: paralysis of the limbs, partial-blindness and other horrors. For his part, Ed didn't give a rat's ass! So, I started saving—ten dollars a week, then twenty, even up to a hundred when sales were good. As luck would have it, my associate stopped trying to woo me as soon his revenues allowed him to court creatures much more appetizing than myself. While prospecting here and there, I noticed that the gambling scene, which I'd first assumed to be a trifling thing not worth getting involved in, not even for a penny, was a kind of lottery parallel to New York City's—they called it the *numbers* and it had everyone enthralled, thanks to the gigantic pots of cash they could win. When I looked into it more, I realized that numbers, also called *policy*, only concerned Harlem and no other neighborhood. It was an unofficial lottery, but apparently tolerated, since the gambling collectors continuously solicited me right in broad daylight. Even Sergeant Fitzroy submitted bets to it, but with less and less conviction.

"I've never met anybody who got rich playing the numbers, Stéphanie. But the bankers, the guys collecting all the bets, those are the fellas with full pockets, I suppose," he answered when I pried him for intelligence about the subject. "Some of them even roll in gold-plated automobiles!"

That very day, I made a promise in my brazen little head to one day become a banker, even if it seemed like a cockamamie scheme coming from someone who was not only a woman, but a foreigner to boot. I set about studying the system and followed around even the shadiest of collectors and bankers who lingered on our street. I decided to give gambling a try, to see what it'd be like. Oh, nothing crazy! Just a few dollars. As my landlord predicted, I didn't win a cent, nor on the day after, nor the day after that. I wondered why people kept investing their dimes in an obvious rip-off, but I came across the answer the day I saw a woman dancing like crazy in the street, twisting and gyrating all over herself, hurling her voice into the sky, her eyes bulging. She'd just won twenty thousand dollars. True, it was after losing almost daily for a solid dozen or so years. I recalled a bittersweet sentence that my mother loved to repeat, "Hope keeps you alive." I realized that hope was the basis, the foundation, of Harlem's illegal lottery.

I'd become a banker no matter what the cost! It was decided.

Better yet — but now this was a stretch toward megalomania — I'd reorganize everything and name a boss, or more precisely a bosslady: me, Stéphanie St. Clair. Every banker worked for himself and had a dozen or so bet collectors. I'd change all of that by erecting a pyramid, and at the top, of course, would be me. Right below me, I'd have four or five deputy bankers in charge of controlling the swarm of subaltern bankers, who'd be charged in turn with leading the horde of bet collectors. Even to me, this scaffolding was delirium-making, but Stéphanie St. Clair was never afraid of any challenge. When I'd managed to save a tidy thirty thousand dollars, I quit that racket to Ed's great displeasure — that poor shmuck thought he'd be living the good life ad vitam aeternam. It must be said that *monsieur* never read the newspapers or listened to the radio. Did he even know the name of New York's mayor? I doubted it.

"Stephie!" he implored. "You can't do this to me, darling. Don't you see how smoothly things run between us? Is there something you need? Ahh, I see, I promised to marry you back then. It's true, I can't deny that. Well, if that's what's crawled up your skirt, let's go see Pastor Roberts! Even if you're Catholic, I'm sure it'll be no inconvenience to him...."

"Marry a yokel like you?! That must be one your stupid jokes!"

"D'you hear how you're talking to me, Stephie? What did I do to deserve this kinda treatment? Not *once* did I ever try to swindle you, though god knows how many chances I had... please, I'm begging you! Don't abandon me like this, Stephie!"

And right there, I swung him one of the very first insults I learned when I landed in America and that, later, I'd come to use in the same kind of circumstances, "Go fuck yourself, Ed!"

In an instant, the oaf changed completely. The ardent, bashful lover — phony as he might've been — transformed into a ferocious beast who charged me and dealt a violent blow to my head. I staggered and nearly lost consciousness. We were in his flea-ridden apartment that day. My face hit that filthy, unswept floor and, before I could get up, he landed a kick in my stomach. I couldn't breathe. Ed howled, totally outside himself, "Dirty black bitch! I'll destroy your smelly French ass."

I have no idea where the reserve of strength came from, but I grabbed one of his legs, staggered to my knees and knocked him down hard. Turned out he'd reached the end of his luck: As he fell, his head smashed against the edge of a table, breaking his neck. I sat stock-still for a long minute. A heavy silence reigned over the apartment. I didn't know how to react. Killing for a second time in my relatively young life was nothing to delight in, even if I'd acted in legitimate self-defense and had never intended to send my associate from life to the hereafter. But I came to grips quick, fixed my hair and clothes and fled the building. Once in the street, I acted casual, tried not to look over my shoulder too much and walked with a quick step. Ed's body wasn't discovered till three days later and the police concluded that it was a burglar attack, which was completely plausible. Sergeant Fitzroy, convinced that I was in love with the dead man, presented me with his sincerest condolences. I couldn't help but laugh to myself. That small time malandrin-crook was just an uninteresting episode in the life I'd promised myself to lead. Dust in the wind that left no trace on my path.

I put ten thousand dollars in the bank for my first lottery on April twelfth of 1917. It was down on 143rd Street, where the gamblers and bankers were all plentiful. They all looked askew at me, but it didn't take me long to bring them to heel, which I'll explain in just a moment, my dear Frédéric....

Second Note

I never cared much for moonlit skies
I never wink back at fireflies
But now that the stars are in your eyes
I am beginning to see the light
I never went in for afterglow
Or candlelight on the mistletoe….

—Duke Ellington (1927)

Chapter Five

At the transatlantic company, no one believed Stéphanie when she asked where she could by a ticket for En-France. Despite her twenty-six years, she had a childlike air, undoubtedly because of her lithe body and high-pitched voice. And, perhaps, it was also because women of all ages had been lining up to try to get enlisted as coal haulers since daybreak. Dressed in raggedy old clothes that they'd given up trying to keep clean, their faces smudged with soot, they hummed under their breaths to rally their courage while awaiting the commander's arrival. That brutal-mannered Mulatto, who'd never bestow a *hello* upon anyone, seated himself behind a wobbly table in his workman's hut and began consulting a hardbacked notebook in which he'd written down the names of the lucky few who, in the preceding days, had received approval to cross the docks toward the bellies of enormous ships filled with charcoal by means of a gangway ladder so unstable that they'd be retching by the end of three trips. In truth, *trip* was too benign a word, too lovely even, to describe that crossing from the En-Ville port up toward the Levassor canal, along the Levee boulevard, lugging enormous baskets on their heads under a villainous sun, the whole process of which would have to be repeated at least ten times over to make even a pittance. See, each coal hauler had gaggles of marmy-scamps (often numbering up to eight or nine) trailing behind her since the male spawners (those raildogs) of said progeny had long ago abandoned them without so much as a thank-you-good-bye. In the very beginning of the new century, twentieth by name, misery roved mercilessly throughout the neighborhoods of the suffering Lowblacks, accompanied by an array of death-door-knocking illness: flu, yellow fever, pertussis, small pox and plenty more.

Ever since she'd been fired from her servant job at the Verneuils', Stéphanie had worked a fair share of vocations,

96

but she'd sworn she'd never degrade herself by becoming a coal hauler, which she saw as a task reserved for humanity's lowliest dregs. But soon enough, circumstances forced her to leave Breadfruit Alley after a knockdown dispute with Louisiane, her mother's neighbor who imagined herself capable of assuming the latter's role and who figured it was her life mission to remind Stéphanie how her mother had sweated blood and water to assure her a good family. Only to go and waste her own future.

"Pis ou konpwann ou vini gran fanm, pwan kay-ou!" Louisiane yelled at her, daring to suggest that young Stéphanie's adulthood claims were betrayed by her rather unadult behavior. In fact, as Louisiane added, all of her mother's possessions had been sold to relieve her debts at the neighborhood boutique and to cover her funeral services.

Louisiane had negotiated with the soon-to-be buyer and managed to convince him to give Stéphanie some time to find a new place to live. But the mamzelle was milking it for all it was worth! That night, Stéphanie slept under a blanket of stars, an ironic expression if ever there was one, especially considering that it was the middle of winter and, as such, violent gushes of icy rain showered down on En-Ville at intervals. Her meager possessions tucked into a caraïbe, she'd first wandered along the Démothène bridge, then headed toward Carenage, before ending up at the Levassor canal, where she found refuge in a boat shack. She'd eaten nothing but one lousy plate of red beans seasoned with salted pig tail, which she'd purchased from a street vender at the edge of the Grand Marché. Her stomach grumbled. Although she'd managed to find a weather-proofed shelter, her arms and legs were still being worked over by squadrons of mosquitos, making even the idea of rest an impossibility. Bord de Canal, the neighborhood's far edge, was plunged in mortal-sin darkness, which in no way impeded the stray dogs from howling and prowling every which way. Arming herself with a heavy round rock, Stéphanie decided to venture to the delta, where she hoped the sea wind would make her stay less arduous. And indeed, the mosquito's rampaging subsided and the noise from the backwash, faint at that late hour, reassured her. It was a clear enough night that Stéphanie could see well into the distance and spotted a shack filled with boating equipment, in which she sought shelter. Suddenly, a cry tore through the night, a sort of half-human, half-animal yowl that sent a deep trembling down the girl's body. It was coming from the shore, but even with her eyes wide open, Stéphanie could see no creature. No sooner had she looked away than an old woman materialized not far from her and started sniggering maliciously. She was in a seated position, but there was no chair supporting her, which iced Stéphanie's blood.

"Yéééé yééléé! Yééélélé!" the woman, who could be nothing but an ally of the devil, a quimbois-sorceress, intoned.

Stéphanie had a deep desire to flee, but her legs had become gelatinous and a light trembling had settled in the rest of her body. And that's when the old black woman tranquilly removed her head, placed it on her knees and began to groom and delouse her frizzy hair, gleefully gulping down each bug she trapped between her fingers. Mauve flashes of lightning streaked the sky above the ocean, which started to rumble even while the surface appeared calm. Stéphanie wanted to pray to the Good Lord but having paid little attention during catechism—not to mention that she'd jabbered gibberish nightly when her mother used to nudge her to her knees beside her bed-pallet in order to recite Our Father – her lips were paralyzed.

"Vini'w pa isiya, ti mafi! Fok pa ou pè nennenn, non!" the old woman's head cried out, urging young Stéphanie closer and insisting she had nothing to fear from the old granny whose head rested calmly on the lap of the demon's ally.

To her immense surprise, Stéphanie felt the fear that had

immobilized her there, smack in the middle of the cold night, begin to dissipate. Inexplicably. She felt her body moving toward the shoreline as her feet felt their way over the stones so as not to lose her balance. The quimbois-sorceress, imperturbable, set her head back onto her neck and called out to Stéphanie with a large toothless smile. Her eyes were two dark holes and, in them, Stéphanie saw the glowing embers of minuscule red points. She then gestured mysteriously toward the waves, which immediately stopped.

"You haven't come here by accident, young lady," the creature said. "Nothing's an accident, despite what those imbecilic humans might believe. As for me, I who went up to Galilee the day after slavery was abolished, it's been a long time since the light of the sun was anything more than a memory. But I've been making the journey between the hereafter and the here and now ever since. A mission was confided to me, to protect those for whom the higher forces have forged a destiny. What's your name?"

"Stéphanie... Stéphanie Sainte-Claire...."

"Pretty.... Yes! A very pretty name, indeed. You were born under a lucky star, my beautiful. Understand, not everyone is blessed with a destiny! Most people in the here and now live perfectly ordinary lives, from cradle to grave, even those who strut about, taking themselves to be more highfalutin than they are. Well, come here! Sit down beside me. I'm going to fix your hair...."

The night was growing darker, enormous clouds obscuring the skies. En-Ville was just a shapeless mass of darkness in the distance, pierced only by the blue-green light of the occasional streetlamp. The young girl obeyed. Without the slightest apprehension. The sand was moist under her skirt. The quimbois-sorceress unwound her hair, which was tied up in a madras-coco-zaloye scarf, the solid-colored kind worn around the house while doing one's chores. Stéphanie only wore her one very beautiful red-yellow-green madras, which her mother had given her the day she was hired by the Verneuils, for very important occasions. The young girl suddenly felt a strange vibration in her hair. A luminous comb was straightening her hair with stupefying speed. At least ten times faster than the hot iron her mother used to set over hot coals every Saturday afternoon. The young girl hated that ritual that almost every woman down Breadfruit Alley underwent with the goal, as they put it, of beautifying themselves for the men who wouldn't bat an eye toward crimpy-haired ladies. Having neither smooth nor crimped hair, Stéphanie had no need to burn it, and the smell that resulted from the operation made her retch. It turned her liver, *lui soulevait le foie*, as she'd say in her creolized French of the time. The old sorceress passed and repassed the comb through her hair in a cursory way, sometimes scraping her scalp as she shaped her hair into a curiously conical style, which she was eager to see in a mirror. As if that woman, who had the power to remove her head from her body like an ordinary hat, had read the girl's mind, she put the palm of her left hand in front of her eyes. Stéphanie gave out a little cry. She saw herself there, elegantly dressed in a shimmering gown, decked out like a stage actress, seated nonchalantly in a plush armchair, dragging on a long cigarette holder. Well, it wasn't quite her, but her in a dozen, maybe even twenty years from now! Yes, it was certainly her, but older. She was recognizable by the sharp mongoose smile, the sly-seeking eyes, her slightly serious forehead, her café-au-lait color (though more coffee than milk).

"Mi kon sa ou ké yé!" the sorceress murmured, alluding to Stéphanie's future self. Then, she coiled herself up with a rustling sound and wisped up toward the firmament.

Stéphanie was speechless until daybreak, convinced it had all been a dream. Then, pulling herself together, she walked toward the city's newest neighborhood, Terres-Sainville, which was a sort of swamp that was becoming progressively filled up by people who'd come up from the countryside. No precise intention guided her steps. Arriving at the door of a barbershop, she was whistled at by the proprietor, who'd been waiting in vain for customers.

"Has the charming little mamzelle lost her way or what? I know her, but she doesn't know me. Ha ha ha!"

"Tjip!" Stéphanie hissed.

"Come on, no need to be short with me, please! What's your name? I see you pass by on the Levee boulevard pretty often, you know. I can help you if you want...."

Stéphanie was about to turn back, but a sixth sense compelled her to lend an ear to the charmer. He was well into his forties and wore a beautiful goatee groomed with exquisite care. The man, who introduced himself as Philibert, invited her in so ceremoniously that she started to loosen up a little. He sat her down on the swiveling chair that normally hosted his clients and set about fixing up her hair, all while pardoning himself for not knowing his way around a lady's hairdo, which is, after all, a much more delicate science than that of men's. He talked and talked and talked until Stéphanie's head started to spin. Exhausted from her agitated night, she ended up dozing off. When she awoke, she was laying on the clean sheets of some bed while the barber, who was seated at her bedside, fanned her with a newspaper. Although the windows of the salon were all wide open, a heavy heat filled the place. Philibert was shirtless. He began fondling her neck, then her breasts, before venturing toward her belly, all with a gentleness so extraordinary that she shivered. Normally, she would have shrunk back and brushed off the stranger's hand, but something prevented her from doing so. He carried on for a good hour or so, until spasms seized the girl and sent her arms flying up around his neck. He laid himself on top of her carefully and started making love to her, neglecting no part of her body. Stéphanie was convinced that she had gone on up to heaven. She didn't know whether it was day or night anymore, having lost any notion of time, her mind now emptied of its shadowy chimeras, a soft moaning escaping from her lips. The couple remained entwined for quite a time, until Philibert finally lifted himself up and went off to the bathroom. Stéphanie could hear him bathing noisily. Out the window, the amber afternoon sky gradually became painted with ribbons of pearl-gray clouds.

"Will you live with me?" the barber's deep voice made her jump. It seemed to have aged a bit since he first called out to her, but the extreme kindness in his eyes, which had immediately captivated the girl, was unchanged.

"We don't know each other, monsieur...." she stammered.

"Don't call me *monsieur* anymore, please! I'm Philibert. Maybe you don't know me, but I know you. As I said, I've often seen you pass by on Saturdays, looking so proud, walking so upright, so indifferent to everyone. I've admired how you carry yourself, your head held high, but I suspect you have quite some character, don't you? Ha ha ha!"

The barber sat at the edge of the bed. He seemed hypnotized by Stéphanie's naked body, even after she pulled the sheet up to her belly button. He repeated his request in a firmer tone.

"I'm going to leave, monsieur... I mean, Philibert. I'm leaving this country for good."

"Ha ha ha! You make me laugh, you know. And you're going where, if it's not too indiscreet of me?"

"To America...."

"Oh, I see! America, that's all anybody's talking about these days. They swear it's paradise-on-earth or something near it. But don't you think we live well here in Martinique?"

Stéphanie made no response. In sum, Stéphanie spent thirteen days with Philibert, a skilled barber whose salon was truly abuzz with clients starting at nine in the morning. Thirteen days of innocent and crazy love, of total happiness, of mutual intoxication, of sweet folly, of total stark-ravingness. Every night, the barber asked the same question, and Stéphanie gave the same reply. He dwelled between despair and fatalism. She'd watch as he rose just before daybreak, quietly opened the window and leaned there, his eyes fixed to the sky as if he were waiting for some higher being to come to his aid. When, one fine morning, Stéphanie announced that she'd purchased her ticket for the boat and that she was planning to cross the Atlantic, he was struck dumb. When the time came for her departure, he pushed an envelope into her hand filled with wad of cash and handed her—who would've guessed—a brand-new razor.

"Life's hard in America, or so they say. Take this! The customs agents won't take it from you if you put it in a satchel with a brush and comb. Tell them you're a hair stylist and voila!"

Chapter Six

That sonofabitch Dutch Schultz, I always knew he wouldn't waltz his stooped carcass around this Bondié goodlord's land for long, not with that Yiddish-speak of his spewing from his giant angry gob of a mouth. I used that idiotic *Bondié* expression because, after twenty-some odd years in America, it's almost all I have left of my native land, my Martinique. At this point, I can jabber through a little Irish, I've got my English and Italian down pretty well, and I can chat my way through Yiddish and Spanish, too. But I've almost lost my Creole, my own Creole, because there's no one here to talk to. Only at night, when thoughts of my land bubble up in me, do I find myself galloping back home; other than that, I can't get to it anymore. My open-sesame has been French, a language that impresses the riffraff as much as the well-to-do's, especially when it comes leaping from the mouth of a Negress! Whenever it fell on me to call one of my bankers or bet collectors (that is, if I suspected them of giving me the shaft), I'd first speak in a very reasonable English, passing them pleasantries about the weather and asking them about their little families. Then once the fish was hobnailed and I'd assembled the necessary facts to prove that the imbecile had tried to cheat me, I, Queenie, queen of Harlem's numbers racket, would burst into French. Like the time when—that was back in 1921, if memory serves—a tall and lanky Negro (long kon Mississippi, like we say in Creole) named Terence, who officiated between 137th and 140th in a shabby spot fixed up to some semblance of a restaurant, started bringing back two times less, then three, then ten times less than the usual wagers.

"The war's barely over, Madam St. Clair," he mumbled. "The Negroes were already strapped for cash, now they're flat broke! We got to wait till things get better, ma'am...."

Terence was a cheeky liar. Oh, it's true enough that their

diabolic war—whose first cannon blast had gone whistling into silence—had turned our lives completely upside down, and many enterprising young people had lost theirs in it, but at no point had the lottery stopped. Neither the official lottery we'd taken the liberty of copycatting (although, more often than not, we took our numbers from the New York Stock Exchange), nor ours. Our damned *policy game*, as the Negroes called it when they felt like fluffing their feathers, or just *the numbers*, as the cloak-and-dagger types referred to it. No matter what you called it, it had held out for four long, conflicted years because it was a just-for-kicks kind of gambling. You didn't need but a fistful of change to get in on the game, and even that could mean the difference between sinking into ruin and living flush. Terence normally brought in about three thousand dollars, plus an extra thousand on Thursdays and Saturdays, and I'd keep half. But one fine day he showed up with the most idiotic expression imaginable plastered across his face, babbling on about how nothing was going off in his sector anymore, then handed over four hundred lousy fivers rolled up in a wad of newspaper.

"And why is that, hmm?" I asked him, chewing on the end of my cigarette-holder.

"Miss Queenie, it's got me beat, I just don't know...."

He tried those theatrics on me the next day, and then again the day after, assuming a dopier and dopier face at every turn, thinking that a foreigner like me wouldn't know a thing about the monkeyshine Negroes put on in front of their superiors when they're screwing them over. In Martinique, it's called doing the black-rhesus-macaque. Back in slave times, it was used on the white plantation masters who controlled everything, the Békés, that is. Over here, in Harlem, they saved it for the leaders of black gangs and, by extension, me (the only member of the supposed fairer sex who dared stand up to that band of ruffians who thought women nothing but a pair of tits and a fat ass). Terence never knew where I came from, and if he'd known, he would've been utterly incapable of locating my island on a map. And even if he managed to do that, it's highly improbable that an illiterate like him would ever have known that slavery existed back there, nigh longer and more savagely than it ever did in his country. The few times he'd heard French escape my lips (and to tell the truth, it was a rarity around him), he'd fix me with a downright bewildered look. One glance was enough to know exactly what was running through his mind, "Where on earth did she come from? What a weird old Negress!"

As it happens, the bastard was screwing me over. At least that's what I was convinced of, so I cut him down to size, but in my own language—French, of course, "Terence you little shit, what d'you take me for, huh? You think you can double-cross Madam Queen, back me up against a wall, that's what you think? Get out of my sight and watch your Negro ass—if you bring me a shitty little wad like that again tomorrow, just see what happens. Beat it on out of here and take your low-grade pennies!"

I tossed Terence's measly wad to the ground and turned my back to him while he cut his eyes over to Bumpy for back-up (he was my newest bodyguard and squeeze, and also the man with whom that little shit debased himself in the speakeasies during that time of Prohibition). My 140th Street banker picked up the money strewn across the ground, shamefaced, and tiptoed out of the room. He must've been as afraid of elevators as I was because that beastly contraption's old whine never rang out when he disappeared from my sight.

"Frenchie, we got a problem. A big problem...."

Bumpy's voice was abnormally calm and that was never a good sign. Like the time I sent him off to bawl out Brandon, one of my dingbat collectors, because he'd been declaring fewer wagers than he'd been taking in. I caught wind of it from his bookie, who couldn't produce the ticket belonging to a garbage man who claimed to have hit the winning numbers. Brandon never handed over the ticket! The winner was enraged and almost beat my bookie to a bloody pulp. That thief Brandon had to be made to pay, and that's when I turned to Bumpy. I knew that, in general, he didn't pussyfoot around his business, but when he came home after inflicting the corrective procedure that Brandon deserved, he simply served himself a triple scotch, as usual, turned on the radio and laid himself out on the couch in the salon.

"Rough day, Queenie," he yawned.

"Mission accomplished?"

"What?"

"Brandon. Come on, man!"

My man propped himself up and shrugged his shoulders, distracted.

"Oh yeah, I forgot all about that, dumb sonofabitch. Sure, I helped him see the error of his ways...."

I didn't dwell on it. I'd already put the incident out of mind when I came across a headline the following day, page two of the Amsterdam News, "Number Runner's Body Found in Harlem River."

The article explained how he'd been fished out of the East River between Harlem and the Bronx in a pitiable state: shattered skull, crushed spine and so on. I knew right away it was old Brandon, though the paper didn't give a name. My 137th Street bookie, the one who'd been in charge of supervising that overbold runner, in addition to a dozen others, told me he was down one man, but offered no further details. That's how they lived and died in dirty Black Harlem. With a knife planted between the shoulder blades or a bullet to the head. Nothing could stir any sympathy or rouse those NYPD pigs to action. Quite to the contrary, they took a perverse pleasure in trying to provoke me at any chance they got. But they wouldn't dare arrest me on Edgecombe Avenue— especially since, as white-skinned as they all were, not a one of them could've afforded an apartment as opulent as mine—but they could always ferret me out in the neighborhood or even at the Lafayette Street bar where I'd meet up with my troops, or I mean to say, my associates.

Yes, indeed, the tone Bumpy used to talk about Terence's demise was completely bizarre. I sat next to him on the couch, enraged but gnawed by a mild astonishment, too, because I'd always prided myself a total awareness of all the goings-on in my neighborhood. I had a servant, Annah, and a driver, Andrew, at my beck and call, along with a fair number of spies, whom I promoted or demoted according to the quality of information they provided. Any intelligence concerning the cops was handsomely compensated. So, everything was under my thumb, and I kept close tabs on each cop's wicked villainy and private immoralities. A number of them delivered barrel after barrel of whisky to their police stations under the cover of night; others chased after women, plundered whores or bribed barely-nubile Negresses; still others maintained solid under-the-table relationships with the Irish, Jewish and Italian gangs, filching money to keep their eyes turned away from their respective trafficking enterprises. My sights were riveted on Harlem's chief-of-police, but we never managed to catch that Puritan skirting the law in any kind of way, he who never opened his mouth, save to bark orders at his subordinates.

"What's the big problem, Bumpy?" I asked, incredulous.

My man got up to fetch a beer from the kitchen and returned nervously clearing his throat. He was coming unglued to say the least, and that was nothing like the Bumpy I knew. "You know, Queenie," he finally declared, somewhat hesitantly, "now that alcohol's legal again, this business ain't lucrative anymore... it's just not bringing it in like it used to...."

"Well, we Negroes never messed with bootlegging, far as I know. We didn't traffic, either, and we didn't give a damn about it, did we?

"You forgetting about your Jamaican Ginger?"

"Knock off your bullshitting, Bumpy! That was just to survive, it wasn't a bona fide business...."

I was lying right through my teeth. It was Jamaican Ginger that had lifted me from my hellhole and allowed me to amass, penny by penny, the staggering sum (at least in my eyes, at least in those days) of thirty thousand dollars. The sum that got me my start as a banker in the numbers racket. For a while, I worked as a run-of-the-mill bet collector for a boss on 142nd Street, as thankless a job as there could be, but I did well enough. Gritted my teeth, I did. Traipsing across the streets of Harlem in dead winter trying to hook a few wagers really took it out of me. The wind was particularly loathsome, coming in gusts that seemed to take a keen pleasure in playing hide-and-seek between the buildings, before slashing its icy claws through any kind of coat, no matter how tightly buttoned.

"Alright, alright, you've got a point, Queenie," Bumpy soliloquized.

In any case, my man had managed to find himself soaked in a damned bath of trouble. That much was obvious from the way the monumental bump on the back of his head was quivering. He'd packed on a few pounds since I'd hired him, but he hadn't gone obese like so many of the small-time bosses who became rich raking it in from brothels and heroin traffic. And I'd managed to smooth down his rough edges—even if he'd never read a single book in his life, he at least knew how to decipher the newspaper. He complained all the time, "Queenie, what're all those books good for, anyway? They giving you anything? Why don't you throw them out after you read them? They're just a waste of space. Okay, okay, I know... Madam connoiters with poets...."

As a girl, I hadn't had any books, as you well know now, dear Frédéric, nephew of mine, but after my mother sent me off to work at the Verneuils', my curiosity drew me ineluctably toward those fat, gilt-bound encyclopedias I dusted clean in their library every afternoon. I know, I know, I'm rambling on! But see, I'd read on the sly, you know, just the beginnings of the endless books the mistress of the house devoured day after day. My mind had already begun to wander far, far from Martinique. I always knew I'd leave my island and that it'd be for good. Once I'd made it to America and managed to worm my way into the Forty Thieves, I realized books were all but alien to the henchmen and second-fiddles I was surrounded by. It wasn't until I'd set up my own business, reinvented myself as the queen of Harlem's numbers game and bought my fancy place on Edgecombe Avenue that I got a taste of the mysterious universe of High Culture. Straightaway, those bearded Negroes made quite the impression on me, bespectacled in their thick horn-rimmed glasses and decked out in three-pieced suits with cravats or bow ties. Well, I say Negroes, though in truth a lot of them were Mulattos, but here in America, the Mulatto didn't exist: not in the eyes of the white world, nor of the black world for that matter. That was one of my first lessons in this country where there's something new to learn every day.

"Fine, Bumpy. Lay it on me," I told him in a casual tone while peering into my compact mirror, a habit I still can't shake, though I know it's turned into joke for everyone. I always knew I was no beauty, but neither was I an ogre. I suspected that, despite my body's stubborn scrawniness, I was closer to beauty than homeliness, so I tried to make up the difference by taking extreme care of my clothes—everyone complimented me on my elegance, à la française. My Black American friends—Mysti, Annabelle and especially Shortie—asked me for advice whenever they had a party or a wedding coming up. I surrounded myself with French magazines, which always impressed them, especially when I'd read such or such article out loud in that enchanting language no one could understand a single traitor word of. They'd express their admiration with exclamations like, "You're so French, Queenie!" which put me at ease. I'll point out that I was the one and only client of 5th Avenue's best-stocked boutique, Au Charme de Paris, which was run by a man from Quebec whom I loved talking to, even if I had to strain my ears to get a grasp on his nasal handling of the language!

"It's some Dutch Schultz bullshit, Queenie, see?" Bumpy grumbled.

No, I saw nothing at all, but the mere mention of his name made me shudder. That con lined his pockets during Prohibition by stocking dive joints on Manhattan Island, and Harlem included. They (the drunkards, I mean to say) all swore his bootleg moonshine was beyond better than the competition's on account of the high-quality Midwest corn he used, unlike the New York distillers who made booze out of any old thing they could get their hands on. The same could be said for those shoddy excuses for chemistry experiments that'd bust you open faster than a blink. In fact, cases of blindness nearly quadrupled in New York because of these traffickings, according to the city's social workers, in any case. OK, fine. I'm not going to play the saint anymore: My Jamaican Ginger's only medicinal power was in its name… and it frequently caused irreversible paralysis in non-stop imbibers of the stuff. I confess: I did have a part to play in that whole disaster. But I had to find a way to climb up from my misery, didn't I? And I had an excuse.… I didn't have a single kinsperson to count on in that city. I was the French Negro Woman, the strange Other, immediately distrusted by the entire world. I never wanted to get mixed up with international booze trafficking. It seemed too vast, too complicated and too dangerous for my small self. So, I left the foul misery the Whites called *moonshine* behind and dreamed about getting into the numbers game. Numbers! Three magic numbers: All you had to do was hit them and your life would be transformed into paradise's antechamber.

"He's one of Lucky Luciano's protégés, Queenie...."

"So? What's that got to do with me?"

"Either we try to make a deal with Dutch Schultz or we're gonna have the Syndicate to answer to!"

"Are you out of your head, man? Does your Dutch Whatsizname have his sights set on Harlem or does he just have a bone to pick with me?"

"It's more complicated than that.... Schultz's been on the prowl lately, looking to expand. His plonk-ass beers bring the house down, don't ask me why."

As I'd heard tell, that Jewish fool (who was, in fact, German and not Dutch in the slightest) had strong-armed all the bars into buying up his doctored alcohol despite their resistance to the stuff. Truth be told, he was just a doltish heavy who'd been locked behind bars on more than one occasion—it was one of his stints that earned him his nickname, Dutch, like the infamous gangster who got colded by a bullet to the head as he was leaving a nightclub after a long night of debauchery. Dutch Shultz the Second quickly erased and replaced all memories of his namesake, at least in most peoples' minds, and as a result, that animal had become utterly unfeeling. The trigger-happy little hoodlum made a reputation for himself by shooting into the sky to unnerve his lunkheaded goons... before taking aim right where it counts—in the genitals! There was nothing that helped a poor chump come to reason like watching his two balls explode.

Was Dutch Schultz (a *beer baron*, in the words of the press) plotting to get his paws on Harlem's numbers game, on my very own business?! Bumpy, that fat fraud, was telling me about it like some lily-livered deserter instead of mustering up some gusto and gathering the troops. No way in hell would we allow the white mobsters to horn in on our turf—after all, they had viciously forbidden us from theirs! Prohibition was an easy scapegoat. And

112

the Great Depression, too. We Negroes had nothing to do with Wall Street's crash; we didn't put our money in their banks. At least I never did! I had a whole room to safeguard my accounts and the records of what my bookies brought in; it was sealed with a metal door, and I alone held the key, which I never took off my person, not even at night. Not even when I'd go out with Shortie and Annabelle to take in a little jazz at the Fulton, where the divine Duke Ellington often presided. The song of his that inspired my deepest admiration for him (dear nephew, no need to tell you why), was his *Creole Love Call*. It went something like this:

> *I never cared much for moonlit skies*
> *I never wink back at fireflies*
> *But now that the stars are in your eyes*
> *I am beginning to see the light*
> *I never went in for afterglow*
> *Or candlelight on the mistletoe…*

Even when I started going to a Baptist church two blocks from Edgecombe Avenue every Saturday in order to spiff up my good Christian image, I'd bring the key to my safe room with me. I became obsessed by a question that Bumpy proved to be incapable of answering: Was Schultz giving up his beer business or did he just want to diversify? The first case would mean out-and-out war. Yes, war! I'd never let him oust me. I'd invested too much of myself, endured too many shunnings and snubs to let a snake like him slither out of his fine white neighborhood and seize control of the organization I'd worked so hard to build up. It required a kind of sixth sense to uncover the right numbers runners and patience to convince the bookies to operate under my protection, to accept me, a nobody foreigner, as their banker-in-chief. And a woman, no less! It took me five years all in all—five long years—and even when they'd all surrendered to their Queenie, I still had the eternal work of keeping my troops in check. At four in the morning without fail, while Bumpy was snoring like a swine, his head lump quivering with each breath, I'd be bent over my account books. I used thick green notebooks with stiff covers to keep track of all my business. I had to rename each column to suit my purposes and cover my tracks, so *revenues* became *donations*—my front was that I ran a charitable organization for my Baptist church, collecting shoes, clothes and cold, hard cash to help Harlem's neediest black families and orphans. The word *expenditures* became *purchases*, seeing as this same organization was in the habit of acquiring baby bottles, cribs and swaddling blankets. Well, suffice it to say that I wasn't careful enough. My front didn't fool the NYPD sleuths for long, but it at least bought me some time. Time enough for my lawyer, Elridge McMurphy, a pure-blooded Irishman as he liked to declare, to come to my rescue, which he'd do ever so diligently each time the cops sank their teeth in. Those cops gave me endless trouble. Their goal was to make my life a living hell, to harass me and to sabotage my business because they knew it would be impossible to launch a raid on my house. Sugar Hill was the fiefdom of the black bourgeoisie, and while it was easy enough to arrest the Central Harlem hoodlums, venturing into Edgecombe Avenue meant risking a scandal—indeed a riot—for the poor Negroes supported the rich Negroes, whom they looked up to as role models and examples to follow. But what did I know? After all, those university professors, renowned writers, talented painters and doctors populating my neighborhood weren't invincible, and their only weapons against white oppression were their enflamed discourse and their learned books—but, of course, most Harlemites had never so much as skimmed the first page of the latter.

Sugar Hill was a well-protected neighborhood, but it would've been foolhardy to imagine it inviolable. I was always on guard.

My bookies started arriving at five-thirty in the morning. I assigned each one a precise time for our rendezvous and under no circumstances were they allowed to stray from it. It was out of the question that they loiter around the area and risk upsetting my dear neighbors with their exceedingly correct English and their thoroughly conventional attire. Some of them were already cutting eyes at me; they had no idea what I was up to or how I was managing to lead such a life. Luxury furs. Ford's latest Model T. A liveried chauffeur. I had every reason to be discreet with the thugs I summoned to my door each morning.

All the bets were collected the night before by an army of numbers runners, who were grandiloquently called *the collectors*, and brought to my various bookies. I must admit that I knew almost none of the runners and they meant nothing to me. They were simply the pawns of the operation—the police bait: harassed, arrested, incarcerated, then soon as they'd been nabbed, brutally beaten to coax out a confession... to get them to admit that they didn't just run errands for some small potatoes banker with a couple of streets under his sway, but for Madam St. Clair herself, the boss of the whole Harlem lottery racket. Only one had ever squealed—a Richmond coward, a Virginian, who'd been caught with twenty betting slips in his hands. I used to prepare those forms myself each midnight in order to give them to my bookies in the morning; they would, in turn, distribute the slips to the runners. It wasn't long before that repetitive task became unbearable, so I ended up hiring two cash-strapped young ladies to come in on Sunday afternoons. It would've been too dangerous to have those little forms—we called them *slips*, my dear nephew—printed. Instead, we were saddled with huge sheets of paper that we'd cut up into small rectangles upon which we'd write the names and addresses of each gambler and the amount they put down. And, of course, the date—which was subject to contestation when the slips got too over-handled. I wasn't just a

115

lazybones bourgeois lady, like some people in Harlem seemed to imagine I was. Running the numbers was a full-time job, and a tedious, complicated one at that, since every gambler put down the sum they wanted, whether it was a couple pennies or a couple hundred (only the rashest played a sum like that). As soon as the New York Stock Exchange quotes came out, I'd get started on tallying up the winners, calculating their shares and preparing their winnings, which I'd conceal in an envelope labeled only with a numeric code in case the bookie who was supposed to pay it out got caught by the police. Mixing up those numbers led straight to disaster: the presumed winner's rage, the suspicion of those who caught wind of it, the diminishment of Madam St. Clair's impeccable reputation, even anonymous tips that would lead to my downfall. So, you see, Frédéric, running the numbers was no cakewalk. I had to be on constant high alert and, on more than one occasion, my insomnia seemed a blessing in disguise.

That bumpkin of a bet collector from his Virginia backwater had cracked. The crafty NYPD had freed him in hopes of catching me the moment I stepped outside the bounds of my protected Sugar Hill home, which I unwittingly did the following Saturday. Shortie had invited me to a nightclub to celebrate her birthday. She lived lavishly as the gal of a rich white mob boss, but I never begrudged her that: Nature had endowed her with curves that could send a saint straight to hell or raise the dead from their resting places. Her single flaw was her height—which is how she got her nickname—but the rest was divine. She was awestruck by her good fortune, and that amused me to no end.

"How many women would kill to be in my place, Stéphanie! Even Whites, even them! Hey, look at what my sweetheart gave me!"

And she'd brandish a gold necklace, a ring set with a precious stone, a vial of the fanciest perfume or a crocodile skin purse. For her birthday, Shortie went big. It wasn't enough for her to have a whole nightclub at her disposal, so she recruited an army of young people, men and women dressed in the latest style, to be at her guests' beck and call. As a birthday gift, her lover had hired the services of the celebrated Harry Carney Orchestra and of Rex Stewart, a trumpeter who had all the New York cabarets fighting over him. Harlem's crème de la crème stampeded the doors. I got a painting for my friend—she'd become one of my closest friends, if not the closest. It was an Aaron Douglas; his work had been praised to the skies by the white bourgeoisie. At first, he was reluctant to let me have it, claiming it was one of his very first canvases and that he was deeply attached to it and couldn't imagine parting with it. What kind of comedy was he playing at? Was he really so vain? I'll never know. I ended up dropping four thousand dollars on the piece of art and, as my perfectly gentle chauffer, Andrew, ferried me down to the club in my Model T, I was riding high. But the second I stepped foot on the sidewalk, twenty cops came out of nowhere and laid me on the ground like a common whore or some drug-addled strumpet while the other guests looked on in shock.

"This time, we're going to lock you away for good, Madam St. Clair," one of the officers gloated. "Forget about calling your lawyer! It'd just be a waste of your ill-earned money."

"And what exactly am I being accused of?"

"Illegal lottery, Madam."

"Never heard of it!"

I didn't lose heart, even if I was plunged into an ocean of shame before the incredulity of my fellow invitees. One of them rushed off to find Shortie, who was resplendent in a black-and-red sequined gown. The scandalized and thoroughly charming young thing (she was barely twenty-nine, while her lover was well into his forties) rained curses upon the brigade, who remained impervious to her abuses. The cops knew who she was and, more importantly, who her protector was. That big man wouldn't have stood for the slightest blunder on their part, especially not in public. They shoved me into their vehicle and rushed me down to the station. To really drive home the point that spinning yarns of hokum would be an utter waste of my saliva, they had my Richmond runner handcuffed to a chair in the depths of the interrogation room. Their ploy had no effect on me. I knew I lived in a merciless world where craftiness competed with ferocity, lies with bad faith. To find a taste of humanity in Harlem, you had either the Apollo Theater or the Cotton Club, where brilliant musicians improvised never-before-heard sounds right before your eyes and left even the greatest minds stupefied. In the white newspapers that I skimmed on occasion, I'd stumbled upon more than one virulent article condemning Duke Ellington or Johnny Hodges as a couple of hodgepodge noisemakers who were incapable of producing true art and who menaced the delicate ears of cultivated men. These assessments made me laugh, even though I wasn't very well-versed in music. I knew those were just the words of those who couldn't bear the thought that the Negroes had a culture of their own, even though hordes of filthy rich white mobsters, members of the white literati, white movie stars and white *artistes* had no problem packing into our Harlem nightclubs every weekend.

On the occasions I was nabbed by the police, I'd recollect a little piece by Duke Ellington that I'd listened and re-listened to ten times, or something from another jazzman, and I'd lose myself in it, I'd retreat into myself, faced with those uniformed stiffs circling in on me, pretending to have all the evidence they needed in-hand, determined to bring me to my downfall. I was aware of their questions, but they seemed to be wrapped in some kind of veil, a halo that must have made my eyes glaze over. Or at least deadened my gaze.

"Richmond, does that mean anything to you, Madam Queen?"

"No, not at all!"

118

"New York and Washington neither, I suppose?" The cop jeered.

"I'm only familiar with Harlem, officer, sir. That's where the people of your race have confined the people of mine."

Then silence. Interminable silence. Until the cop couldn't contain himself anymore, "All right, enough of your little games, Stéphanie St. Clair! This time, we've got you. There's a witness ready to expose your racket before a judge. So, either you tell us everything and we'll show you our gratitude when the time comes, or else stay stubborn and see how badly it ends for you."

"I don't know anybody by the name of Richmond. And I don't know this gentleman here."

"Suit yourself! You'll explain everything to the court, sweetheart, but in my humble opinion, you're making a big mistake.

You see, my dear nephew, I'd had to undergo this type of interrogation so many times I'd lost count. At first, I'd get hot under the collar. I'd start cursing the cops out, first in English and then in French, which always had its effect. Or I'd toss out an insult in Gaelic if I was faced with a green-eyed ginger. They'd let me loose sooner than their other clients, but that didn't stop those dirty scoundrels from writing up nasty reports about me for the judges. I practically had my own official courthouse, the one on 156th Street, which was staffed by white judges who were nearing the end of their careers and still clinging hard to the belief that the Negroid race was "irremediable from a moral point of view," as they liked to put it. An assembly line of the accused emanated from that courthouse: pickpockets, burglars, whores, alcoholics, druggies and, of course, numbers runners and bookies who'd been hustling the illegal lottery. Judge Philips, a bald, rosacea-faced man, afflicted with a pair of enormous glasses and chronic exhaustion, had put me on the witness stand more than once.

"Ah, it's our elegant little French dame again! They don't know how to behave themselves in Paris, eh?" he'd try for pleasantries.

His pronunciation of *Parisss* was already enough to put my nerves on end, so I'd assume a severe face and look him straight in the eyes, though every time I did, my eternally jovial lawyer, Elridge McMurphy, would advise me to keep my head down.

"In Paris, they don't arrest honest people at the drop of a hat, your Honor."

"Who'd have guessed! Madam St. Clair, a paragon of virtue? That's not what your street corner goons have been saying when the police bring them in. Call the witness to the stand!"

Then one or another of my runners—or, on very rare occasions, one of my bookies—would approach the witness stand, handcuffed, halfway between sheer terror and principled resistance, flanked by two cops. I'd shoot him a look and he'd immediately get the message: Either you keep your trap shut, you poor bastard, or you blab—but in that case, you'll be good for a bullet between the eyes when they let you out. They all chose the former option, obviously, swearing up and down that they'd never laid eyes on me before in their life, much less had business with me. That little game invariably exasperated Judge Philips, who wouldn't think twice about threatening the accused (in vain, mind you) with a new and terrifying invention: the electric chair. Truth be told, that contraption was far from humdrum back then, and the *New York Times* had reported a certain number of failed executions, which had deeply disturbed white public opinion, provoking a wave of protest. Electrocuting someone to death just for collecting illegal bets hardly seemed plausible, so without fail the witness would retract his statement, which always worked to provoke the judge.

"Queenie—permit me to use your nickname... that's how you're known in your circle, right?—you're getting off this time, but sooner or later your luck will run dry. I'm not giving up until

I've got you cornered!"

"Go screw yourself, you wimpy old geezer!" I'd mutter in my heart of hearts....

Chapter Seven

Ever since I became the boss of Harlem's illegal lottery bankers, the only woman in the business, which exasperated my colleagues, who'd been progressively transformed into my debtors—the James Warners, the Casper Holsteins, the Wilfred Brandons, the Simeon Francises or, again, the Joseph Isons—I'd been literally assailed by all types of request for aid. How could I refuse giving to the Universal Temple of Christ the Redeemer and its magnificent gospel singers, even if I was still a Catholic (admittedly, I was not a fervent believer) and even if the airs and graces of the pastor and his flock's shouts and cries and their Baptist rollicking had always discomfited me? How could I turn my back to the boxing club on 133rd Street where young, out-of-work Negroes could come vent their frustrations? Anyway, didn't my fortune come from the thousands of poor wretches who, day after day, bet one single penny or a dime or a quarter in the crazy hope of finally and definitively escaping misery? Because everywhere echoed with it: The Whites don't want us, they won't let us eat in their restaurants, watch films in their cinemas, shop in their stores, visit their parks, and even their public toilets are off limits, but they'll put up with a Negro who's been educated or who's made something of his life, and all the more so if he so happened to be endowed with light skin on account of some great-great-grandma who'd cheated with the master or been assaulted by the man. Oh certainly, the Whites didn't mix with them, but they didn't search out trouble over nothing, either. The nothing-Negroes, on the other hand, were endlessly harassed by the police and the Rikers Island prison was overflowing with them.

"Madam Queen is generous," was the word in Central Harlem, "much more generous than the rest of her class, even though she's not even from around here, but some faraway island down in the Caribbean with a hard-to-remember name." In truth, my reputation was richly deserved. After paying my runners and my bankers and squaring up with that day's winners, I had enough left over to feed a whole block for days on end. But I had neither family nor children, even if my lover and associate Ellsworth "Bumpy" Johnson made no secret of his wish that I come live with him. I wasn't nuts! Mixing business and pleasure was like opening the door to a downward spiral and, in my specific case, Bumpy was my employee, nothing more. Well, I'm exaggerating a bit, my dear Frédéric, every now and then I'd let him slip into my bed, you see, on particularly cold New York winter nights, for example. I was neither coquettish nor a spendthrift; I wore the same pearl-gray dresses that brought out the brilliant black of my eyes (or so they said) and I'd wear elegant hats, that's true, but never eccentric ones. Fur coats were the only thing that pushed me overboard, but not for the reasons everyone suspected: Rather than trying to play the role of the elegant Parisian lady, I was quite simply cold. For twenty-six years, the whole first part of my existence, I'd only known a single season—or rather, a single temperature, that of my tropical island, unlike the American Negroes who couldn't understand why I was always cold, even during spring and autumn. My teeth were nearly always clattering, and to keep anyone from noticing it, more often than not I'd chomp on a golden-tipped cigarette holder, even though cigarettes were not my principal vice. I preferred by far a nice glass of Irish whisky.

Nonetheless, among all my customary largesse—which had earned me the respect of those around me—there was one cause that I'd long refused: financing the Universal Negro Improvement Association, a group directed by that ugly-as-three-devils Negro Marcus Garvey, who was positively consumed by pride. He'd never guessed that before becoming Madam Queen, back when I was just a miserous Negress dragging my dreams all across Harlem, I'd listened to him preaching on a couple occasions.

Maybe "preaching" isn't the word. "Cantillating" is probably better, perched as he was on an enormous soapbox, strangely dressed in a bicorn hat embellished with a feather and a Prussian general's uniform. Rain or shine he was there, stoic, exalted and lyrical with that melodious Jamaican accent of his. Some people, back then, took him for one of those crazies who haunted Harlem's seamiest streets, always ready to help you save your supposedly inveterate sinner's soul in exchange for a half dollar or pile of leftovers. His stentorian voice still rings out in my ears.

"My brothers and sisters, listen to me, please lend me your ears! The white world we've been thrown into isn't for us. No, it is a place of perdition for our race. This country is not ours, it cannot be and will never be. Damned is your name, America! My brothers and sisters, open your eyes and realize that our land is none other than mother Africa, the land the Whites have forced us to forget about for almost three centuries, but she lives on in each one of us, an eternal flame...."

Such eloquence—or maybe I should say grandiloquence— moved the bastardscum; they'd stop open-mouthed to drink in Marcus Garvey's words for hours on end (the man was nothing if not voluble). If all that didn't move me one bit, I still admired his vast knowledge, all those works he could quote from at length, those historical events—largely unknown to me—that he remembered down to the smallest detail. I liked his feverishness because it made him a real man, not a two-faced creature like the majority of the American Negroes. Later, after I'd become wealthy and began rubbing shoulders with bigwigs like Du Bois, I came to understand the reason for this difference between us, the island Negroes, and them, the mainland Negroes. In our countries, Jamaica and Martinique, Whites, of course, had practiced slavery, but they were never more than a tiny minority, and there was never a moment we couldn't perfectly well imagine living without them, whereas here, in America, their white counterparts—be

they English, Irish, Dutch, Italian, Russian, or whatever else—
were solidly in the majority. They dominated every aspect of
Negro life, and these latter, in order to survive, had to create a sort
of armor against them. And that's exactly what Garvey wanted to
tear away. When he stepped down from his soapbox, his audience
would rush to him to shake his hand or slap his back, and it wasn't
long before he became a kind of prophet of the return to Africa.
Upon becoming engaged in the numbers business, I lost sight of
him and, for years on end, had only sporadic news of him thanks
to the papers. I knew he'd started a paper of his own, *The Negro
World*, but it was poorly distributed and only rarely found its way
to me. But then, one day, two well-dressed and very polite men
came knocking at my door. After declining my offer to come
in, they declared that as a successful Black, it was my duty to
contribute to the financing of a grandiose project, that of the
Black Star Line, a shipping company founded by Garvey for the
express purpose of repatriating all the American and Caribbean
Blacks to the land of their ancestors, Africa.

I was speechless....

[FATHER NÈG

The first time Stéphanie St. Clair saw him, it was this
expression, "Father Nèg," which her mother had used so often
back in Martinique, that came to mind. He was, in truth, more of
a Mulatto, but that term, she would come to realize, didn't make
much sense in America because of the insurmountable color line
separating Whites from Blacks. "Father" meant, if her memory
of the Creole language still served, something like "learned," or
at least "educated and respectable." Yes, William E. B. Du Bois
was all that, and more so than any other person she'd ever met
(or would ever meet). With his strange hooked nose, he looked
rather like the Jews who ran the corner stores and clothing shops
in Harlem, and his olive complexion was the polar opposite of

Marcus Garvey. Always dressed in a well-cut suit and a bow tie, the tips of his moustache well oiled, his beard neatly trimmed and pointed, his eyes steady and piercing, he was an impressive sight. He also took the stairs at the Edgecombe Avenue building where, just like Stéphanie, he had his apartment, but he—she would learn later—didn't do so out of fear for the elevator, no, he took the stairs to keep his heart in good health. They were bound to cross paths. The first time, he ignored the young lady, his eyes seeming to slip right past her small person, but Bumpy's breathlessness—he who fulminated ceaselessly against Queenie's avoidance of the elevator—made him smile.

"We're just a couple of ignorant Negroes to him…." Stéphanie's bodyguard whispered. "Mr. Du Bois isn't just anyone, Queenie! Even the Whites respect him. He's the one who does that paper… what's it called again? Oh, yeah, *The Crisis*, all filled up with mumbo jumbo. Forget reading about who got killed or what the odds are at the racetrack. Pff!"

Another time, a summer day hot as a thousand devils, Mr. Du Bois had taken off his jacket and was carrying it draped over his shoulder. Stéphanie was, for once, alone (she'd sent Bumpy off to settle a score with one of her West Harlem runners who thought he could dupe her), and, so, he was friendly with her. Gallant, even.

"Good morning, ma'am!"

He had tipped his hat and smiled at her, unless it was just some kind of tic of his. She'd been so stunned that she hadn't managed to peep out a single word. When she'd ordered information about his person, she'd been told that he held a Doctor of Philosophy from Harvard University. He was, in fact, the first Black to have earned that distinction! Stéphanie was obviously in awe in front of such a person, she who'd attended school for no more than five years, but overcome by a sudden impulse, she asked him over for tea (and in French, no less), "Puis-je vous inviter à prendre le thé?"

He looked at her in such a way that she felt overwhelmed by

shame. What she wouldn't have given for some magical power to bury her six feet underground or to vanish her into thin air. Compared to him, she was nothing. They didn't belong to the same world. Hers was the world of illegal bets, bars that sold contraband moonshine and heroin, nightclubs where Blacks and Mulattos with endless legs danced and debased themselves with the highest bidder as soon as the show was over—a world that had nothing at all in common with this other one, this tasteful and refined world inhabited by the eminent Mr. Du Bois. At least that's what Stéphanie was thinking.

"Pourquoi pas?" he calmly concurred in French. "But at my place, if you'll agree."

The young lady was startled because she hadn't known that he—an American at that—had such a mastery of her language, her personal language, the one she isolated herself inside of when she'd had it up to here with this violent country where the Wild West still reigned, despite the fact that the Indians had been definitively beaten and the horse carriage had been exchanged for the automobile. Every now and then, Stéphanie would be seized by a nostalgia so overwhelming that she'd find herself babbling, speaking senselessly, saying things no one could make head or tails of. Always in French, or in any case, a French mongrelized with Creole. That habit, which never left her, always took her lovers aback—especially Bumpy, who'd stop in his tracks and listen open-mouthed until, exasperated, he'd shout, "Hey, Frenchie! What the fuck's going on? Knock off your voodoo!"

Mr. Du Bois's apartment was much bigger than hers, but completely devoid of the knickknacks and trinkets that Stéphanie bought compulsively whenever the lottery had had a good day (in other words, when that week's winners had been few and far between). Her runners and bankers paid her in full, and everyone was happy, except the poor wretches who'd played their last cents. Ah, being the boss lady of that undertaking (which the law declared criminal) was no job for a weak woman! Or rather, no job for someone whose heart was too soft. Everyone knew, from one end of Harlem to the other, that Madam Queenie was hard-as-nails.

The walls of the prestigious professor's apartment were lined with books from floor to ceiling. She'd never seen anything like it, even as a young servant at the Verneuils' Fort-de-France villa. Books everywhere. Some were carefully arrayed in bookcases, others were stacked up here and there. A couple were open on the real leather sofa upon which the eminent professor gestured for her to take a seat.

"So, you're the famous Black Frenchwoman who's imposed herself on the merciless gangsters of Harlem," he asked in a jovial tone that surprised her. "In the end, you and I both defend the same cause, in our own ways, of course."

Aside from the fact that she was deucedly intimidated, Stéphanie couldn't see what he was getting at.

"We're defending the Race, Madam Queen, yes, the Race with a capital R," he added, suddenly serious. "I do so with words and speeches, and you by preventing the Italian and Irish underworld from helping themselves to Harlem."

She'd never seen it like that. As far as she was concerned, she was only defending her own interests. Besides, she hadn't emigrated to America to defend any race but, rather, to make a better future for herself. It was true, though, that since her arrival—about a dozen years prior at that point—she'd heard talk of a certain Booker T. Washington. He was much better known among the Negro underclasses than Du Bois. As Stéphanie understood it, the former had passed an accord with the Whites allowing Blacks to receive vocational training in technical schools before trying to claim high-level offices, and this because the former slaves apparently suffered from a major educational backwardness as compared to their former masters. That theory didn't seem outlandish at all to the majority of the Harlemites in her entourage, so she was careful not to tell them that on her island, on Martinique, after slavery was abolished, people of color (starting with the Mulattos) went straight to school, then university, and it didn't take long before they became doctors, dentists, pharmacists, architects and professors. America is America and Martinique is Martinique, she'd told herself.

"You... you speak French very well," Stéphanie ended up murmuring.

"Well, my name gives that away, doesn't it? Du Bois! Nothing could be more French than that. Ha ha ha!"

She hadn't noticed it because of the Anglo-Saxon pronunciation of his name: *Dyoo Boyse*. The professor revealed to her that his father, Alfred, had been half Haitian and had lived on Martinique's sister island before reaching the continent—Massachusetts, to be precise. And that he himself, William, had never had the opportunity to learn Creole because that man had abandoned him and his family when he was just a baby, but fortunately he'd taken it upon himself to learn French starting from a very early age and he'd managed to perfect that language during his university studies. Stéphanie realized at that moment that, like the majority of Americans, Du Bois didn't understand that French and Creole were two completely different languages and that the latter wasn't simply a type of French, as he truly believed.

Du Bois spoke at length. He asked questions every now and then about what he referred to as Stéphanie's *activities*. Without any extra commentary. Without seeming to disapprove. When the young lady took her leave, he offered her a copy of one of his books, *The Souls of Black Folk*, which he signed for her. That book would never leave her side and, if it didn't quite change her life, it *did* change her way of seeing the relations between Blacks and Whites and between Blacks and Blacks. Or, to be more precise, between Blacks and Mulattos.]

When the men from the Black Star Line returned a few weeks

later, they uttered a word that made me shiver: *lynching*. A word doesn't exist until it reflects something or some event you've seen or experienced. And Stéphanie St. Clair—excuse me, my dear nephew, if I sometime speak of myself in the third person—had heard and read that word often but, having rarely left Harlem, she didn't quite understand what it meant. There had been, of course, that atrocious episode when the bus she'd taken after gouging out Duke's eye was attacked and she was raped by the barbarians of the Ku Klux Klan, but she'd managed to almost completely erase it from memory. She'd graduated, in some way, from her years of American apprenticeship—the hardest years of her life, during which time she'd joined the Irish gang of Forty Thieves and learned to kill a man without batting an eye. The war had ended in early 1919, and hundreds of black draftees had returned from Europe, where they'd seen other faces, been confronted with other moral codes and were no longer so willing to get walked all over. She'd succumbed to the charms—one of the only times in her life such a thing would happen—of a handsome sergeant whose skin was the color of café-au-lait and whose kinky hair would've made him a Câpre back home, according to the racial terminology in use in Martinique—even if such terms made no sense in America, they counted for something in the eyes of the freshly immigrated Stéphanie St. Clair. One day, he suggested they visit the nation's capital, Washington D.C., and the young woman—who was thrilled by the prospect—figured rightly or wrongly that it was to be a kind of trial run for their future honeymoon. On the train, everyone eyeballed Tim on account of his uniform and, most of all, the row of medals decorating his chest. Stéphanie was prideful before the feminine sex for having been chosen by a war hero. Even the white train conductor showed a certain deference toward them. Throughout the whole ride, Stéphanie daydreamed: She had the incredible opportunity to not only get out of Gehenna, but also to become, slowly but surely, a real American. Tim planned to take her to visit his family in Georgia the following month, and she was determined to devote herself—as soon as she had a moment to herself—to improving her pronunciation, especially the *ze* sound she made instead of the proper *th*, which never failed to bring mocking smiles to the faces of the people she spoke to.

In Washington, as soon as they'd descended from the train, the couple was thrust into hell. All along the train platform, rage-drunk Whites were attacking black passengers and the family members and friends who'd come to pick them up. "Bunch of Bolshevists! Niggerscum, get out of here!" they shouted.

The manhunt had even spilled over onto the rails. Stéphanie held back a cry of horror as she watched a young man's brains get blown out while he was trying to flee the scene. He'd been shot at point blank range by two of his pursuers. Blacks were sprawled out on the ground every which way in the station's main hall and all along the stairs that led up to it. The acrid smell of blood filled the air. Tim—a man who'd fought valiantly against the Germans on the battlefields of Europe—was taken aback, but he didn't flinch. Advancing like an automaton, he held a terrorized Stéphanie by her hand. Before long, a group of rioters had encircled them. The most rabid among them yelled, "It's not enough to steal our jobs, huh, you rape our wives, too, you filthy apes! Well, now it's time to pay!"

Miraculously, one of the police patrols that were crisscrossing Washington that evening passed by and came to the couple's aid. They took Stéphanie and Tim down to a police station that was already packed with white rioters and battle-bruised Blacks. The whole place was filled with cries and shouts and slobber and insults, and the police struggled to restrain the two groups. The din of wailing firetrucks tore through the night and was punctuated by gunshots. Tim pressed Stéphanie close in his arms with an infinitely tender gesture that dissipated the terror engulfing her. With a man like him, she was safe from all danger. His uniform, his medals, his Olympian calm would impress themselves on the rioters. These latter seemed to be targeting one man in particular, a Black of about forty whose face was covered with blood and who lay curled up on the floor. Ever more explicit threats were hurled into the air.

"We gonna hang that rapist! Get that niggerbastard!"

The man began moaning and denying the accusations, but the policemen kicked him into silence. Tim detached himself from Stéphanie and rushed to his aid. A bullet to the chest ended the life of that man who had, for the past four years, managed to evade the Teutonic enemy. A bullet shot by one of the group of policemen who'd been halfheartedly guarding the door to the police station. That door was broken down in short order, and the shouting rioters swarmed in. Afterward, it's a gaping hole. Stéphanie woke up in a hospital bed. A couple black nurses were smiling at her. One of them wiped her forehead with a bit of cotton that had been soaked in some stinging liquid. Her lips were moving, but the young lady couldn't understand not a one of her words. Her ears were filled with a buzzing that made her feel ill. She realized part of her head had been bandaged. Little by little, her senses returned to her. As if she was returning to her body after a long absence. She was so totally absorbed by the strangeness of the situation that it seemed like time had stopped and night would never come again. In actual fact, the hospital room was permanently lit by fluorescent lights, which made her eyes ache.

"Young lady, can you hear me?"

The voice came from far away, very far away. Stéphanie managed to rub her eyes and make out a round, coffee-colored face offering up a motherly smile. The nurse clasped her hands in encouragement. That good soul returned to her bedside day in and day out. For weeks on end. Until the young lady was able to sit up in her bed and eat without assistance. The news they had no choice but to give her was devastating: They'd done everything they could to save Tim, but the bullet had pierced through a lung and he'd been brought to the hospital too late. As for her and the other Blacks who'd been found at the station, they'd been attacked by a lynch mob and had only been saved—some of them, anyway—thanks to the intervention of the riot police.

Excuse me for having used the third person, dear nephew, but that's my way of drumming it out of my memory. Of expunging that episode.... I know, I know, I'm mixing everything up again, but I'm sure you'll manage to straighten out the chronology.

Chapter Eight

Finishing off that rotten cloggie-scoundrel by the name of Dutch Schultz had become my bête noir and prime obsession for those early months of 1926. That swine convinced himself he could sink his grimy claws into Harlem's illegal lottery, even though he knew it was a lifeline for thousands of poor Negroes; the ones who sometimes put down a penny, one lousy penny—well, pennies and nickels, anyhow—in the hopes of winning big enough to eat for a couple days. And that's not counting the assistance we bankers gave to all those associations, totally on the up and up, too. We invested in laundromats, corner stores, bakeries, even hotels. I lost count of all the charitable works I contributed to and all the companies I had stock in. Stéphanie St. Clair was a businesswoman and damn proud of it! A woman who *gave back* to her community. No, sir, she didn't just roll around in the millions she raked in from the gambling pot—she knew how to treat her people with compassion, with magnanimity. The way it went, I'd introduce myself to my upper-class Edgecombe Avenue neighbors as a businesswoman, and most of them bought it, aside from a few who mean-morgued me. But Dutch Schultz was a whole other story, nothing more than a predator, just another shameless White with one thing in mind: to squeeze Harlem folks dry till every penny was siphoned out of their neighborhood and into the places they were forbidden to go.

You see, *solidarity* was no empty word for us, even if some people took advantage of it to hustle their benefactors. Most of the time, I kept my generosity quiet to avoid attracting the attention of the narcs; Harlem was swarming with them. Small-time thieves who'd been released before the end of their sentences, druggies who couldn't make it a single day without their bump of heroin, pimps who were left to run the streets or murderers who got away with it because no one could string together enough evidence to lock them away: All those animals were at the NYPD's beck and call. Perhaps instead of saying *generosity*, I should talk about *investments* like the Whites did, but seeing as I saw no kind of return on what I dished out, I'll stick with the former. The word in Harlem was that *Madam Queen's got a big heart*, and not a single week went by that I wasn't called upon to help open a restaurant, a laundromat, a corner store, a newsstand or god-only-knows what other venture. There was even one fellow with the audacity to ring at my door three times in a single year. *Real* crafty, that one: He brought his three young daughters along with him, a trio of darling creatures whose worn-out dresses made my heart ache.

"I'm a hard worker," he'd plead, "but I lost my job at the city hall…. I need help to pick myself up again, to raise these poor children, left motherless now…. She died giving birth to the youngest girl."

He'd play his part so well that I let myself get all softened up and even gave him five thousand dollars to help open his restaurant. If I hadn't pushed him off me hard as I did, he would've kissed my feet till they were soaked through with spit and over-obsequious thank-yous. A little while later, he invited me to the grand opening of his place. If you ask me, the location was bad; it was too far from Central Park. But the food was good and pretty similar to Caribbean food—the man must've been from the South. You can imagine my astonishment when I discovered a woman there, in her late thirties and pretty enough (in any case she was still red-blooded), totally running the show. The newly minted restauranteur introduced her to me as the sister of his dearly deceased wife, but to see how she acted with the girls, I had my doubts.

"You're too soft-hearted," Shortie teased. "That Negro over there pulled the wool right over your eyes. I bet that man already owns two or three different restaurants…."

My compè was right. One night, Annabelle, Mysti, Shortie and me—our little inseparable quartet—had gone out for dinner on the outskirts of the Bronx. We'd heard high praise for the place and decided to check it out. Well, what do you know, there was that famous sister of the deceased at work at the cash register! She nearly jumped out of her skin when she saw us come in, but she recovered quick and managed to maintain a semblance of calm as she came over to us. After an awkward little greeting she announced that every now and then she had to find a side-hustle like this one, since it wasn't easy, no, not easy at all, to feed three growing girls, her three dear nieces. I believed her. Shortie didn't.

On another occasion, I was attending service over at the Colored Methodist Episcopal Church (in fact, to ensure universal goodwill, I attended the Adventist Church, the Baptist Church, the Methodist Church and Lord-knows-which-other services on a rotating basis, though everyone knew I was a Catholic) when a lady claiming to be the Director of Charitable Works approached me near the end of the service to tell me about her project. She claimed to be spearheading the construction of an orphanage on 138th Street. In Harlem, abandoned or orphaned children had become a major epidemic. They'd wander the streets by day, begging or hawking small services for a handful of change and, by night, they'd huddle in the entryways of shuttered buildings or warehouses along the banks of the Harlem River. It was heart wrenching to see them so filthy and skinny, but since everyone was busy living hand to mouth, there weren't many charitable souls taking an interest in those kids. Every now and then, I'd ask Andrew, my chauffeur, to stop at certain corners and hand out some coins. He took care of it, but a horde of scrawny kids would inevitably end up swarming around my Model T to thank me. I was always surprised that they knew about Madam Queen. My popularity throughout Harlem never ceased to shock me. After all, wasn't I a foreigner? Or maybe even a usurper? But I'd correct myself almost immediately and return to my role as the

Priestess of the numbers game, a role that seemed to fit me like a glove, at least in the eyes of most Harlemites. I visited the lot where the lady from the Colored Methodist Episcopal Church hoped to construct her "Refuge for Misfortunate Children," as she'd begun to call it (not without a certain pomp). It was a two-story red-brick Victorian house that had been damaged in a fire some ten years prior; the former owners—a couple of well-heeled doctors—had tragically perished in the flames. It wouldn't require construction so much as rehabbing and modernizing, as the lady (whose name my memory has buried somewhere) explained to me. I, who never had children and who certainly did not want to bring any into the world, was secretly thrilled at the idea of becoming a kind of second mother to the thirty or forty children who were supposed to be welcomed there. I'd surely be able to transform myself from Madam Queen to *Mother Queen* if the undertaking was successful, not to mention the fuzz would be conveniently more circumspect about harassing such a generous, selfless individual. Hell, I'd kill two birds with one stone! Not only would I gain a certain respectability—which would go far in my buttoned-up Sugar Hill neighborhood—but also some welcome peace of mind as concerned my business. After some consideration, I decided to oblige this charitable lady and passed the torch to Bumpy, convinced as I was that a man would necessarily be more well-versed than any woman insofar as overseeing the masons, the tile-layers and the construction workers—a task that, in any case, bored me before it even began. But the lady was a con! She hoodwinked me and made off with my bankroll. It was a lousy idea, and I was a damned chump for taking her bait.

But getting conned by members of my own race left me neither hot nor cold. Because in the end, I'd been adopted (big nobody that I was) into this little corner of Harlem, where outsiders— black-skinned as they might be—weren't always welcomed. I'd been accepted into a place where folks were already slaving for chicken scratch. Around Sugar Hill, no one had ever tried to step on my toes, even when I was just getting started in the numbers game. First a numbers runner, then a middling banker, I ended up reigning sovereign over my own little world. But small as it was, it was a world that the white mafia wanted to sink their teeth into. And to think, that crybaby Bumpy was declaring himself ready to enter into negotiations with them! Sure, they were better armed than us and had the mayor of New York and not a few influential members of Congress in their pockets, but damn! The man was a wimp.

"Queenie, be realistic," he kept harping at me. "They're just too strong. If they want to negotiate, well, then we'll negotiate."

I refused. The next month, that damned Schultz had four of my runners offed and replaced them with his guys. The NYPD didn't lift a finger. So, I had to go back to the drawing board if I didn't want to watch my whole business unravel before my very eyes. Finished were the days of beating the pavement, hawking lottery slips to the first passerby! I asked my bankers to draw up lists of regular wagerers so that my runners could make direct appointments, a tactic that would undoubtedly cut my clientele in half. Some of the gamesters were suspicious and couldn't understand the reasoning behind this new way of doing business; others didn't have a steady address and knocked about from woman to woman or were in a delicate situation with the law and didn't want anyone to know exactly where they stayed. It took Schultz four whole months to figure out what was going on, especially since I'd started the rumor that I'd earned enough with the numbers game and was ready to retire and return to my Martinique.

"Swell! St. Clair's going back home to Africa!" he'd shouted from the rooftops. "I really wonder how that pidgin-speaking bag of bones ever managed to claim Harlem, anyway."

When he finally caught wind of what we were up to, he lost it and rubbed out two of my bankers on their way to my house with the bet money early one morning. Murders were a real rarity in Sugar Hill, and the black press milked it for all it was worth and dragged me into it, too, though they didn't name me directly (but *the French Negro woman* wasn't the vaguest allusion out there). It brought the worried and contemptuous regard of my Edgecombe Avenue neighbors down on me. And overnight, the mysterious grande dame with the *delicious* accent turned into a lady gangster who was threatening the peace in the only *decent* part of Harlem, the one where you'd always been able to walk without fear. And despite everything, that half-wit Bumpy was still talking about a truce! A cease-fire! He was completely ignoring the fact that it was Dutch Schultz who crossed turf lines and disrespected me on my own street, who started the war in the first place, going after my runners first and then my bankers!

"That goddammed Dutchman could come after me and you wouldn't even bat an eye, Bumpy!" I was frozen with icy rage and starting to see my companion in a new light. He reminded me of a bad taste I thought I'd washed out my mouth by then: Duke, that small-time goon who fancied himself a boss till I was forced to gouge one of his eyes out, poor bastard. Ah, the Harlem Negroes all talk big when they're fighting with their own kind, but they turn to cream puffs as soon as a White gets involved! Why should I have given a damn if Shultz had a whole armada at his command? We were under no obligation to wage war, and we were smart enough to lay traps for him and to make his life so miserable that he'd lose heart and retreat. Yes, indeed, it was within our means to do that!

Bumpy wasn't convinced. Organized crime filled him with an almost holy terror. Those notorious names—Al Capone, Lucky Luciano, Meyer Lansky—intimidated him so much he didn't dare pronounce them aloud, preferring to refer to *the big Sicilian boss*, *the Chicago chief, the Yiddish outlaw*, and other circumlocutions of the sort that got me all worked up.

"If that's how it's going to be, Bumpy," I challenged him, "I'll go it alone! Get out of my house, y'hear! Beat it! I don't ever want to see your big sissy ass around here again!"

And he scrammed for good, right then and there. His celerity surprised me. I'd believed—wrongly, it turned out—that he'd grown rather attached to my person....

[RECOLLECTION

The strange news had reached Madam St. Clair in the most improbable of ways. If she was in the habit of devouring newspapers and, to a lesser extent, books, she nonetheless took no interest in any article that did not directly concern her—in other words, that did not deal with gang wars. During that distant era of her life, way back in the late 1910s, the only names that got her attention were those of Al Capone and Lucky Luciano, and tales of their exploits always thrilled her. Once she finally broke with the Irish gang of Forty Thieves, she dreamed of cutting herself loose from the evanescent and un-hierarchical associations of black connivers that had always seen her as a kind of dredged-up nether creature, a bizarre animal on account of her accent. Stéphanie liked order, careful work, discipline, dedication, in short, everything that was unbearable to the men she'd taken to calling *nutjobs*, in other words, perfect imbeciles. One day, she'd set up a gang of her own and rule over it with an iron fist, and that's why she pored over every detail of the confrontations between the New York mafias, that's why she followed their vendettas, studied their operations, tried to read between the lines, at least, what she could glean from the papers.

It had been a couple months since the war *over there* (in Europe) had ended—welcome news for those forced to suspend their illegal activities. The fervor of patriotism and the ever-increasing enlistment of young men (including those of color) had put a stopper on the flow of business. As such, the year of 1919 was heralded as a kind of renaissance. Of what? The edges were not yet clear, but the world *must* have been headed for decades of peace. Stéphanie St. Clair had taken a job as a numbers runner for a banker on 147th Street, a job that was more than a little thankless. The brunt of the work consisted of convincing poor sods to wager the little they earned by dangling the promise of splendorous paybacks, the likes of which would make them set for life. In reality, three times out of four these were nothing but pipedreams. Stéphanie's boss—a fedora-wearing, Cuban-cigar-chomping, blowfish of a banker named Watson—had approached her one evening as she was leaving the Cotton Club. She could always rely on that joint to toss her a bone when times were tough, and this time she got a spot there as a cleaning lady. Stéphanie despised this particular genre of work—it reminded her of her childhood in Fort-de-France when her villain-of-a-mother had placed her with the Verneuils, that high-ranking family whose daily habits were the perfect illustration of that old Creole saying, "As soon as a Mulatto becomes the owner of just one horse, he forgets his mother was black."

She had to *make it* in Harlem, a place where, even though you were among people of your own race, no one gave anything away to anyone. And especially not to a woman, and a foreign woman who mangled the English language at that. She started her shift at seven p.m. along with a handful of companions in misery: women from the Deep South with coarse accents who were always cutting up. Together, they'd sweep the floors for the umpteenth time, polish the woodwork till their fingers were raw, beat the seat cushions and curtains and keep a vigilant eye out for any threat of a smudge or hint of cigarette ash, which would inevitably offend and horrify the Cotton Club's particular clientele. The crowds were made up of middle-aged Whites who always sat in the front rows, their arms draped around ethereally beautiful creatures of the feminine sex— blondes with their hair à la garçonne, swathed in pink tulle, heeled so extravagantly that sometimes they were set a good head taller than their companions, and coquettishly dangling cigarette holders from their delicate fingertips. Even during Prohibition, alcohol flowed freely there and, before long, it became the best known of the reckless clubs that dared to mix with whisky and rum. They'd climb onto the tables and shimmy grotesquely as the orchestra tried to drown out their drunken eructation and as the colored dancers continued their numbers up on the stage. Sometimes they'd extract wads of dollars from their pockets and toss them into the air, which never failed to provoke rioting among the Club's horde of servers, all of whom were black. Stéphanie kept her distance from all that monkeying just like she rebuffed the advances of the men who came stag strictly to luxuriate in the black flesh that they otherwise claimed to abhor.

"Don't mind them. Whities are nutcases!" the women who offered themselves up for the charade would guffaw as they shamelessly displayed the gold rings and necklaces their one-night-lovers had given them.

Watson had waited outside the club's service entrance in the glacial cold, stomping his feet against the ground to try to warm himself up a little, and he had offered her a wide smile. Stéphanie wasn't marketing her charms to the Negro clientele because, back then, she was still hoping to find true love (though disillusionment had already begun to shadow what remained of her romantic bent). Anyhow, that oaf of a banker in the doorway didn't do anything for her. When he approached, she turned her back to him and hurried her footsteps.

"Hey, sister! I got a better job for you! Don't turn up your nose at me young lady, I'm only trying to help a sister out."

"What kind of job?" Stéphanie mumbled without stopping.

"Something that'll really be worth your while, darling...."

"Ha! I'm no five-buck harlot. Did you get a good look at me, you big sap?"

"Cool it, lady! Gee, you got a funny way of talking, sister. Where're you from, talking like that?"

The Martinican lady (as the Yiddish gangsters insisted on calling her) scowled, curled her hands into fists and got ready to fight. Watson burst into laughter, but his half-rotten teeth weren't on display very long. An uppercut knocked three of them out before the man fell to his knees on the grimy sidewalk, incredulous as his mug ran with blood and frothing saliva. The people passing by only stopped for an instant, convinced that they were watching a domestic squabble or, more likely, a lovers' spat—a rather banal event in Harlem where Negroes spent their time screwing their women and chasing skirts. As soon as he'd pulled himself back together, Watson wiped his face with the back of his sleeve and sniggered.

"All right now, you're exactly the kind of woman we need in our business. What's your name?"

Right then and there, Stéphanie accepted the banker's proposition: He'd give her a list of gamesters, some fifty names and addresses, and it'd be up to her to wake up in the afore-day of each dawn the damn goodlord granted, rain or sleet, chilblains-cold or scorchingly hot, and knock at the doors of the unlicensed lottery's regulars or, failing that, track them down at their workplaces just before their shifts started. It'd be up to her to have enough change in her pockets since bets were normally placed in small shares. Pennies and nickels, almost never bills. It'd be up to her to nimbly hide the bet rolls each time a patrol of cops prowled past. It didn't take Stéphanie long to learn her job as a numbers runner. And one day, she swore, she'd make it as a banker in her own right.]

Eventually, I had to make a choice. Stop dawdling around. Dutch Schultz's territory was growing day in and day out; meanwhile, mine was shrinking away fast. My arm was so twisted I even convened a veritable war council at my apartment.

Normally, I forbade my henchmen to step foot beyond my threshold. As for my top bankers, they were permitted to come only in the earliest hours, before my venerable neighborhood began to stir, bet rolls in hand, and again at the very end of the afternoon, when they came to collect the winnings of those rare gamesters graced by a touch of fate. Those two operations didn't take long, so I'd offer them neither seat nor drink. I never let my face betray me in any way; I'd stare those men down with my polished anthracite eyes (that was how one of my nicest neighbors, the famous painter Aaron Douglas, referred to them, anyhow). Each of my bankers took care of three or four streets and oversaw an army of number runners. I wrote out all the so-called slips by hand, but it got so tedious and time-consuming when my business really took off that I could no longer rely on the out-of-luck kids I'd gotten in the habit of plucking from the street, so I was obliged to hire a secretary. Of course, I couldn't just call upon one of those well-to-do young ladies from the good Sugar Hill families, those scatterbrains who walked with their eyes cast down to avoid the men's lustful eyes and who always spoke in whispers—their silly straightened hair (as soon as I'd arrived in America, I'd rejected that barbaric custom, defying the disapproving looks of the Negresses and the mockery of the Whites), their dresses and many-layered underthings hiding their figures—*they* were learning to become white ladies. Second-class white ladies, but Whites nonetheless. So, I had to turn to the Lowblacks, and, amongst them, a pearl like that—I mean, a young girl who knew how to read, write and type—was a real rarity. After scavenging all of Harlem, I managed to find two and invited them for interviews. The first one, a real dummy who couldn't even figure out the elevator and ended up climbing up to my tenth-floor apartment (and it must have been quite an undertaking for her, mind you, seeing as she was bona-fide obese) and positively collapsed at my feet.

"Madam St. Clair, I admire you very much, I would be so honored to work for you. I'm available to start right now, I can work all hours, for whatever you're willing to pay me. I used to work for a newspaper, but it shut down six months ago, my boss wrote me a letter of recommendation, I—"

"Enough! That's enough, I got it."

Her rapid-fire words annoyed me. The girl wasn't totally in control of herself and in the kind of business that I practiced, keeping a cool head was do-or-die. She was so piteous that I got a thousand dollars from the W.C. and gave it to her, promising her that I'd get back to her in a couple days. She stared at me—her eyes and mouth formed a perfect triumvirate of three round Os—as if she had found herself in front of Jesus as he was turning water into wine. A wet-behind-the-ears fool like that would get suckered off by the first wastrel to cross her way; she'd end up bringing a kid into the world just to get knocked up by another man and so on and so on until she ended up with a tattered and malnourished flock at her heels. When she left, a cold rage filled my body. I was mad at myself, mostly. I needed to cut my over-sympathetic bullshit and just shout at that heap of quivering fat, make her feel the shame that she brought to our race, "Get your fat Negro ass moving, girl! Don't just come here to piss and moan. Seize your first chance you get! The first job in reach! Work hard, put something aside, figure out a damned goal!" As you know well by now, that's what I, Stéphanie St. Clair, had done! And, my word, it worked out pretty well, didn't it?

The second candidate was a real ironing board, which was already a plus in my eyes. And secondly, she didn't have that hangdog way about her, so common in Harlem among women who've given up too soon. I loved her name right away: Charleyne. It had a little *je ne sais quoi* that went well with the girl's calm—or rather, with her studied cool. We reached an agreement almost right away: She'd come over three times a week in the afternoon to help me make the lottery tickets for the next two days, take dictation for my letters (most of them were addressed to the mayor or the courts), file my documents and help me get dressed if I was going out in the evening. Eight hundred dollars a month was a good salary and she didn't try to negotiate it. As for anything to do with my accounts, no one other than Stéphanie St. Clair had or would ever have the right to do the books. If I was sick—a rare occurrence outside of the coldest days of winter, when I'd get carried away and go outside without being sufficiently bundled up—all bets were off for a couple days. It'd afford a little break to the handful of bankers who'd so far resisted working for me and who still had a couple corners to call their own in Harlem. I'd thought about eliminating them, but Bumpy convinced me that it wouldn't be very prudent to become the police's one and only target. Besides, those bankers were practically decoys, much easier to catch than I was, so arresting them would give the cops some fish to fry. My bodyguard was right for once. And in any case, it wouldn't ruin me to give them a couple days to claw up some extra clams while I was stuck in bed with a sore throat or a no-joke cold (or, more pedestrianly, with cramps, although my periods normally weren't much of a bother). So, I was the only one who had a key to the W.C. and the only one who knew the sum that was stored in there, hidden behind the veritable wall of books and old papers I'd carelessly piled up to make it look natural.

The day I convened my war council, I asked Charleyne to record my decisions because what with my advancing age, my memory wasn't always as sharp as it'd been, and it was getting to be a chore keeping tabs on my vendettas against those associates who'd rubbed me the wrong way from the very beginning. Their mugs all blended together in my mind's eye. And now that we'd found ourselves at war, each man would have to carry out my plan to the letter in order to barricade that cursed white mafia. I had a half-dozen armed men at my disposal who'd oversee the number runners—they were a small troupe of delinquents and criminals who all answered to Bumpy. Two thirds of them had killed their women, another hung his own father high and dry over a question of inheritance (a pittance: some old shack in Alabama), another had raped a couple girls who were on their way to school. I preferred not to know their identities. Instead, I'd given them a kind of registration code composed of a letter and a number—but that got troublesome after I took Bumpy (who had recruited them) off commission. I managed rather craftily to extract A2's name from him—he was called Charlie—and from C7, who went by the nickname Budd, and I was stunned that they looked quite less sinister than I'd imagined. B4—I mean Dick—got on my nerves as soon as the council had been called into session.

"Madam Queen, with all due respect, those Whites answer with their Tommy guns first and discuss it afterward. Those guys make my blood curdle!"

A majority of the council nodded their heads. I was flabbergasted! So, these were the toughs Bumpy had been bragging about, the heavies who supposedly weren't afraid of anyone! They were the ones in charge of enforcing the law and order I, the Digit Queen of Harlem, had established. I was so enraged that I had to stifle the urge to crush B4's balls with my high-heeled foot. With those shoes on, he would've gotten what he deserved, that big sissy! I couldn't help but unleash a torrent of exasperation.

"I'll show you how to keep hold of the game, you bunch of niggers! I'll show them what a fight is. I'll teach that Dutch Schultz better than to think he can just muscle in and take the numbers away from us like that. Sure, they killed Harris. But I ain't scared and they know it. I ain't like those niggers!"

A deathly silence fell over my living room, in which I was the only person seated. I looked for my cigarette holder on the coffee table where I normally left it, but it wasn't there. I must've left it in my room—strictly off limits to all—even though I had charged myself with keeping it tobacco-free, just like the W.C. Even Annah, my maid, had formal orders to keep out, and I always cleaned it myself. My occasional lovers after Duke and then Bumpy only were allowed in when I deigned to let them make love to me, otherwise they kept to their own rooms at the opposite end of my apartment. I always maintained a private bedroom because I despised conjugal intimacy, someone else's body pressed against yours, their breath on your neck, their unappealing sweat and their foul-smelling gas. If I really think about it, maybe that came from my adolescence, back when Eugène Verneuil would slip into my bed around midnight, quietly rape me and then tip-toe away thirty minutes later.

The one called Charlie, a.k.a. A2, was the first to react.

"With all due respect, Madam, we're all niggers in this room, even if you come from Martinique. I understand you're angry, but—"

"Shut up, you bastard! I'm not from Martinique as you believe; I am from France. I am a Black Frenchwoman, you hear me?"

"Yes, ma'am."

"We… we're ready to follow your orders, Queenie," the one called Dick finally stuttered out. "Say the word and it's good as done."

I ordered the immediate executions of three Black Judases who'd succumbed to the siren call of the white mafia. They'd started shaking down the 134th Street stores where I had stakes and threatening my number-runners with a pistol to the temple in way of—those bastards!—a first warning. Just who did they take themselves for, those race-traitors? They were a low-life bunch of burn-outs, hideously swaggering with pride to have been recruited by Dutch Schultz's gang, scrambling like pigs at the trough to grease his lousing palms. Ha! They'd see what they were in for.

Then I demanded that someone settle accounts with two little sluts working at the Savoy Ballroom, a well-known club where the Charleston reigned supreme. Apparently these two kept Schultz informed of my comings and goings by worming the information out of Bumpy. And though the man wasn't any more swayed by tender flesh than the average gorilla, he'd complain about my lackadaisical negligence and would go to bed with other women from time to time, not without my tacit approval. It didn't matter to me if that half-wit, who'd always crawl back to me after eating his humble pie, emptied his load into their pussies, but the fact that he loosened his tongue was putting me in danger and was no mere trifle to be ignored. Back before Dutch Schultz got his heart set on claiming Harlem for himself, it wouldn't have been a problem, but now I was at war. I couldn't tolerate the slightest indiscretion from my associates and certainly not from my right-hand man. Once my war plan had been laid out and my orders given, I asked Charleyne to sit at the typewriter and in one breath I dictated the following letter to the editor-in-chief of the *New York Amsterdam News*:

> To the Editor of the New York Amsterdam News,
>   In your issue of last week, you wrote, "It is believed that the slain banker was one of a group of Negro operators whom the 'Policy Queen' has been trying to draw into a union to support her in her active crusade against the usurpers," and further that "the finger has been placed" on me.
>   This letter is to let you know that Martin L. Harris was in no way connected with any activity in which I may have been engaged. I assure you that had he been affiliated with me in any way, he would never have come to such an untimely and ill-fated end. The gangsters who killed Harris know better than to molest me or my associates.
> Yours sincerely,

The Martin L. Harris that the police had found on the docks with a bullet between his eyes had, in fact, long worked for me. First as a simple numbers runner, then as a banker. He was among those whom I trusted the most. In the morning when he'd report to my place and hand over the bets he'd collected in his designated streets, I'd ask him for news of his little family and especially of his daughter, a charming eleven-year-old whom he'd often take out for a stroll in Central Park, right at the edge of Harlem. What went through his head to make him—like others before him—stop believing in Madam Queen's omniscience? How'd he get the balls to try and double-cross me? What had Dutch Schultz whispered into the ear of one of my best associates? I'll probably never know. The main thing was to nip it in the bud. As I say, when an arm or leg grows gangrene, you amputate or perish. I had no other option after Harris's betrayal than to send him to the sweet hereafter. And that's what I ordered without the slightest hesitation. But at the same time, I needed to maintain a certain upstanding public-image and swiftly tamper down the innuendos and allegations spread like contaminate by those scandal-hungry journalists. Madam Queen and the numbers game had always been a juicy topic for them—I'm sure my name kept their presses hot. I made sure to clear away any shadow cast in my direction and would publish refutations whenever I deemed it necessary.

Except that I'd come to realize that the enemy was right in front of me. Bumpy, my Bumpy, had turned on me, or at least had renounced my determination to refuse any kind of negotiation with the enemy….

Third Note

With two white roses on her breasts,
White candles at head and feet,
Dark Madonna of the grave she rests;
Lord Death has found her sweet

Her mother pawned her wedding ring
To lay her out in white;
She'd be so proud she'd dance and sing
To see herself tonight.

—Countee Cullen

Chapter Nine

"You're a total mystery, Madam!" the poet Countee Cullen would chuckle at me each time we met up, whether at Roseland or Small's Paradise—the famous concert halls of the day, always well-stocked with what the press called the "giants of the new music straight out of New Orleans, jazz, a miraculous mixture of African rhythms and European instruments," in other words, the Duke Ellingtons, the Fats Wallers and the Louis Armstrongs. In truth, I much preferred blues to jazz; the blues reminded me of the slow sadness of Martinique's bel air music, but here, up north, it was seen as a kind of barbaric noise, too rural to enchant the delicate ears of the big city dwellers in New York. But, as it happened, I'd run into Countee Cullen every now and then in a cabaret flowing with alcohol (under the table, of course) despite the shroud Prohibition tried to throw over the merriment. I'm circling back to that damned period again, dear Frédéric. I'm sorry! You'll set everything in order afterward, won't you? Some crazy Whites had decided to ban alcohol, and so, police all across the country were spending half their time chasing down clandestine distilleries. Except in Harlem! Every night hordes of tipplers would brave the invisible frontiers separating our neighborhood from the Bronx to come wet their whistles. Bad whisky was produced in Harlem, a kind of rot-gut that would've knocked out a cow—nothing on earth could've compelled me to touch my lips to that stuff. Everybody knew that the Black Frenchwoman named Stéphanie St. Clair only drank champagne. To tell the honest truth, that was all just trickery because, while I did appreciate Irish whisky, what I really missed was rum. Real rum! Not that bitter, red-hued stuff they imported under cover from Jamaica, but the kind that's clear as water. When I had to take leave of my position at the Verneuils, I hung around the Levassor canal for days on end, sleeping in fishermen's shacks and eating the scraps left behind at the hodge-podge market that'd improvisationally appear every other day. Back then, sugar-cane alcohol kept me *good* company. Or, rather, a band of soaks had taken me under their wings, and they gave me a taste for that alcohol, and let me say: No young lady—even one who's living in utter insecurity—would be mis-advised to avoid the stuff. Fortunately, I held my booze well and not once did I ever lose control of myself. Especially since the old quimbois-sorceress' prediction was still echoing in my head—and that lady's ability to detach her head from her neck like some old hat was well known. I'd go far, very far, not only off to some distant country, but in life, too. Philibert, the barber, the first man to awaken my senses, agreed.

"Mysterious lady!" Countee Cullen would sigh. I'd listen to him wax poetic over my *Frenchie* accent and he'd ask me thousands of questions about *the land of Victor Hugo*, questions I'd avoid because, after all, I'd only lived there for a total of seven months.

It was that very young poet (he was only in his twenties back then) who opened the doors of the black intelligentsia to me. They tolerated a certain lack of culture (at least in women). In my case, it was more a question of ignorance, since I'd only spent a couple years behind a school desk before my mother had gotten it in her mind to find me a place with the Verneuils. The thing that saved me, I believe, was my voracious appetite for reading, and I was quite serious when it came to it. My mother's Bible, old newspapers from here or there, battered books I stole from my bosses or their encyclopedias and atlases that I'd consult in secret, little white magic books like the *Grand Albert* that the junk-sellers sold under wraps. Countee, who had a curious way of pronouncing his name, with an *ay* instead of an *ee*, as if it were a French word, realized my fondness for books and, at first, found it amusing. Sure, he was a brilliant Harvard man, but that didn't keep him from hobnobbing with his old pals in Harlem, and it was a cabaret boss who introduced us—in 1927, if memory serves. Our relationship never got anyone's eyes crossed. I was pegged as too old and not pretty enough for him, according to the beauty standards pedaled by the so-called black community, and that suited us fine. We were friends, nothing more! A rare thing, a real rarity between a man and a woman, but a thing that was possible and he and I were the living proof. Back then, he was bursting with energy and an appetite for life—he didn't suspect his would be brief. He possessed a boundless veneration for an Africa he didn't know and sang that land's praises in his poems. Now and then, he'd invite me to a mass at the Salem Episcopal Methodist Church, the church whose pastor had taken him under its wing back when he was an orphan child on the verge of joining a gang.

Countee's reputation was already imposing when I met him; he'd won a couple poetry contests at New York University, where he'd been accepted—a real rarity for a Black. The first time I heard him reciting verses from his collection, *The Ballad of the Brown Girl*, I was literally transfixed. His baby face and his affected diction clashed with the weight of his deceptively simple words—simple because I understood all of them. I suspected there was a hidden meaning, a double sense, a tenderness to be found or, at least, something to be shared. I learned "A Brown Girl Dead" by heart, and I'd recite it to myself whenever a feeling of loneliness threatened to overtake me because, even though a swarm of folks depended on me for the damned numbers, even if others counted on my generosity to keep them afloat in this or that business (legal businesses, I mean), none of that did anything to make me feel less different from the people around me. I was a prisoner with no chance of parole in what they called my *Frenchness*. But during my adolescence and my childhood back in Martinique, I'd never felt French. The masses were too busy trying to wrest themselves from misery to have the leisure to wonder about who or what they were. We lived on an island where native-born Whites, Blacks and Mulattos all lived together, and the foreign-borns came from a country we couldn't imagine, a country the schoolteachers regaled as our mother land and that others likened to a kind of Holy Virgin. We learned to love France, to tremble upon hearing the melody of the *Marseillaise* or seeing the tricolor flag flying, we learned to venerate its grand authors—Victor Hugo and Lamartine above all—but, in truth, it was a platonic love (a term I obviously didn't know back then). No, I'd never been French. Never *felt* French; not even once I'd finally decided to set off to discover France at the age of twenty-six. The minute our ship made landing in the heavy grayness of Le Havre, I rushed toward more hospitable climes—island dweller as I was—but setting my suitcases down in sunny Marseille, I *still* couldn't deceive myself into being French. Besides, I was never considered as such by the natives. In their eyes, I was a slightly civilized African, probably the daughter of some kinglet on a pleasure trip to mainland France, who enjoyed wandering along La Canebière. It wasn't until I landed in the United States that the question of who I really was arose. Imposed itself upon me would be more accurate. I was somehow compelled to define myself because if my skin color wasn't a giveaway, my accent and my hesitant English, my way of wearing my hair, my clothes, even my laugh—everything else indicated a non-American origin. Most often, they'd classify me as *the Black Frenchwoman*: Almost no one was aware of Martinique's existence, not in Five Points (where I first lived) and not in Harlem. And my word, that designation—to my great surprise—didn't displease me in the slightest. On the contrary, it was often a succor for me. Take, for example, those occasions in which the cops would arrest me for one reason or another and send me to court. The judges, all Whites, would observe me with perplexed eyes, ask me to repeat this or that mispronounced word (in truth, many of my mispronunciations were intentional) and would inevitably end the procedure by handing down a lighter sentence than my lawyer had feared.

"Thankfully you're French, Madam St. Clair!" my lawyer, Elridge McMurphy, would breathe out, relief twisting a little smile into the corners of his mouth.

So that's how Countee Cullen—that brilliant, young Negro who'd managed to make his way from a squalid school in the Bronx to New York University and then on to Harvard, following in the footsteps of W.E.B. Du Bois himself—ended up taking a friendly interest in my person. He'd been granted a scholarship to study in France and had apparently spent enough time there to be enchanted. Each time he'd bring up the subject, I'd respond evasively to his questions because undoubtedly his knowledge of "my" country was more accurate and vaster than my own. Countee had travelled and lived in the real France; as for me, aside from my brief stay in Marseille, I only knew the France of books. To keep him from noticing my shortcomings on the subject I'd beg him to read his poems to me and, being in possession of a more virtuosic memory than most everyone else, I'd have them committed to heart after no more than two or three recitations. We used to go strolling along the banks of the Harlem River in late afternoon when it was practically deserted—in the summertime, it would stay mostly deserted till it was dark out. That the sun shone until eleven at night had always stunned the tropics-gal that I was, having spent twenty-six years watching night fall like a guillotine blade at six p.m. Each time summer returned, I had to consciously remind myself that it was possible to perambulate and even to noctambulate without seeing a single illuminated street lamp. Countee, snazzy no matter the day of the week, would attract infinite feminine regards as soon as we neared Central Park—and this despite the overly-serious expression that was permanently etched across his face. I could see in those women's eyes a certain disdain, as they had certainly deemed me an old whore (I was in my early forties) trying to sink her claws into a young man from a good family. Sometimes he'd leap on a park bench and recite one of his poems and I'd jokingly imitate him, which shocked the passersby even more. I loved reciting the cryptic "A Brown Girl Dead."

> With two white roses on her breasts,
> White candles at head and feet,
> Dark Madonna of the grave she rests;
> Lord Death has found her sweet.
>
> Her mother pawned her wedding ring
> To lay her out in white;
> She'd be so proud she'd dance and sing
> To see herself tonight.

The poem told the story of a young girl who passed away before her wedding, a Black Madonna as the poet wrote. Her mother gives up her ring to buy the girl beautiful funeral clothes. The fact that death seemed to be venerated as *Lord Death* and even, perhaps, desired, troubled me. At no moment of my existence had I ever succumbed to wishing for death—not even at the worst of times, not even when I was raped by those thugs from the Ku Klux Klan who'd stopped our bus in the middle of the night on an abandoned stretch of highway. I wasn't afraid of Basile, the name we give in Creole to the specter who comes to knock at your door to announce that your last hour has arrived. I simply didn't think of it. I'd always been too busy trying to survive and surmount the obstacles that lined my path. Maybe that poem touched me because it contained an image of the mother I'd always wanted. Maybe. Then again, I must admit that I never had any strong feelings toward my mother. Neither love nor hate.

She was just there beside me because she was the one who'd brought me into this world, her and a man whose face and name she couldn't remember, and she took care of me simply because that was her duty. But I was bothered by the presence of the word *white* in Countee Cullen's poem: The young woman had two white roses at her breasts and white candles had been placed beside her head and feet. And her mother had wanted to dress her in white for her final journey. Did that color symbolize purity like so many people believed?

Countee smiled and suddenly stopped walking. The part of Central Park reserved for Blacks—or rather, the part they'd overrun—would start emptying out little by little toward the late afternoon, whereas the Whites' part of the park would grow more and more animated as the day progressed. The Blacks hurried home at nightfall because it wasn't good to dawdle around. Darkness was an ally of the underworld and permitted trafficking both minor and rather more major in the poorly-lit streets of Harlem.

"No, Madam St. Clair, white is the color of mourning for many people of Africa. It's the color of sadness, of suffering, of despair...."

Countee was a kind of professor for me. By talking with him, I learned something new every day, even if he was surprised by how much I knew, me, the creature he saw (rightly, I might add) as a gangster in heels who was almost entirely consumed with running the numbers game. He'd even asked me to place a bet on his behalf once, just once. To see. But I refused. I didn't mix my criminal undertakings with the educated Negroes living on Edgecombe Avenue. They'd been to university, earned advanced diplomas, had prestigious careers and seemed to be respected by the Whites; as for me, I was forged by the wind and my whims, from Martinique to Marseille, from Marseille to New York, and who knows? Maybe tomorrow I'd set off for Mexico without

160

ever looking back. They were established, settled in their lives, whereas I was a wisp of straw constantly fighting against the formidable gusts that threatened to carry me off. Countee Cullen heard news of the war that damned Dutch Schultz was waging against me to get his hands on the numbers and he reassured me, "I know you'll never let yourself get overtaken. You don't have the right, anyhow! The Whites penned us up in Harlem and now they'd better leave Harlem to us!"

Those swaggering words didn't jive with the character of the young man who was naturally reserved, almost shy. The jealous types would even describe him as effeminate, something I hadn't really noticed, especially as the tomboy-labeled woman that I was. They said my voice was too husky, my gaze too steady, my manners to brusque, my face and body too angular. My girlfriends were always trying to soften me, as they said. Mysti would get me all dolled up and Annabelle would paint my face whenever we were going out to some cabaret, but nothing doing. I remained an androgynous creature—I learned that fancy word from Countee— that the men (including even the hardest gangster) approached with dread-fear. Well, I mean the black gangsters, not the ones from the mob. Not that sonofabitch Dutch Schultz.

"Madam Stéphanie, I'm going to marry Yolanda... soon, very soon," the brilliant young man had whispered mid-conversation one day.

"Oh, that's wonderful news! Congratulations, dear friend! I was afraid you might follow my bad example. After forty, a woman can no longer hope for her Prince Charming to sweep her off her feet, can she? Of course, it's not the same for you men...."

"The survival of our race must be ensured. Ha ha ha!"

"And when will I have the pleasure of meeting the—I assume—beautiful young Yolanda?"

"But... you already know who she is!"

I was speechless. Never had I imagined she might be the very same daughter of W.E.B. Du Bois. True, he'd briefly served as a kind of mentor to Countee, he'd probably helped him get into New York University and then Harvard, but from that to offering him his daughter's hand, well, that sure was a leap. Du Bois was from a grand family with a prestigious name and very light skin. The kind of light-skinned people that the black masses worshipped because they were considered to be at the forefront of their fight for emancipation. On the other hand, Countee was black as night and came from nothing. From the Bronx rabble. Endowed with an extraordinary brain, he'd managed to wrest himself from them, but that still didn't mean he could count himself among the *grand monde*.

"I... I don't suit her?" the poet stuttered out, wounded by my shock.

"No, no, no, that's not what I meant.... Look, Yolanda is a very timid girl, she's never set foot outside without a chaperon and, well...."

"Well, then it's high time she breaks out of her cocoon! That she be confronted with the hardships of our existence... isn't that what real life is?"

I doubted the young creature with long auburn hair and nearly transparent skin that I crossed daily in the hallway of my building could for one single instant bear seeing a man's head burst open by a bullet down the block, much less watch those bands of miserous Negresses trollop along 142nd Street for three dollars without an ounce of shame, so commonplace back then. Yolanda Du Bois had been raised in an enchanted world, that of Sugar Hill, the only part of Harlem you could wander around in peace all night long. She went to an upper-class school where all the students had light skin—and, paradoxically, it was the students of that school the white press labelled as our *future black leaders*. In reality, those people were Negroes in name only, or rather, they'd been so designated because the United States lived in thrall of the one-drop law. A single drop of black blood in your veins and voila: You'd be classified as a Negro even if you were white-skinned and blue-eyed! As for me, I'd always harbored a certain distrust for the people who would've been able to *pass*—another accepted expression—simply by moving to a different state. From being a Negro in Virginia or Georgia, they'd turn into a Caucasian in Maine or Massachusetts. There were plenty of them in Sugar Hill, especially on my street. I could tell, whenever I passed them on the sidewalk or in my building's lobby, that in their eyes I, a too-dark Negress, was an intruder and had invaded their little world of café-au-lait-colored folk, closer to milk than to coffee.

One morning, the phone rang. I tell you now, I never did hear that noise without trembling. Lord knew I had no love lost for those damned machines of modernity, but a couple of my main bankers had managed to convince me to install the contraption. As they demonstrated, it'd allow them to warn me if one of our moles—planted in one or another precinct—tipped them off to a major operation that was getting underway. Which is to say, when two dozen coppers armed to the teeth, under the orders of a boss and brandishing wolf-dogs and paddywagons, came to round up my numbers runners in the three or four block radius around my headquarters. Six or seven thousand dollars' worth of bets up in smoke! And that's not counting the five or nine hundred to make bail the next morning or the morning after that. And the legal troubles. For the NYPD, any reason was reason enough to hassle Stéphanie St. Clair. But sometimes the information was wrong, and the operation would target other blocks instead of the ones I'd been warned about. I guess the police knew that some of their men were corrupt; narcs, to put it crudely. As a result, I was filled with dread even before I picked up the phone.

"Madam St. Clair, am I interrupting?"

I was so anxious I didn't recognize the voice on the other end at first. It was my closest neighbor, W.E.B. Du Bois, that intellectual, so immensely revered, even by those who couldn't read. He'd always treated me with utmost respect, I, who'd had such difficulty accepting the sidelong stares of a certain number of my neighbors. Of course, *he* was perfectly aware of the illicit nature of my business.

"May I stop over for a moment?"

I acquiesced, a bit confused. What on earth could he (a man so highly regarded by the black intelligentsia, who always got a column in every major paper—including the *New York Times*—whenever he had a new book out) want with me? What was I (a lady gangster, after all) compared to his eminence? Du Bois came over in a housecoat and slippers; he had the exhausted eyes of someone who hadn't got a wink of sleep.

"Countee Cullen is your friend, isn't he?" he asked in a hushed voice as soon as I'd offered him a seat in the living room. He probably thought I wasn't alone. That my man was lurking in the next room. Or, anyhow, the latest model. I was no paragon of morality in that regard. I allowed myself to have whomever I wanted or needed, and my officials at the various periods of my life—the Dukes, the Bumpy Johnsons and the Lewises—had no say in the matter. I answered Du Bois with a nod of the head, bowled over by finding myself on almost intimate terms with the man whom I'd always seen dressed in suit and tie. He'd invited me over to his place twice—once to introduce me to his daughter, Yolanda—but that was the first time he'd come to my place.

"You… you haven't noticed anything?"

"You mean here, in this building?"

"I mean with Countee…."

"Hmm… no, nothing comes to mind Dr. Du Bois. Why do you ask?

He stroked his goatee, a mannerism surely intended to hide his nerves. You could just tell he was trying to work up to something he didn't dare say aloud.

"Are things not going well with Yolanda and Countee?" I guessed, then instantly regretted involving myself in other people's business.

I'd hit the nail right on the head, of course. That was the first time I'd been confronted with a father's distress and, by the same token, with that man's love for his daughter. I had never known the warmth of paternal arms, and it touched me deeply. Feeling like quite the dawdle-head, I forced myself to hold back my tears. I hadn't exchanged more than two or three pleasantries with Yolanda, but it was just as well. I didn't dare stick my nose any further in whatever dispute it was that had pitted her against Countee. To tell the truth, I was surprised to hear it because, unlike the vast majority of Harlemites of the masculine sex, the young poet was no nighthawk. Far from it! While Bumpy shamelessly ogled the first fine-figured woman we passed out on the street—without any regard for my person—Countee seemed to live in his own little world. Unless he was just distracted. I never quite knew how to take it. He was a man whom you could never quite see through, though he overflowed with kindness and a rich sort of altruism for others, and especially for me, who was always ready to lend him an ear. Without exactly admitting it, he'd become a kind of son to me. But he worried me a little because the more his literary reputation grew, the less he seemed to feel easy with himself. Something was tormenting him, some very old wound or some unfulfilled desire that he never spoke to anyone about. Not even to me, the trusted confidant that I'd become.

"Yo... Yolanda found something out...." Du Bois stammered out. He'd sunk into deep thought and had practically forgotten I was there.

"Nothing serious, I hope... they're such a handsome couple!"

"She wants a divorce."

"What? So soon? But it's unthinkable, Dr. Du Bois!"

I was sincerely shocked. I liked Countee a great deal, and to know that his marriage was turning to vinegar was unbearable. I begged Du Bois to try to speak with his daughter, to explain to her that nowadays it was no easy task to find a man like her husband, that she'd end up short-changed, that she'd regret it until the day she died. An inexorable flood of beseeching words rushed from my lips and I couldn't stop myself. They were like the words of a mother pleading her beloved son's case. Du Bois looked at me with a dazed expression and rested one grief-stricken hand on my shoulder. To tell it like it was, Du Bois was devastated.

"Madam St. Clair, I… well, this is rather awkward, but… well, it's that Countee prefers men."

Chapter Ten

How did that sonofabitch Bumpy end up falling under the spell of that sewer-rat-faced Italian Lucky Luciano after letting his drawers down for Dutch Schultz? Birds of a feather flock together, as they say. Except that my Bumpy was black and stumpy-legged and the other one was white and lanky. Except that my Bumpy had already woken up in jail cells in Harlem or down on Rikers Island at least thirty times over, and the other guy, that filthy wop, had never once been bothered by the police. At least to my knowledge. Except that Bumpy and even I were small-timers compared to Luciano. Alright, fine, those two thugs did have one thing in common: The first had a fleshy lump protruding from the back of his head that made him look like an alien from behind (although he was a more-or-less appealing man from the front) and the second had a chronic lazy eye—a droopy souvenir from an episode with the infamous mob boss Salvatore Maranzo. One night, Luciano got kidnapped and was nearly beaten to death, and after that he couldn't open his eye all the way anymore, so he seemed to be constantly surveilling someone on the sly. Every now and then he'd tear through Harlem in a brand-new Model T driven by a black chauffeur in white cap and gloves, but he'd never stop anywhere. The Lowblacks would applaud when he passed by—some of them believed he was the President of the United States of America.

In any case, after that beer baron Dutch Schultz got whacked (clutching the now famous telegram I'd sent him as he lay on his deathbed—famous because the press milked it for all it was worth, reprinting it in entirety: *As ye sow, so shall ye reap*), Lucky Luciano came along to try and crush me under his heel. His gripe with me couldn't have been about business: His specialty was heroin dealing, and that racket brought in a hundred times more than the numbers game. The man pissed me off! Hadn't he made enough money during Prohibition? Didn't he make a killing with his Canadian and Caribbean imports? Back then, I used to send Duke to one of Schultz's speakeasies on the edge of the Bronx to stock up, and that was how I discovered that what the American Negro called rum had nothing—truly nothing!—to do with what we French Blackfolk called rum. The first time the stuff came my way, I ended up having a truly memorable fight with my man-of-the-moment who was feeling so proud of the gift he'd offered his *honey*—I never could stand that term... it was just too concrete. Stéphanie St. Clair is more vinegar than honey, and she'll certainly never be any man's tootsie! Anyhow, my man brought me a bottle of Jamaican rum. Right away, I was taken aback by the color of the liquid—it was an orangey-brown that reminded me of whisky. I brought a glass to my lips but spit that foulness out reflexively, furious.

"What the hell is this, Duke? Shitty bourbon, huh? Doctored-up cognac? Whisky from the Midwest?"

"Madam, it's... it's rum. I swear it is!"

"You big lunkhead! Rum is clear as water."

Lucky Luciano's feats had been known to me since day one, when my Irish family and I, freshly arrived in America, first set our bags down in Five Points. They made him out to be a real terror, and some would only utter his name in sotto voce, with no end of furtive glances in every direction. His gang didn't deal in the realms where I'd managed to stake out a claim for myself, the notorious Forty Thieves, for example—oh, I still miss them even today, dear nephew, but my chatter must be starting to bore you. Back then, I was free of all responsibility, nothing weighed on my shoulders. I was just a small-timer, a look-out charged with alerting the heavies when the police were nearby or with keeping an eye on the business owners who balked at giving us our cut. I even helped their old sourpuss cook in the kitchen, too, and I'd deliver their meals discreetly while our men were dealing with one sensitive operation or another. Well, maybe *sensitive operation* is too grandiose. Most of the time, the Forty Thieves organized raids that barely lasted half an hour and then they'd lay low till the next operation. But I cut my teeth with them. And cut my first men. That's where I learned how to wield authority, how to establish such exacting rules with my subordinates that not a one dared disobey me—any scrap of disobedience was deemed an act of high treason, and everyone knows the consequences of that crime. The brute who was our boss, O'Reilly, the one whose balls I ended up slicing off, had no qualms about gunning down anyone guilty of the slightest deviation. Little by little, handling a gun became almost second nature to me, and the obsessive fear that their very presence had stirred in me began to dissipate. That's how this scrawny-zoklet woman who'd never laid finger on a gun back in Martinique or in France became an American.

Back then, Luciano was a fortunate man—that's where that nickname "Lucky" came from. He had, or so they said, eluded no fewer than five assassination attempts (the work of rival gangs), which was the basis of his legendary status. After I left Five Points and settled myself in Harlem, I stopped hearing about him, except every now and then when the tabloids would sensationalize his *exploits*. During Prohibition, he'd managed to amass a colossal fortune that made my pathetic Jamaican Ginger money seem like a joke. According to the press, he'd managed to fall in with the boss of all bosses, the *capo degli capi*, Mr. Al Capone himself, the Emperor of the Chicago Underworld. In Cuba, where a Yiddish Mafioso named Meyer Lansky (Capone's childhood friend) was hiding out, Luciano had become a partner in a chain of luxury hotels and brothels. I'd fixed my sights on him from the moment he got the idea into his head—an absurd idea, if you ask me— of taking over Harlem. Why did those white mafiosos rich as Croesus suddenly come up with the ridiculous (to say the least) plan of taking over the poorest part of New York? Why were they so interested in our under-the-table numbers game that, compared to their business ventures, brought in no more than a pittance?

"Stéphanie, you ought to... meet Lucky Luciano," Bumpy said offhandedly to me one day, as I was railing against the nth killing of my numbers runners.

"Never! You hear me, n-e-v-e-r! You already tried to get me to kneel down to your Dutch Schultz scum and look at what came of it!"

"There's a lot to gain from getting in league with him. After Al Capone, he's the second biggest man on the scene, isn't he?"

"What do you mean, get in league with him? What are you talking about, you dope?"

Ellsworth Johnson—who wasn't proud of his lump and hated when I'd call him Bumpy (he preferred "Ells")—poured himself a whisky, a habit that seized him whenever his mind was troubled with thought. Although he had his full share of vices, notoriously overdoing it with the prostitutes he protected (he thought I was oblivious to that), wasting his money at the racetrack and sending for heroin the second my back was turned, he was, in truth, a relatively sober individual. Long after I'd taken up with him, and without wishing to pry, I learned that when he was a teenager, his mother had scared him by telling him that the more he drank, the bigger his lump would grow. I drank much more than he did, even if I only rarely filled my glass.

"You're always out with those hot-shot intellectuals... Du Bois, Countee Cullen, Langston Hughes, just to name a few, but Madam wants me to explain what *in league with* means. Ha ha ha!" he guffawed.

I absolutely despised it when men tried to make an ass of me, especially since all the men I was in contact with were dependent upon me, upon my goodwill, upon my good fortune, and that was certainly the case with Bumpy. Besides, I'd already thrown him out once, and *monsieur* had wandered lost through Harlem for weeks on end, incapable of lifting himself up again, abandoned by everyone—including his ladies of the night—he came back to me like a beaten dog and begged me on his knees to take him back. He started his campaign of redemption by hanging around my building (he knew my usual comings and goings), but I ignored him haughtily. I'd recruited a pretty young man as my new bodyguard and, although there was nothing physical between us, he was devoted to my person. Lewis was an abandoned boy who'd been shuttled from orphanage to orphanage before being hired as a servant for some rich Sugar Hill family. As I understood it—I didn't try to clarify—he'd been seduced by or tried to seduce his boss's wife and was promptly fired. He'd approached me ever-so timidly one evening at the Lafayette (the bar I'd go to when I needed new perspective).

"Excuse me for bothering you, Madam Queen, but may I have a moment of your time, please?"

"Spit it out, boy!"

I hadn't even glanced at him before speaking; I was so accustomed (exasperating as it was) to being assailed by all types of people who wanted me to help them financially or to invest in their businesses. I still hadn't gotten over the fact that I, a little island Blackwoman with no friends or family in Harlem or anywhere else in all of America, had turned out to be the one at whose feet everyone groveled. When they were face to face with me, they thought I was hard as nails or, as a lady who wanted to borrow two thousand dollars for I-don't-know-what once put it, *a real ice queen*, but deep down I was a real worrier. Not shaky, but full of the feeling that I was living in a waking dream, that at any moment the wonderful existence I'd worked so hard to create could collapse around me. Strangely, the Creole translation of "collapse" just came to mind: "to spank yourself against the earth."

"I... I admire you very much," the pretty young thing

murmured.

"And why is that, if my question's not too indiscreet?"

"In Harlem, it's you who's the real mayor... or rather, the queen, I mean, our queen.... We'd be nothing without you."

"Alright young man! Quit beating around the bush. What do you want? Money? What for?"

The young man's face grew wet with tears, which were at odds with his herculean stature. Although he was at least a head taller than me, he looked like a boy caught red-handed and even though I was caught up in worries—well, in one major worry, that shitty wop Lucky Luciano who'd gotten it in his head to lay his filthy hands on my territory—I let him get to me. Maybe you could even say he seduced me, because as soon as I'd decided to hire Lewis as a bodyguard, he started teaching me the Charleston (he loved to dance). Music had never been in my blood and I rarely went to the cabarets and nightclubs, unless I had some business or other to check up on or if I needed to catch up on the latest fad—those things changed like lightning in Harlem, and I liked to keep myself up-to-date. Or sometimes I'd come around to keep my friends Shortie and Annabelle company. My powers, omnipotent as they may have seemed, were in the cross-hairs of a staggering number of envious individuals. Many of the small-time black mobsters couldn't swallow the fact that a woman ran the numbers. And a skinny woman at that, not even a mamma. In other words, an unintimidating creature—unintimidating, that is, aside from her icy gray eyes (according to Duke) and her French accent, which she apparently made no effort to hide. And then there was the NYPD—all those white cops who found a perverse pleasure in harassing me, in arresting me on some minor infraction or even just a rumor, in putting me in jail longer than the law allowed, then sending me in front of a judge. And now, I had this latest plot to deal with. The white mafia wanted to bring me to heel, that fucking mob that took itself to be more powerful than the Holy Father!

"Let's dance this one, Madam Queen," my new bodyguard said in a cheerful but respectful voice no sooner than we'd set foot in the nightclub. I let him lead me to the dance floor without really knowing why. My first time on a dancefloor! And my word, I found the bizarre gyrations of the Charleston rather amusing. Leaping with all your weight from one leg to the other can knock you right over, even if you're not large, because you have to swing your hips in while bending your knees as you flail all around. That acrobatic dance (to say the least) was responsible—according to the papers—for the success of a certain Josephine Baker, a Black American lady who performed with the *Revue Nègre* at a theater on the Champs-Élysées.

I eagerly read all the stories on her in the white press, read about her tumultuous life, her love affairs, her escapades. But I was not a fan of her banana skirt—she'd dangle bunches of bananas from her hips when she took to the stage. I even started comparing our two lives: she an American lady, the descendant of slaves, who'd found success in France, and I, the Frenchwoman, likewise a descendant of slaves, who'd done the same in America. But no one had ever made that parallel and no one ever would for the simple reason that Josephine Baker lived in the limelight permanently, positively seeking it out, whereas I, Stéphanie St. Clair, attempted to live as discreetly as possible, preferring the shadows to the spotlights. Without you, Frédéric, dear nephew, without that letter of yours that miraculously made it all the way from Martinique to me, I bet you that all memory of Queenie, the little sovereigness of Harlem's numbers racket, would've ended up vanishing like the smoke from a wood fire beneath the clear sky of summer. Ah, how I love the summertime. It goes so quickly in New York; three months, three and a half, depends on the year, but it's worth it. I say summer in New York is better than all twelve months of heat in our native Martinique.

[LETTER FROM MARTINIQUE

Dear Aunt,

You don't know who I am because you left our island a couple months before I was born. My name is Frédéric, and I'm the oldest son of Edmire, the sister of your mother, Félicienne. There are sixteen years between our mothers, mine being the youngest of her family, and many more years separate you from me. That's why, even if you are my cousin, I prefer to respectfully call you "aunt." I would never have even known of your existence, except that one of my English teachers at the school in Schoelcher gave a lecture on the Harlem Renaissance, that magical time you lived through and for which I envy you. After listing off all the major black intellectuals, poets, musicians and scholars, he alluded to the gang warfare back then and, without lingering on it, he mentioned— among others—a certain Stéphanie Sainte-Claire who went on to become the queen of Harlem's clandestine lottery. I was startled. That lady had the same last name as me! Pure coincidence? Was I somehow related to her? I wanted to get to the bottom of it, so I started hanging around the Schoelcher library, which got a few American newspapers in every now and then. But my grasp of English was too tenuous to make much sense of the articles. I ended up—I admit it—forgetting about you. The second stage of my baccalauréat was approaching and my mother was counting on me. Oh, I forgot to tell you that my mother, unlike yours, never left the Vauclin countryside for the capital city. So, when I won a scholarship to study in Fort-de-France, I ended up boarding with an old lady there.

In the end, baccalauréat in hand, I resisted my vocation as a teacher (as prestigious as it might have been) because, just like you, I suppose, I had a taste for adventure. I wanted to travel, to see the world. Except I didn't have a cent to my name! I accepted a clerical position with a rich White Creole who exported livestock and salted meat to the English islands surrounding Martinique. Every now and then, I'd accompany him to Jamaica, the Virgin Islands, Barbados or Trinidad. My English improved rapidly. And it was on that last island that I stumbled upon an article from an American magazine that sketched out a portrait of you. I was as bowled over as I was delighted. Back then, I wasn't sure if we were actually related, but seeing the name of St. Clair—for some reason, it'd been abbreviated to "St." and the final "e" had been dropped—printed in bold letters across the pages of the most powerful country in the world's press swelled me with pride.

It was my mother who chased away my uncertainties. "Stéphanie Sainte-Claire? She was the daughter of my sister Félicienne who lived in Fort-de-France," she told me without giving it a second thought. "I think she left for France in 1910 or 1912, I'm not quite sure of the year." I showed her your photo in the magazine and she almost fell out. Her hands shook and tears rolled down her cheeks. She cried out that Stéphanie was the spitting image of her own mother, who passed away before I was born. Her spitting image! She clipped out your photo, framed it and kept it on her night table.

I bought a subscription to that American magazine and, even if it took three weeks for the issues to reach me, I learned so much about you, my dear Aunt. I read all about your exploits, right down to the smallest details, and I assure you I am very proud of you! Proud to be your nephew. I want so badly to get to know you in person, that's why I am writing this letter. I'd like to write your story. It's much too thrilling to end up forgotten one day. To do so, may I come to New York to interview you? I'm no writer—I'm much better at numbers—but I have a friend who'll know what to do with what I bring him.

I hope this letter, which I admit is much too long and stilted, will make it to you and that you'll accept my proposition. I hope you are well, my dear Aunt, and I am eager to hear from you.

Frédéric Sainte-Claire

26, Boulevard de la Levée
Fort-de-France
Martinique (French West Indies)]

What was it that finally convinced me to go to Cuba to meet Meyer Lansky, that infamous Yiddish criminal? You know, according to word on the street, Lansky owned a veritable empire on that island, and apparently, there was no definite border separating the legal from the illegal. Maybe it was because we'd immigrated to America at almost exactly the same time. Him in 1911 and me, the following year. Or maybe it was because of the research I'd done into his background: I was moved by the fact that his family had been subjected to horrors (the *pogroms*, as the press called them, although that term was unfamiliar to me back then) in their native Russia. As the descendant of slaves, I could understand what Meyer and his family had been through. But it's more likely that my tumultuous dealings with the Yiddish Black Hand, back when I worked for the Irish gang of Forty Thieves, had strongly influenced my decision. Taking my first steps into the New World then, I'd narrowly escaped adopting the prejudices—you could even say hatred—that our boss, O'Reilly, had for them. To embolden his men, he used to shout crazy stuff in the heat of the moment. For example, "Never forget that those shitty yids killed our lord Jesus Christ! They crucified him and for two thousand years, they haven't regretted their disgusting crime, not even for one second!"

Our gang would get whipped up into a fury, which would be rained down on honest and peaceable Jewish businessmen; we'd extort money from them, we'd argue with those crooked yarmulke-wearers over rigged bets at the racetrack and start fights over moonshine. Although we respected certain limits when it came to the Italian mafia, whose activities we simply sought to limit to the docks, we had no scruples at all when it came to shooting a yid in the back. We ended up using a word from their own language to refer to them: *khazer*, which means "pig." It was a way of mocking their religion's ban on eating pork. Could you imagine, my dear nephew, our succulent Creole cuisine without boudin? Pas possible! Oh, O'Reilly had taken it upon himself to teach us a whole sentence that, according to him, we were supposed to shout whenever we ran into a Yiddish gangster: *Hent in di luft!* He claimed it meant "hands up!"

"But," our slightly muddle-headed boss would add right away, "you gotta pull the trigger while you're still talking because that race has more than one trick up their sleeves."

When I left the Forty Thieves after castrating O'Reilly, we were already losing the war. The wops had managed to impose their own law over the port, and the sidelocks (we called them that, too) had gotten the upper hand on the rigged bets at the racetrack. The Irish mafia, despite a couple repartees here and there, were beating a retreat. Later, during Prohibition, when I put all my energy into selling Jamaican Ginger (that alcoholic pseudomedicine) the last of the Irish mobsters finally gave up the ghost. What I mean is that their clandestine distilleries were mercilessly attacked by the Italians, their stills destroyed, and their delivery trucks overturned, even if they were admittedly the best and most expert at distilling whisky. I was able to follow that war from afar thanks to the papers, busy as I was with my investment in the numbers game over in Harlem. The white mafia figured our neighborhood was too poor to bother wasting their time with it. Their bosses, whether they were big bananas or just small-timers, preferred Harlem by night—they came around to visit cabarets like the Cotton Club or the Savoy Ballroom and to listen to jazz or get laid by shameless Negresses. So, we were taking it easy.

As soon as Prohibition was struck down, the wops and the yids got their hearts set on Harlem. In the meantime, they'd signed some kind of peace treaty, or at least that was the rumor, and it was supposedly all thanks to Meyer Lansky—the same man who'd organized the mass killings of a number of mafia bosses in the early 1930s. He had promised Lucky Luciano—or convinced him, in any case—that he'd liquidate his rivals, starting with the two big bosses, the capi, Joe Masseria and Salvatore Maranzano, and indeed he did. From that moment on, there was a single mafia—only one mob with any importance, I mean—and that was the Italian-Yiddish mafia. Who could've believed it? Luciano and Lansky were suddenly blood brothers and they shared all their territory: at first, New York, Chicago and Boston; then Florida and Cuba. It was an impressive organization, and they'd decided to get their hands on Harlem and our numbers game, to dethrone Madam St. Clair without the least consideration for all she'd done! Now, dear nephew, I can understand who I was up against. At the time, though, I couldn't see things clearly; if I had, I surely wouldn't have refused to cooperate with that Hydra, and I'd have given in to Bumpy Johnson's arguments.

So, a rendezvous with Meyer Lansky was arranged. I was to meet him in a fancy hotel in Miami. I hadn't been back to the tropics for years, and Florida's hot sun felt very fine. I felt light, euphoric even, and I was sure I'd manage to convince that khazer Lansky that he'd better keep out of New York's black ghetto, otherwise he'd really have it coming. I had my head in the clouds! My petty power had gotten to me. After all, the queen of Harlem was a far cry from the queen of America. Ruler of the black underworld, as prestigious as the title might sound, was nothing compared to being boss of the Italian-Yiddish mafia. Meyer Lansky owned hotels, casinos and racetracks; he dined with Florida's bigwig politicians and even with the Cuban president, Fulgencio Batista. My authority, on the other hand, reached no further than Harlem, and even that wasn't always a given! Some of the numbers game bankers—not many of them, but some nonetheless—refused to submit to me. In the end, when I had to face off against Lansky, my queendom was only a facade, and he was doing me a favor by accepting to meet me face to face. He could have just as easily sent a commando to cut me down right in front of my Edgecombe Avenue apartment, and no one would have had a second thought for the strange Black Frenchwoman who'd had the gall to think she could impose her law in Harlem.

At the hotel, I took the elevator up to the fourth floor to Lansky's suite, nervous as ever to be trapped in that damned mechanical contraption. As soon as I stepped out into the foyer, I was met by a command that sent me flashing back to my first years in Five Points.

"Hent in di luft!"

Two heavies had their revolvers trained on my person. They advanced toward me with measured steps and then unceremoniously began to search me as if I had no natural sense of modesty. I swallowed down my rage, but my humiliation swelled when Meyer Lansky, fresh from the bath, greeted me in his underwear with these words, "So, you've come to sign your surrender? That's fine, Queenie... just fine."

Chapter Eleven

He'd set up a ladder at the corner of 125th Street, a perilous stepladder at least twenty rungs high, and he was perched at the top, dressed in a cape and a kind of purple-colored turban. An oriental-looking dagger hung across his chest, its blade glimmering in the pale light of the wintery morning. Madam St. Clair stopped in her tracks. She'd seen all kinds of preachers and other self-proclaimed saviors of all humanity since moving to Harlem twenty-five years before, but that man radiated an extraordinary force. Nothing like the flamboyancy—one could almost say grotesquerie—of a Marcus Garvey whose get-ups made him look like a chubby-cheeked buffoon and who was always soaked in sweat, no matter the season. Nothing like the haughty cool that emanated from the big black Sugar Hill intellectuals like W.E.B. Du Bois or Countee Cullen. His Holiness Bishop Amiru Al-Mu-Minin Sufi A. Hamid, as the sign propped against the feet of his ladder indicated, was a real character. The queen of the numbers racket was smitten right away. She thought her heart had been hardened to all feelings regarding the masculine species, which she nonetheless did not despise, seeing as she considered herself to be at least a partial member of their kind. When men reacted in shock after seeing how she stood up to the meanest gangsters, how she pounded on the table with her fists, how she brandished the tiny pistol she kept in her elegant handbag with such vehemence, she would carefully articulate a single sentence, taking care to clearly pronounce each syllable, "I'm half man myself, and don't you ever forget it! That's why the white press calls me *the Lady Gangster*. At least they know what I am."

Is this the love at first sight everyone's always talking about, Madam St. Clair asked herself, heart a-flutter. As if to protect herself, she instinctively clutched the collar of her fur coat with both hands and tried to catch her breath. That character had a funny name and she wasn't sure she could place it: African? Arab? Indian? In any case, it certainly wasn't Gaelic or English or Yiddish or Polish or Italian, and it definitely was not French; it was unlike anything she'd known up to then. Besides, it was such a long name that she couldn't quite memorize it all and only managed to remember the second half: Sufi Abdul Hamid. That was during the Great Depression, just as it was really starting to make itself felt in Harlem. At first, the Blacks—who'd been accustomed to living with very little—hadn't noticed (unlike the Whites) any difference between the days leading up to Black Thursday and the days that followed it. Some of them asked in mocking tones, "What's the color of our skin got to do with that damned Thursday? It's *their* banks that suddenly went under, isn't it? Their businesses and their factories that closed overnight. The rest of us, we don't have any of that, so we got nothing to lose."

Except that Harlem was far from being an oasis, and it was slowly but surely taken over by the same disaster that had hit the white world. First of all, the Whites—or, rather, the richest among them—stopped visiting the Cotton Club or the Savoy Ballroom with any real frequency, and the owners of those exclusive cabarets were forced to fire their dancers. Then the servers and the valets. The ladies of the night began to cry out in misery having found themselves incapable of doing business with the men of their own race—they were too accustomed to doing it with potbellied and aging Whites. The Great Depression had landed in Harlem, and Sufi Abdul Hamid, a convert to a religion—Islam— that no one had ever heard anything about, was off on a crusade against what he referred to as *the Jewish Profiteers*.

"Brothers and sisters," he'd shout at the crowd, unperturbed when a strong gust of wind threatened to blow his ladder down or when a sudden downpour would send all the passersby running to shelter. "Those people who run the shops and corner stores in our neighborhood, those people we've always mingled with, imagining them to be different from the Christian Whites, well, listen up! It's me, the Commander of the Faithful, who is assuring you, they are even worse than the Christian Whites! Oh yes, a thousand times worse! In truth, they've sucked our blood from the very start and paid us back with wide smiles and a pat on the back, but once their doors are closed, know that they don't give a damn about us. We've seen the proof of this today! Far from holding out a hand, helping us to forge on ahead, they're firing their Negro employees and replacing them with people of their kind, even if these replacements already had work. My brothers and sisters, the Jew only cares for the Jew. Open your eyes! I, Amiru Al-Mu-Minin Sufi Abdul Hamid, have been sent on a mission by Allah to end the terrible injustice of which we are the victims. The Jews will hire our children or get straight out of Harlem!"

Day after day (but discreetly) Madam St. Clair—excuse me, Frédéric for using the third-person again—would contrive a way to walk down 125th Street. She'd ask her chauffeur to drop her off on one end and then wait an hour or so, time enough to do some window shopping. Double-checking her outfit, repinning her sophisticated hat à la française, dangling a cigarette-holder from her lips, she'd walk with seemingly insouciant steps, her fur coat half open, pretending to linger at the storefronts. When she was no more than a couple steps from the Muslim preacher's stepladder, she'd toss furtive glances in his direction while drinking his words in, and suddenly she'd feel the same overwhelming emotion that she'd felt the very first time. Her throat would turn dry, her fingers would stiffen for no reason, her heart would start to gallop like a wild horse, her knees would wobble—was it love? More like infatuation. Madam Queen was vaguely irritated because, for the first time since she'd come to America, she felt like she was in a position of weakness and desperately vulnerable. What had saved her each time up till then was that she'd never let her guard down for anyone, not even for those vile Ku Klux Klansmen when they'd raped her. Certainly, she'd been momentarily overwhelmed, but she'd pulled herself together in no time flat. Arriving as a penniless black immigrant, she'd turned herself into the queen of the Harlem numbers racket and that, well, *that* was nothing to sniff at. Over the course of her life, she'd never allowed feelings of love to interfere with her business; she in no way lived the life of a racketeer, even if some of her Edgecombe Avenue neighbors would have said so—no, she lived like a real businesswoman. The numbers game required a precisely organized operation and strict discipline from top to bottom, that is, from her (the big boss) all the way down to the last numbers runner, without forgetting about her bankers, her bodyguards and her chauffeur. Everyone knew his or her role, and there was no question of even the slightest deviation, which would have led to immediate expulsion. Or execution, in the case of dirty business. "Queenie's goodhearted with those who obey her," was the word on the streets of Harlem, "but she's stone cold with those who double-cross her."

He was right, that character perched on his ladder: Ever since the Great Depression—the press came up with that expression— the Jewish shopkeepers only employed their brethren, and the Negroes, who generally had no business sense at all, found themselves left out in the cold. One fine day, the gamesters informed my bankers that competition had been moving in on Harlem. A strange gentleman who prayed in a mysterious language and who prostrated himself on a rug that he rolled out right on the sidewalk was wheedling dollars from the out-of-work, allegedly for some organization, a kind of union to be more precise, called the Negro Industrial Clerical Alliance.

"Never heard of it!" Queenie snapped at the guy who told her about it. "What are they promising?"

"To organize protests in front of the Jewish shops."

"Yeah, and?"

"To force them to hire colored people…."

"No kidding!"

She asked Bumpy to figure out what was at the bottom of it all, she was convinced that it was some kind of new racket, a trick being pulled by some bunch of shysters who wanted to screw over the wretches and wring out their last pennies. In any case, it was of utmost importance to put an end to whatever it was because each person who gave their change to the abovementioned union was one gamester fewer for the numbers racket. Her bodyguard returned a few days later, bowled over by the words of that mysterious organization's boss. Certainly, he had a funny get-up on, his name was impossible to pronounce, and he was taking advantage of the out-of-work to try converting them to a bizarre religion, but what he said made perfect sense: Picket the Jewish shops to persuade the Blacks to boycott them so long as the shopkeepers refused to hire Harlemites. Right away, I understood it was the man who preached at the corner of 125th Street. The one who'd made my heart race for the first time in all my life, even though I still hadn't seen him up close and we hadn't trucked the slightest word. Sufi Abdul Hamid! Yes, indeed, it was him, and, my word, the action he was planning was perfectly sensible. On Edgecombe Avenue, the majority of the shops and corner stores belonged to the Yiddish, which had never been a problem in my eyes. In any case, they were the only white-skinned people who could move through Harlem day or night without fear of being attacked by thugs. It was risky enough for us Blacks, but they seemed to benefit from some kind of impunity, or better, from a perpetual laissez-passer. Maybe the Harlemites were secretly flattered that those Whites treated them like human beings and mixed with them without holding their noses. But what do I know? The only Jews who'd interested me up till then were the ones in the Yiddish mafia. From the first moment I got involved with the Irish gang of Forty Thieves, I'd had to deal with them, but not because of their religion. Because they wanted to move in on our territory in Five Points. We had to deal with the wops and the Poles, too! In the end, I'd fallen out of touch with those gangsters who didn't work on the Sabbath day—that really confounded us, given that we, Christian as we might have been, didn't take any break, neither on Saturday for the Protestants nor on Sunday for the Catholics.

The only Jew I'd heard about after that was the mob boss Meyer Lansky, whose reputation had preceded him all the way to New York, even while he was displaying his skills in Florida and Cuba. Speaking of him, it had happened that in my moments of doubt, when that damned Dutch Schultz started to make life difficult for me and I could sense Bumpy was ready to knuckle under, I began to imagine a retreat to the big island. After all, it wasn't so far from my native Martinique, and at least I wouldn't be cold anymore. Everyone thought Stéphanie St. Clair wore thick fur coats to play at being the bourgeoisie, but the truth was more prosaic: I never got accustomed to winters. Or to the brutal temperature drops. As soon as it got below freezing, I'd shut myself away in my apartment and give free rein to my so-called associates. Of course, in all the twenty-five years I spent struggling to make a place for myself in North America, I never admitted that to anyone. Not a one of my three bodyguards-cum-lovers—Duke, Bumpy and Lewis—none of them ever had any inkling that Queenie, after a short period of wonderment (a time during which she could never have imagined that she'd become a queen one day), feared the arrival of that season that she, at least, considered as cursed. I kept going out to the nightclubs, the restaurants and the churches, but I avoided walking in the streets. My Model T would await me just outside my building and would drop me off exactly where I wished to go, thus sparing me from the New York cold.

His Holiness Bishop Amiru Al-Mu-Minin Sufi Abdul Hamid was no bluffer. No fewer than a dozen picket lines were set up under his supervision, blocking off entry to the main Jewish businesses in Harlem. He'd patrol the streets, haranguing the passersby with a stentorian voice and ordering them, in the name of Allah, his personal god, not to shop there. I wanted to see it with my own eyes, so I got dressed in rather plain clothes, knotted a scarf over my hair and, a battered old shopping bag in hand, headed off to Moshe Kahane's corner store. Kahane was a pudgy, bearded guy who could smooth-talk you into buying anything. Peruvian honey that would heal rheumatism, Palestinian olive oil that was precisely the same variety that was used in the time of Moses, Chinese prayer books in case of headache, dried hippopotamus imported from Patagonia for lovesickness. You'd go in looking for some rice, some butter, a piece of salt pork or a bottle of wine and you'd leave with some improbable product that you knew at first glance you wouldn't dare to imbibe. But you couldn't refuse that jovial Mr. Kahane, you had to show him your appreciation for his good-naturedness toward the Blacks! But that day when I went to his shop to observe Sufi Abdul Hamid's goings-on, I discovered another man entirely. He was fuming at the entrance to his utterly empty store, which normally would have been packed at that time of day.

"Beat it! Beat it you bunch of apes! I have nothing to do with your sob stories. You think it's my fault that this country's all messed up? Huh? I'm just a simple shopkeeper and I've never owned a bank or played the stocks. Go on, get out of here, leave my customers in peace!"

That very short, disheveled man looked pathetic with his red-checked apron tied tightly under his potbelly. Sufi Abdul Hamid walked toward him with warlike steps, sending the Jewish shopkeeper scrambling into his shop like a crab into his hole, and, as a crowd of rubberneckers gathered around, Sufi unfolded his stepladder—he carried it in one hand, although it looked mighty heavy to me—and climbed the rungs four at a time until he'd reached the top. From there, dressed as he was, he looked like an Oriental prince. I could feel the shivers starting to run down my body again. I couldn't tear my eyes off him. Each of his words echoed inside me, "Listen to me, brothers, I am the messenger of Allah—Exalted and Majestic is He—and I've come to tell you that the time of Jewish domination over our people is coming to an end. For century after century, that cursed race has sucked the blood of other nations, infiltrating everywhere, stealing the best-kept secrets, governing in the shadows, amassing colossal fortunes and, now, my brothers, yes, now it's time to put an end to it. Right here, in Harlem, an end to the world's Jewish control is being proclaimed! None of us will buy anything from them anymore!"

Suddenly, a squad of policemen appeared and encircled Sufi Abdul Hamid and his followers, handcuffing them with no other formalities. The cops went after Sufi with clubs, and he fought back, shouting that they were White Christian swine and that the end of *their* domination was written in Allah's book, too. He'd gotten me right in the heart. I could no longer lie to myself: I'd fallen in love. At fifty-two years old! As the end of my life was dawning over me. It was almost impossible to believe, and if the feeling provoked a deliciously upsetting sensation in me, I had to fight against it with all I had because the line of work I was in required an utter absence of sentimentalism. To love meant becoming dependent on someone else. What was happening to me, I who had never counted on anyone, I who defied the whole world? Why should such a curse—a pestilence, to use a turn of phrase from Martinique, my dear nephew—have suddenly befallen me? I tried to rid myself of his image, and I was fairly content to read an article on Sufi Abdul Hamid a few days later and see him referred to as *the Black Hitler*. The war—the second in less than a century!—was getting going in Europe, but we'd only heard a few faint echoes. Not one gunshot (except from the local delinquents), not one cannon blast, not one aerial bombardment. An ever so distant war, just like the first one had been, the whole affair personified by one single man, a man whose face was both comical (on account of his strange little moustache) and troubling. I'd seen that face a couple times when I'd gone to the cinema, seeing as there was always a newsreel before the film. Hitler's crimes, of which we wouldn't know the extent until after the war had ended, seemed unreal to us. So, when Sufi was referred to as the Black Hitler, it seemed to imply more that he was some kind of buffoon than a dangerous person. And how could I, Stéphanie St. Clair, have fallen in love with someone like that? If he'd been some big heavy, a gun-wielding trafficker of heroin or alcohol, a clandestine cabaret or brothel racketeer, well then… but this! It was quite simply incomprehensible. Impossible. And yet, it was the bare truth! The bare truth. How could a woman in full bloom, the queen of the Harlem lottery, fall for a joke of a prophet who wanted to convert the Harlemites to some religion that no one was quite sure actually existed or if it was just some figment of his deranged imagination?

I went to wait for him outside the jailhouse, as did the whole swarm of his followers, and, forcing my way through the little crowd, I shouted at him straight away, "Black Mufti, let's work together! We're fighting for the same cause."

That expression, which no one but he and I understood, had come from my adolescence, back when I'd distract myself from my tedious work as a servant by paging through my bosses' atlases and books while they were out. I'd tried to locate the famous Holy Land that the preacher filled our ears with during mass, and I'd stumbled upon the face of a bearded man who'd proclaimed himself the Grand Mufti of Jerusalem. Besides, I'd already gathered up knowledge about the religion of the man who made my heart race in the only library worthy of that name in all of Harlem, which was, of course, in Sugar Hill. Stunned, the militant stared at me, sizing me up with his eyes and, after muttering a phrase in a language that must have been Arabic, added this in English, "Madam St. Clair, I know of you, and I accept your proposition. Allah—Exalted and Majestic is He—caused our fates to cross. I am certain we will accomplish great things together."

There was a smattering of applause among Sufi Abdul Hamid's followers, but also a few perplexed looks. A rather beautiful woman (younger than I) who was dressed à la orientale froze like a pillar of salt, as if she'd been hypnotized by my person. Taking me at my word, the Muslim preacher installed himself in my home that very afternoon, without asking my opinion of it. When I asked him where he was living, he waved his hands evasively, "Wherever Allah—Glory to Him, the Exalted—wants me to live, Samia!"

He'd debaptized and converted me. In other words, my dear nephew, my transformation into a good Muslim had begun with my name change. I thought it had a nice sound. In Martinique, they'd have called a man like him a devil in a tin box. He was always in movement, always doing something, preparing for this or that operation targeting what he referred to as *the oppression of the light-skinned devils*. He was constantly juggling an incredible number of ideas that he desperately wanted me to adopt as my own. Then he'd calm down all of a sudden when it was time for one of his five daily prayers. He'd unroll his rug in my living room, turn toward the east and begin to pray with his hands outstretched. Sufi Abdul Hamid was a permanent spectacle, and the longer I lived beside him, the more he awed me. He wasn't difficult about eating or money or sex. Such a frugal man was truly a rare pearl in Harlem, and it was out of the question that I let him slip through my fingers, especially since the converts of the feminine sex were beginning to rush into the Universal Holy Temple of Tranquility, the mosque he'd established on the ground floor of a modest four-story building on 143th Street. In fact, Sufi gave me the best protection imaginable: marriage. Before him, a whole swarm of men—Bumpy and Duke in particular—had wanted to put a ring on my finger—ah, I forgot all about the very first one! Philibert, the Fort-de-France barber—but I'd turned them all down without mincing words. Forget about chaining down Stéphanie St. Clair, not even with a wedding ring. I was a free woman, free to want what I wanted and to go where I saw fit, free to say anything and to believe what I believed. In my eyes, marriage was not a prison—that would be an exaggeration—but a kind of house arrest. I'd never permitted any of my lovers to ask why I was going out or when I'd be back or even whom I'd seen during the day or night. Why, then, did I give in to that gentleman who'd taken it upon himself to convince the Harlemites to renounce Jesus Christ in favor of a certain Muhammad, whom they'd never even heard of before? I wanted to get to the bottom of it. The best thing would be to just ask him directly. Perhaps that way, I'd be able to get a clearer vision of things. In the late afternoon, we'd slip off to my room and, when he wasn't making love to me, he'd plunge into his religion's holy book, the Quran, which he'd read in a whisper.

"Sufi Abdul Hamid, I want to know something," I asked in a wavering voice.

Putting his book down, he looked into my eyes in a troubling way, "About my religion?"

"No, about you.... I saw that you're called Eugene Brown on your IDs and...."

"A slave name, Samia! A name that was given to me against my will, just like yours, by the slave masters. We have to cast those names off so we can begin to recover our true identities."

With those words, I was right back to the arguments I'd already heard from the mouths of two very different people: the big Harvard-diploma-holding intellectual W.E.B. Du Bois, my neighbor on Edgecombe Avenue, and Marcus Garvey, the prophet of the return of the American Negroes to mother Africa, who'd claimed a patch of Central Park where hundreds of the miserous came to drink in his words. But neither of them had seen fit to change their names. On this point, Sufi was very self-assured.

"Samia, there were Muslims among the slaves transported to America. Our religion reached Africa long before Christianity did. Sure, I know some people accuse Islam of having condoned slavery. But they're forgetting that it only affected those who refused to convert to the way of Allah, blessed be his name, Whites or Blacks, Christians or pagans.... The author of *Don Quixote*—you've heard of that famous Spanish book—that is, Cervantes, well, he, too, was a prisoner in Algiers for five years. Muslims crossed the Mediterranean Sea and the Sahara to spread the truth of our Holy Quran...."

Sufi Abdul Hamid wasn't an imposter. He was a truly cultivated man; he devoured books, although he didn't much appreciate the books in *my* library. He was filled with a kind of serenity that radiated from him and that, day in and day out, won over new followers. God only permitted cohabitation in times of war, so we'd have to get married in order to not betray His will. And so, I, Stéphanie St. Clair, had to become Samia Abdul Hamid! I didn't dare tell him that I'd searched the depth of my heart and my mind, but I couldn't find any trace of his god (or of any other, for that matter). While chatting with the young poet Countee Cullen one day, he explained to me that I was an *atheist*, a highbrow word that I thought sounded ugly. But for my first love—I'm almost ashamed to use that expression because I was already in my fifties—I was willing to make an effort. After all, what proof was there that all those people filling up the Adventist churches,

Baptist churches, Pentecostal churches or Catholic churches every Saturday or Sunday actually believed in a Supreme Being? I accepted the marriage proposal of the man who'd styled himself as *the first modern Muslim in the United States of America.*

"Yes, modern, because the moment the slave traders caught our ancestors worshipping Allah, they'd kill them and then throw their bodies overboard. Some managed to hide their religion and, after reaching the plantations of America, fomented revolts. One day you'll have to read the epic tale of the Saint Domingo revolution, Samia. It began with an uprising led by a slave called Bookman—a living book. That book was none other than our Holy Quran…."

I had no reason to doubt the man I loved, especially since the feeling was so new to me that it chased all my worries away and filled me with a lightness—a kind of euphoria—that quickly became indispensable to me. I'd met the man of my dreams. So, the romance novels had been right about their Prince Charmings after all. On the other hand, I didn't get to have the pomp of a Christian wedding because Sufi insisted that our ceremony take place in the strictest intimacy. An Egyptian imam who'd come all the way from Boston blessed our union in front of thirty guests, half of whom I'd invited and half of whom he'd invited. My three forever friends, Shortie, Annabelle and Mysti, were on my guest list, but were refused entrance into the mosque because their outfits had been deemed indecent by two of Sufi's followers! Freshly converted despite all outward appearances, those two men were utterly devoted to Sufi and demonstrated a zeal that, in other circumstances, would've been hilarious.

"Don't forget that from this moment on you are Muslim, Samia!" Sufi hissed at me when he noticed that I was getting irritated.

My conversion to Islam was a thousand times faster than I'd imagined it would be: All I had to do was repeat a phrase (*There is no God but God, and Muhammad is His messenger*) in Arabic and then again in English. The night before, Sufi had made me practice saying it in the prophet's language and was astonished by my rapid progress. If I had a single gift in this life, it must have been the gift of language. Creole, French, English, Gaelic, Italian, a little Yiddish and a few words of Polish. Each of those languages had been useful at a crucial moment of my life, and I liked them all, although, understandably, I preferred French. My friends stood stock-still on the sidewalk outside the Universal Holy Temple of Tranquility, still reeling from the shock of their almost forcible ejection and shot me looks of commiseration as I exited the temple.

"Those three... forget about hanging around with them anymore," my husband said, speaking as if it were a given rather than a command.

From that day forth, I became a double-faced creature: When I was taking care of my numbers business, supervising my runners and my bankers, I was Stéphanie St. Clair. I hadn't changed one iota, but when Sufi came home, I changed into a submissive housewife, attentive to his every desire—in other words, I became Samia Abdul Hamid. It ended up turning into a game, and I became an expert at it. But I had to make a choice when New York's scummy mayor, Fiorello LaGuardia, had my man arrested after a group of important Jewish businessmen filed a complaint. The crisis had finally hit Harlem, and almost half of the working-age population was sitting idle, twiddling their thumbs. Young people, unbelievers for the most part, joined the picket lines that Sufi organized outside the Jewish shops, and the moment the owners dared to raise their voices, scuffles and brawls would break out. They had to make an example by arresting the leader of the movement, and he sure didn't hide who he was. Without giving up the lottery, I dedicated myself to getting him released, organizing sit-ins in front of the courthouse and publishing virulent articles in the papers.

Stéphanie St. Clair had become a high-flying activist.

Chapter Twelve

I still remember the day—even the hour!—when the cops dared show up at my home as if it were some ragged, bombed-out block of Central Harlem and not my well-heeled building on Edgecombe Avenue in elegant Sugar Hill. It was the very day the press would later anoint as *Black Thursday*. Black like the days that followed, plunging the country—and then the whole world—into an outright crisis. The Great Depression of 1929, that's what we call that period nowadays. At the time, I was furious that they had chosen the adjective "black" because we had nothing to do with the New York Stock Exchange's crash, and for one very simple reason. Simpler than simplicity itself, as we say in Creole. There wasn't a single Negro who bought or sold stocks in the temple of the Holy Dollar. It wasn't that none of us had the means to devote ourselves to that activity, but rather, those who did were kept at arm's length by the white world. In any case, the really rich Negroes were all involved in illegal activities like heroin trafficking, prostitution or speakeasies—those were the clandestine cabarets in which you could drink doctored moonshine during the Prohibition. Or some of them were in league with the Italian or Irish gangs, serving as strongarms in the poor white neighborhoods. Yes, and it was those so-called *black days* that caught my black intelligentsia friends off-guard. Before the crash, they'd lived more-or-less comfortably thanks to their university-degree professions; but, like me, they knew little of financial management. Generally, our attention was elsewhere, until large numbers of shops, factories and businesses began closing their doors. There'd already been a few scares in the past, little panics among the stock market players, but they'd never lasted more than two or three days. This was different. Black workers with decent enough jobs in the white neighborhoods found themselves out of work overnight and, in little more than five months, all of

195

Harlem was in the thick of it. My numbers runners came back in the early afternoon with paltry sums because no one had any hope for the future anymore. In truth, what the fuck did we care about all those extravagant words the Whites were constantly repeating, words like *the Dow Jones index* or *stock market crisis* or *monetary policy* or *banking system* or *reduced market activity*? We kept our money at home, where it was safe and warm. Hidden under a mattress or a floorboard for the poorest, in a safe for the most fortunate. As for me, true to my little idiosyncrasies, my stash was in a room marked *W.C.*, an ungodly (and adequately deceptive) mess of overflowing newspapers and books—it even had a toilet inside. I didn't ever use it, but to keep up the illusion, I'd stocked it with a couple rolls of toilet paper, a brush and a dustpan. I didn't bother cleaning that room too often, but I did make sure to brush away the spider webs.

So, on that famous Black Thursday, I'd convened—exceptionally—my bankers and a couple major runners all at once, around dawn. I'd prepared a little speech for them in which I'd explain that the market crash wouldn't affect us Negroes, and that, in fact, it could even be a way of outwitting our oppressors. They'd put all their money in the banks, taken out loans, bought stocks, all things that were alien to us. But when you really thought about it, I could've named my enterprise the St. Clair International Bank because I was, in truth, a kind of moneylender (certainly no pawnbroker!). I simply sought to demonstrate the confidence I had in my black brothers and sisters. They always turned up, imploring. "Madam Queen, I'm in a real bind, could you do something for me, please? I'm begging you!" Sometimes women with four or five kids who'd been abandoned by their bastard boyfriends would come to me for help to stay afloat until they'd found steady work. Other times, it would be the owner of a bar or restaurant or cobbler shop or this-or-that-repair service who'd hit a bad patch and needed a little financial aid. Now don't get me wrong: Madam St. Clair was no bitch. Far from it! Obviously, I didn't wear my heart on my sleeve (if I had, someone would have snapped it up long ago), but I didn't take any pleasure in miserliness, either. I helped my brethren. I came to my race's aid. It was the natural thing to do. Of course, if some asshole imagined he could scam me, I'd turn the case over to Duke or Bumpy or Lewis, depending on which one was my bodyguard at the time, and in the blink of an eye, the problem would find its solution. It might only take a verbal threat or a little thrashing, but the most recalcitrant among them sometimes ended up with a bullet between the eyes. I didn't have any qualms because I had the feeling that I was cleaning up our community that way. We had to stick together against the Whites, and any misunderstanding between our kind could end up being deadly. Weakening us, I mean, my dear Frédéric.

The speech I had in mind and that I planned to offer to my men was clear: Don't fear the rotten news being spread by the big papers. Don't lose your heads at the sight of all these banks collapsing like so many houses of cards in the wake of this infamous Black Thursday. Make Harlem a place of strength by continuing to live as if nothing's happened. I ended with these lofty words, "*Market bubble*—does that mean anything to you? No, nothing? Fine! We don't give a damn about *their* fucking Wall Street!

Several bankers (a funny title, given the situation) brought me wads of crumpled bills as per usual, and that was the irrefutable proof that everything was going fine with the numbers game. They listened to me with an almost religious fervor, kind of like those who gulped in the inflammatory words of Marcus Garvey every Saturday morning in Central Park. That Black Jamaican had gotten it into his head to bring all the American Negroes back to their ancestral Africa. That idea had always struck me as a bit daffy, but even I ended up (thanks to my friend Annabelle's insistence) paying my share for the creation of the Black Star Line, the future boat company that would be responsible for the titanic transshipment. I liked to live with the idea that I'd already paid my fare, even if they never gave me a ticket, and that, in case of a hard knock, I could always make a quick exit to one of those countries — Mali, Ghana, Ethiopia — names that kindled the imaginations of many-a-Harlemite. After all, as the prophet of the Great Return never tired of reminding us, "The Whites don't need us in this country anymore, not since slavery's been abolished. They're furious at the idea of having to pay Negro workers, even if they pay them on the scraps of their white counterparts. In the South, there are all sorts of groups that have it out for our people, not just the Klan's vermin. Burning houses down, destroying their churches, raping their daughters or simply prohibiting them from accessing the same places as the Whites… yes, of course, we're in the North here, and it might seem different, but my brothers, it's all illusion. Sooner or later, they're going to force us all out of America. Our future is in mother Africa!"

Marcus Garvey was a peerless orator. His eloquence captivated even the bums who dreamed of a paradise on Earth, from which the slave ships had torn their distant ancestors when they brought them captive to the New World. I liked to revel in his pleas, but I didn't share his pessimism. I was sure that by fighting, by keeping our chins up, by harboring lofty ambitions, our people would ultimately find their place in this country; after all, it didn't belong only to the Whites. I'll never forget the shock that overtook me on my way to a clothing store in the Bronx that didn't deny their services to Negroes (provided these latter were in the money). I'd glimpsed a Redskin panhandling across the street. I was so taken aback that it took me a long time to cross the street. His dignity intimidated me. He was still as marble. Not even his eyelashes fluttered. He had a long braid that was adorned with two red feathers and wore a tunic made of animal skin. He seemed unmoved by the din and the fumes from the automobiles. He wasn't holding out his hand. He was sitting on the ground, and he'd spread a colorful rug out beside him, onto which passersby threw coins. Strangely, he didn't make any effort to gather the coins up like the beggars—both black and white—did. I was so intimidated that I couldn't bring myself to hand him the five-dollar bill I was clutching. In the end, I simply passed him by and never saw another Redskin. Apparently, the Whites have confined them to reservations in the Far West and, particularly, to a region with a convoluted name: Oklahoma.

But on that evil Thursday, I had not yet begun to harangue my men (focused as I was on finally managing to pronounce the *th* as correctly as possible) when a barrage of fists rang out against my door. Instinctively, several of my bankers reached for their guns; others rushed to the windows—poor saps!—only to realize it would be impossible to jump from the tenth floor.

"Madam St. Clair, it's the New York police. Open up or we'll have to use force!"

I recognized the voice of the 147th Street chief, a man steeped in hatred for all people of color. Someone must've betrayed me. Impossible to know who because I didn't deal directly with all the numbers runners; there were simply too many of them and, in any case, those derelicts (no matter how senior) wouldn't dream of ever setting foot in Madam Queen's home. If I were to open the door, I'd be finished: The police would have a singular opportunity to lock up my main men, who, as soon as they'd been handcuffed, wouldn't hesitate a second to sell me out. To cough up everything about the mean old Black Frenchwoman who ruled over Harlem's clandestine lottery with an iron fist. Negroes are traitors or became traitors because of the centuries of slavery. They'd sell out their own mothers to save their skin. Whether they're American or Martinican, it's the same thing. I had no illusions about my subordinates' fidelity, not even Bumpy's, that idiot who wanted to negotiate away our profits to the white mafia. The pounding on my door grew more insistent, and I was seized by sudden inspiration. I ran to hide the wads of dollars in my infamous W.C.-cum-safe and ordered the dozen or so terrified Negroes to get down on their knees. I lit candles all around the room and pulled the curtains closed as I shouted, "Please, give me five minutes! I just woke up." Then I whispered to my associates to hum church songs. Any old songs! And to hold their hands up toward the heavens with their eyes closed. I had just the time to turn the key in the lock before the cops could start kicking the door down.

"What's this bullshit? What's going on in here?" the 147th Street police chief shouted, stupefied.

"You are disturbing a religious ceremony, sir," I responded as calmly as possible. "It is unacceptable."

Disconcerted, the man and his henchmen weren't sure how to react, especially since my bankers and runners were going all out, some were even rolling on the floor in a very realistic manner. If I hadn't known it was a comedy act—or, rather, a bunch of monkey business—I would've been fooled. To tell the truth, their songs were no more than cacophony because each man was humming the first song that had come to mind, but for the Whites, it surely was more than that. The lack of synchronicity simply passed for savagery. My men had put on their most handsome suits because they knew they were coming over to my home, and Madam Queen—who was known for her French elegance— didn't tolerate careless dress. So, they really seemed like they'd come for a religious service, albeit one in my home rather than a temple or church. Louisiana voodoo was practiced in certain parts of Harlem, so our little service wasn't that out of the ordinary.

"Stop! Knock it off!" the police chief barked, having pulled himself back together. "Everyone on your feet, hands up and stop this commotion!"

Two of my runners suddenly went into a trance. They started writhing on the floor, mouths frothing and eyes rolling. The cops, aside from their chief, seemed to be in a state of shock and, in any case, were little inclined to interfere. Two of them had even opened the front door, as if they were ready to leave. Not a one of them had unholstered a gun as they normally did whenever they were trying to deal with unruly Blacks.

"I'm going to search your apartment," the chief declared in what he must've meant to be a professional tone. "Either tell me where you hide your cash, or we'll have to tear everything apart. It's your choice, sweetheart!"

"Do you have a search warrant?"

"Don't fuck with me! A search warrant now that the country's been turned upside down! Now that the banks are crumbling one after the other! As factories and stores are closing! You really think the law has time to waste with bureaucracy?"

The noose was tightening. I wasn't simply in danger of catching a few days in a jail cell as usual. No, this time it would be a multiyear sentence if those swine managed to find my cache. So, from the very depths of my being, rising up from the centuries of slavery that my ancestors had endured in the sugar plantations back on Martinique, I channeled a lunatic rage that was transformed into an outright fury. I started screaming, stamping my feet, spewing up a bunch of gibberish that became increasingly horrifying, now in Creole, now in French, now in English, in Gaelic, in Italian, until, petrified, the cops beat a hasty retreat. Their chief remained alone with the witch I'd suddenly become. Incapable of uttering a single word. Instinctively, my men took up their religious songs again, voices throbbing, and that White ended up backing out of my apartment, one foot behind the other until he rejoined his colleagues in the hallway, all jeering at my neighbors as they peeked their heads out to investigate the source of the ruckus. The pigs fled down the stairs.

"You're unbeatable, Madam Queen!" my men cheered, still not over the shock of my efforts to get us out of that mess.

That episode—a grotesque one, I'll admit—reinforced my power over those who were determined to glorify me as a voodoo priestess. I abandoned the speech I'd prepared and invited my men—a truly rare occurrence—to have a seat in my living room where, with infinite patience, I explained to them that the massive crisis shaking up the White world didn't concern us, or anyway, only very little. Unlike them, we were used to living with almost nothing; we couldn't be dragged any lower then we already were. In the end, what would much later come to be called the Great Depression of 1929 only affected the lives of us Harlemites very moderately, and it certainly had no effect on the numbers racket. Well, the quantity of bets and their monetary sums probably decreased, but not enough to drastically affect my business. The country was in the throes of the crisis. The whole world, Whites and Blacks, had to live with less. But for once, it was the former who would pay the lion's share.

In any case, Madam Queen made it through the Great Depression if not in total tranquility, at least in relative serenity....

Fourth Note

MI VOTU E MI RIVOTU

Mi votu e mi rivotu suspirannu,
Passu la notti 'ntera senza sonnu
E li bidizzi toi jeu cuntimplannu
Mi passa di la notti sino a ghiornu

Pria tia non pozzu n'ura ripusari,
Paci non have chiù st'affritu cori.
Lo sai quannu jeu t'haju a lassari?
Quannu la vita mia finisce… e mori….

—Sicilian love song

(I toss and turn in sighs,
I spend the whole night sleepless
Contemplating your beauties
As night turns into day.

Because of you I can't rest even an hour
Peace has not afflicted this heart.
Do you know when I'll have to leave you?
When my life has ended… and when I die….)

Chapter Thirteen

I admit I never imagined I'd live so long! A septuagenarian, that's what I am now! When I left my native Martinique in 1912, at twenty-six years old, for a trip that I knew (and hoped) would be a one-way, I had it in mind that my existence would necessarily be short. A young black woman on her own, without resources and unable to speak a single foreign language just couldn't hope to succeed in the big-ol' world. I'd gotten aboard a ship bound for France—the country reverentially referred to by everyone on my island as the *Motherland*—and although a love for those distant shores had been instilled in me from my earliest childhood, I nonetheless had an inkling that my stay there would be brief. Of course, I was awestruck by Paris, and the unmarred blue sky of Marseille bewitched me—the Mediterranean did, too. On our island (of course, I'm not telling you anything you don't know, dear nephew) the sky is always dotted with clouds, even when the sun is shining, and its color is paler and almost faded, which necessarily affects the color of the sea. On the other hand, during that summer I stayed at a modest hotel in Marseille a few blocks from the old port, and the blue of the Mediterranean never ceased to steal away my breath. What motionless beauty! The whirlwind love I felt for that handsome Neapolitan Roberto had something of the same awe, but even in that, I didn't let myself get hoodwinked by vain illusions: That love simply wasn't real. It wouldn't last and, in fact, three months later, I left for America. But, even I'll admit, those were seven months of daily enchantment.

Every morning, I'd wander through the old port, observing the ships that had come from the world over to drop anchor there. I'd try to guess which country they were from based on the flags they flew (those, too, I was able to recognize thanks to the Verneuils' library), I'd exchange a couple words with the sailors who were making merry, then we'd go our separate ways. I had no desire to get my leg over anyone, even if some of them promised me the sun, moon and stars. The tidy little sum my Fort-de-France barber man had given me was vanishing fast, and I was going to have to make a decision about my future. Either I'd stay in France and look for work or I'd leave for other lands. I wasn't too hot on the first option because it wouldn't let me put enough distance between Martinique and me; the second option quite simply terrified me. I was in a state of unbearable uncertainty when I met that old man whom I've already told you about, dear nephew, the one who'd never left the city but who knew the whole universe like the back of his hand. He strongly recommended America without ever guessing an old photo of a New York street that I'd glimpsed years prior in some book had already ignited an interest in me. It was an image of a tubby black man in his fifties or so, standing in front of a candy shop. He was wearing a top hat and was advertising a dentist's office just next door. Why would something like that have struck me so, dear Frédéric? I'll probably never know. It's just one of the mysteries of the human mind, I suppose.

To get back to Marseille, I'd given myself until the end of 1912 to make a decision. In the meantime, I got a job as a waitress in a rather shabby sailors' bar to keep from landing on my ass before the year's end. My room in the equally shabby hotel was just a couple blocks away in the Panier neighborhood, and every morning I'd have to walk down a street barely wide enough for two passersby to cross. That's how Roberto and I ended up running into each other. Quite literally. The colossus knocked me over. I was rushing that morning, and he took the time to hold out a hand and help me to my feet. Our eyes met furtively. He mumbled a *scusi, signorina!* before hurrying off, his guitar slung over his shoulder. I didn't see him again for several days and, then, one morning, I found him standing in the same twisty street that the sun struggled to reach, leaning against the wall of a house with shuttered windows, strumming at his guitar. I smiled as I passed him but didn't slow down for much else.

"Little Vesuvian flower, what's your name? Come on, don't be afraid of Roberto! We Neapolitans ain't so bad, darling, no matter what these rotten Marseille men say...."

I didn't turn back, but I heard him sing a few scales in his language and make the strings of his instrument vibrate. From that day forth, he'd post himself up right there and, unabashed, never deterred by the face of indifference I would affect, he tried to entice me with sweet nothings and romantic songs. I never scowled at him, but I did my best to show him that no matter how long he kept at it, he'd only be losing his time with Stéphanie Sainte-Claire. I had a very bad impression of European sailors, watching them disembark back in Fort-de-France and scramble over to the poor neighborhoods in search of tender flesh. Breadfruit Alley, where I lived with my mother, seemed to be their place of predilection. Too many young black women desperate for money fresh from the mint would spread their legs for them without precaution, and nine months later, they'd be birthing a baby with skin too light for anyone to doubt for one single instant that the father was some nameless sailor-stranger. Love between a black woman and a white man seemed completely unrealistic to me. I was mistaken. Without losing heart, Roberto—he'd shouted his name as I walked away one day—continued to pester me. I ended up getting annoyed with his act, but one afternoon as I was returning to my hotel to rest, he grabbed me by the arm, pressed his face against mine and whispered, "We Corsicans have a lot of patience, but this is too much, my bella! I know you've got feelings for me, so what's the problem?"

Had he forgotten that he'd already told me he was Neapolitan? Was that part of his game of seduction? In any case, I rose to the bait and agreed to go drink an anisette with him. He'd already chosen for me! He, on the other hand, ordered a pastis. Without

208

letting me get a single word out, he started recounting how he'd come to leave his homeland (which one was it?), bored as he was with working as a mason for a miserable wage, how he'd landed in France because he didn't want to be too far from his family, how he'd failed in several professions; he even offered up a funny anecdote about training bears for a circus in Toulon. As he slathered me with flatteries, he started surreptitiously fiddling with my fingers. It took me a while to realize what he was up to. That strange gesture, unfamiliar to me at least, turned out to be so pleasant that I didn't pull my hands back. He noticed my reaction and instantly started adding an *amore mio* at the end of each sentence, then finished that off with a discreet kiss on my ear, which gave me quite the start. Back then, dear nephew, I was not used to being courted (or, as you'd probably say, being flirted with). All I'd ever known were the assaults of my bosses' eldest son, that rather brilliant but extremely withdrawn Verneuil boy whose family standing would, nonetheless, assure his future. You remember the one.

Roberto took advantage of my naiveté, that bastard! He led me to a shack he'd rented, a stone's throw from a pretty beach whose water was too chilly for my taste. We spent dreamy days there, followed by nights of wild fornication. We lived on love and sweet water, as the idiotic saying goes; it always struck me as pretty dumb, anyhow. Except that he'd stopped singing in the bars and restaurants, and I'd abandoned my job as a waitress without so much as a toodle-oo to my boss. We started living off of what I had left of the money I'd borrowed from Philibert, that Fort-de-France barber who'd fallen madly in love with me. Up to that point, it'd been enough to buy passage from Martinique to Le Havre, to take a train from Le Havre to Paris and, finally, from the capital of the north to the capital of the south (Marseille, of course). A sum that I'd dipped into to rent that hotel room and to keep myself afloat until I'd found my job waiting tables.

A sum that was now close to vanishing at the hands of my unscrupulous proclivities with Roberto in our isolated little shack. At first, I'd been so bewitched by his Neapolitan vocalizations (or Corsican...) that I'd forgotten about the rest of the world. I was in a kind of bubble of happiness and never suspected that it might well burst. In the evening, after making love, I often had trouble falling asleep (insomniac that I was), so I'd watch my lover as he breathed with his mouth half open, his angelic face glistening with perspiration. Did I love him? Was that really love, that forgetting of daily existence, that indifference toward tomorrow, that feeling that we had all of eternity before us? After sounding the depths of my heart, I discovered to my great surprise that it wasn't thrashing in my chest but, rather, that it was thanking the person beside me for simply being there. It could have been another man, handsome in a different way, obliging and devoted to my person but in a different way, and I probably would have felt the very same way.

It bothered me a great deal and gave me something to think about.

Of course, I realized that no one on Earth was indispensable and that everyone could eventually get over even the greatest sorrow. That there's a cure for every ailment. That the ultimate cure is none other than death. All of this was known to me since early childhood, and I never needed anyone to teach it to me. But to be personally confronted with the tempest of carnal love for the first time in my life... well, that led me to make a radical decision. One afternoon, I pretended that I had to go into the city to buy provisions, a task we normally did together, our little corner of the beach being no more than four or five kilometers from the old port. On the way, we'd normally run into some compassionate cart owner who'd offer us a ride. Roberto didn't suspect anything. He said he'd take advantage of my absence to go fishing at a nearby inlet. Unbeknownst to him, I'd put some clothes and my passport in my bag. I didn't want to give him a last kiss, so I just offered him a simple *see you soon, honey!* to which he replied with a smile. I hurried to the port and asked for the first boat heading anywhere at all. Oh, they laughed in my face! There were forms to fill out no matter what the destination and, at best, I might be able to embark in two days. Nervous, I returned to my hotel, where I begged the owner not to reveal my presence to anyone, and then I locked myself away in my room with a few provisions. Two days later, I ran straight to the port via the famous twisty, narrow street where Roberto had courted me. There he was! Leaning against a wall, strumming his guitar, his hat on the ground beside him to collect the coins the passersby would toss his way. Impossible to turn back! I walked straight ahead, looking neither right nor left, terrified by the idea that Roberto might grab onto me. He didn't even try to! Quite the opposite, as I passed by, he simply called out, "Bon voyage, my bella! The Virginie is an excellent ship."

And so, to try for the nth time to get back to my story, in this country that sets the whole world dreaming (America, that is), I've experienced the worst personal tragedies, I've been cold (winter can be awful in New York, which is not that far from Canada after all), I've suffered from hunger, from the distrust of Black Americans, from the contempt of Whites, I was raped by the Ku Klux Klan, I cut off violent men's balls and gouged out their eyes, I ordered the elimination of anyone who opposed my reign over Harlem's clandestine lottery, I survived the First World War, the Prohibition, the Great Depression and the Second World War and then, one fine day, I decided to turn my back on all that agitation. To sell my beautiful Edgecombe Avenue apartment, to scrape all my savings together and—this was back in the early 1960s—to discreetly withdraw to a new neighborhood, Queens, a place where Blacks and Whites mixed for the first time. To vanish, if you like!

I'd never imagined that such a thing would happen one day. I admired the battles being waged by W.E.B. Du Bois and Countee Cullen and the other black artists and intellectuals; I was even proud that, starting in the 1950s, they'd begun referring to the period between the 1920s and 1930s as the Black Renaissance because I liked to think, though I was neither a writer nor a musician nor a painter nor a dancer, that I'd made my own little contribution. The affirmation of blackness wasn't limited to elegant salons and university lecture halls; it was out on the street. Hadn't I fought tooth and nail against the mafia's attempts to take over the Harlem business? Certainly, I'd been obliged, in the end, to sign a profit-sharing agreement with the head of the white mafia—back then, that would've been Lucky Luciano— but did I completely cave? No. Back then, I was convinced that Negroes would never manage to establish themselves outside of the neighborhoods they'd been allotted, but I was wrong. Wrong on all accounts. The NAACP, which had saved me from ruination after the episode with the Klan, had grown over the years, and other black movements had begun to emerge and were much more audacious in their demands for the unthinkable. The unheard of, even. I mean, complete equality with the Whites?! I would've loved to be a part of that enormous wave that seemed to turn everything upside down in its wake, sweeping away the most well-anchored prejudices, changing the way Whites saw Negroes and the way Negroes saw themselves. In short, reinventing a brand-new America.... But I felt too old. Oh, I would've loved to participate in the March on Selma, and I nurtured an unmeasurable admiration for Rosa Parks, who'd refused to give up her seat. I heard Reverend Martin Luther King's magnificent sermon on the radio and the now-famous words he pronounced not far from the Capitol. They still echo in me like a payback for the lynch mob that Tim and I had witnessed in Washington. The cold-blooded assassination of my handsome officer had completely transformed me without my even realizing it, turning me into someone who was both there and not there. Present and absent all at once. You've probably noticed that already, Frédéric. My sixties had come and gone, and I figured it was high time to withdraw from the world and contemplate the time I had left on this Earth.

Overnight—or almost—I left Sugar Hill and moved into a pretty house in Queens where my next-door neighbors were Whites. Neither rich nor poor, they were so friendly toward me that, at first, it made me uncomfortable. You see, in the black neighborhood, aside from the Jewish shopkeepers, always holed up in the darkest depths of their shops, the White was an invisible creature. In charge, the maker of rules. You knew that the mayor of New York, the governor of the state and the president of the United States were all Whites, but that was about it. No daily contact that might have allowed us to better understand their behavior; in any case, we feared their remorselessness, which was probably left over from the time of slavery. When I think back on my life in America, I realize that, in reality, perception of color is largely linked to whether your pockets are filled with the breeze or whether you're the owner of a fat bank account. The very first people I'd met over here, once I'd made it out of Ellis Island, was that distraught Irish family whose kids I looked after. And you know, at the time, I didn't consider the Mulryans to be white. I didn't feel they were Whites to be more precise. Their skin was no darker than an aspirin pill, they had freckles and red hair, but I never felt any real difference between them and me. Then, when I joined the Forty Thieves, that notorious gang of Irishmen, it was more the woman they teased than the Negress. Every time their boss, O'Reilly, or one of his men gave me a mission, they always had to add, "Watch out, Stéphanie! You know how scatterbrained you women are."

When did I start to notice a difference between the Whites and me? Paradoxically enough, I think it was when I set my bags down in Harlem and threw myself into the numbers game. From that day forth, I lost practically all contact with them, their world, their way of speaking—well, except for the times when those shitty cops took me down to the station. They obviously had it in for me, they suspected that I was earning four or five times what they did, and they weren't wrong. My car and my full-time chauffeur, my bodyguards, my investments in various legal affairs, the calm confidence I exuded; it was absolutely unbearable for them. But my arrests never lasted very long, and I'd return to the world of Blacks, my own little universe, my habits, my friends and my lovers. When I think back over my whole life, dear Frédéric, I realize that neither during the Prohibition nor during the Great Depression did I have any prolonged contact with the Whites. The mafia controlled the traffic of alcohol from Canada and Europe in its entirety, leaving us in Harlem only our piddling little Jamaican Ginger trade, but all the same, that was enough for me to amass a nest egg big enough to open my first bank for clandestine betting. As for the crisis of 1929, it didn't really hit Harlem because we were used to hustling to get by. We just hunched over and let the storm blow by.

Anyway, I'm tired today and I can tell that my stories are even more mixed up than usual. Thank you for your patience, dear nephew! I want you to know how much I miss our dear Martinique. You'll tell me that it's not too late for me to visit one last time. I don't disagree, but how would I be received there? I could go incognito, but all it would take would be one nosy journalist to discover who I am, and then the whole trip would become uncomfortable for me. The bourgeois Mulattos wouldn't miss the chance to harrumph the presence of a lady gangster on their island, a criminal, a dealer of this or that, a gadder with doubtful morals and so on. Don't try to convince me otherwise! I know that island like the back of my hand. I saw those scornful Mulattos in action when I was a servant to the Verneuils. Unless

214

there was some miracle, I doubt they've given up their prejudices. Obsequious toward the Békés, contemptuous toward the Blacks and the Indians, that's how I know them! I've still got this horrible image in mind that's never left me, even after all these years. Back then, all the street sweepers in Fort-de-France were Indians—we called them *Coolies*—and they lived in unspeakable misery. A lot of them were waiting to be repatriated to India as they'd been promised, but the government didn't give a shit. Those poor bastards devoted themselves to jobs no one wanted: tin can collectors, djobeurs, road menders, street sweepers. The people who passed early in the morning by rue Victor Hugo—the street where the Verneuils lived—were almost as skinny as the brooms they wielded. My mistress—a very dignified woman, excessively proud of her social status—would regularly lean out her window to urge them to sweep faster; she wanted to be spared the sight of their filthy piss-stinking faces around her house. I can still hear her shouting down to them, "Bann Kouli santi pisa, brennen kò-zot balié lari-a vitman-présé pou sa disparet douvan kay-mwen an!"

My dear Frédéric, I hope that's changed by now. But I admit I have no desire to go verify it for myself....

Chapter Fourteen

The New York police force was a band of uniform-stuffed sonsabitches. Well, I'm going backwards again, dear nephew, an old lady's quirk, I suppose. Not a day went by that they didn't harass my runners or take them down to the station, which obliged me to intervene and which upset the business because they'd seize and destroy the bet records, and all the maniacal precision that had gone into carefully recording the names of everyone who'd shelled out—even if only a couple cents—would've been for naught. As if those poor bastards who dreamed of a sunny future thanks to some sudden good luck were actually dangerous criminals. I'd call up Officer Brian (that wasn't really his name, but he insisted I call him that) to find out what was going on, and that lowlife White had the nerve to jeer at me, "We picked up two of your boys, Madam St. Clair. It'll be five hundred bucks a piece."

"Three hundred...."

"No, five hundred or your boys go nowhere. It was three hundred last week, but life's getting more expensive by the day, Queenie. You already know that, don't you? The guy you got driving your fabulous Model T hasn't asked for a raise? Hmm, that's strange.... Ha ha ha! And how about your two bodyguards, they didn't either? Why, you lucky devil, you!"

And that asshole would laugh in my face, regardless of the thick wad of hundreds I stuffed into an envelope for him every two weeks so he'd leave me in peace. And it wasn't just him: Officer Bobby, too, and a cop from the 147th Street precinct by the name of Robertson. And sometimes a whole heap of other NYPD guys puffed up like proud little blue penguins. It was either that or else the bets would dry up overnight, and that would've snuffed Harlem out for good. Or else the lottery would've been taken over by the white mafia. They'd been scoping it out since the end of the Prohibition and figured it was a veritable gold mine. Well, it's true I'd been clearing about two hundred thousand dollars a year since 1921, but that was the result of round-the-clock work. The numbers didn't leave a moment to spare! You had to keep your eyes peeled day and night because at any moment some sonofabitch Negro would get clever with a little bettor's bank of his own and try to sheist you out of the whole game. Especially as I, a French Negress, was already badly seen by the five bankers who controlled Harlem. Badly seen because I was a woman and because no Black American lady had shown half as much nerve as I. To give orders to crooks with loose trigger fingers and a view on creatures of the feminine sex as nothing more than bodies to throw a leg around… well, that was quite an exploit. Badly seen because I was a *Frenchie* and that nationality didn't mean anything to anyone. They only vaguely knew of that country's existence. For them, it was all marquises luxuriating in châteaux and leading fairy-tale lives in some faraway (and therefore, unimaginable) land. The whole extent of their knowledge of France was that it had a capital called Paris. In any case, I never got used to pronouncing it in the English way with all those hissing s's at the end: *Parisss*. But, oh well, I'd never be—even after ten years, twenty years and, now, over forty years as a resident here—a true American, even if I did try. I suspect the cops tolerated me because of my foreignness. When I'd go bail out my runners, Brian would hustle me into the station and lead me straight to his office.

"Comment allez-vous, madame?" he liked to cajole me in a French that surprised me every time. In fact, it was just an act. He didn't know my language. He'd learned that phrase by heart, he'd probably repeated it at least thirty-two thousand times so it would sound natural when he said it to me, but if I answered in French, he'd instantly go back to speaking in his own language, insisting I go back to English, too, before barking out at me,

"Madam Queen, stop ruining my ears with your *ze*! So, things are going well for you these days? They say you control 124nd Street now, is that right?"

"Control is a mighty big word...."

"Ha ha ha! Still as secretive as ever, huh? The police have eyes and ears all over. You can be as crafty as you like—very, very crafty—but we still know everything you're up to."

I'd open my bag and, as if I were a French duchess, take out my cigarette holder and my gold cigarette case, and I'd stare Officer Brian right in his eyes, which always managed to make him terribly uncomfortable. He was asthmatic and couldn't bear the smoke, so he'd practically beg me to put my paraphernalia away. I'd lean in and murmur in a voice low enough that they couldn't hear me in the adjoining room, "How much this time? For you, I mean...."

He'd hold out his two hands, opening and closing his fists as many times as necessary. See not, hear not. In addition to the bail for my runners, I'd have to grease Sergeant Brian's palm, too, even though he was regularly paid off to keep his eyes shut. Damn police extorting money from honest citizens! Because if you looked at things clearly, I wasn't stealing from anyone. People wanted to bet on the New York stock exchange numbers and that's all it was! The ones who won were paid out in full. Those who lost—the majority, true, but how's that any different than the official lottery, the city lottery?—well, they'd just have to try their luck again the next day or the day after that. That's life! Oh, they'd object—this was Officer Robertson's old song and dance—that I was breaking the law because I wasn't paying any taxes to the state of New York. I don't deny it, but we Negroes had already suffered through slavery in this fucking country, we'd sweated out every drop of water from our bodies in the cotton fields of Virginia, Louisiana, Alabama and Mississippi. We'd muled away for the Whites, and now this one had the cheek to expect us to pay taxes! Well, fuck you, Whitey!

The police who paraded down the streets taking potshots were just a bunch of crooks, rotten to the bone. To protect and to serve, my ass! They were amoral scoundrels, and everyone knew that they were in league with the mafia, all of them, even at the top. Even the mayor of New York! The Sicilians, the Yiddish and what was left of the Irish had plagued the city by distributing tons of money to anyone who could've put a spanner in the works. In comparison to their trafficking in heroin, alcohol and cigarettes and their innumerable clandestine brothels, my numbers racket was a big nothing, even if, for a Negress who'd escaped her island, who'd learned English in the streets, it really was something. There's no point in denying that I lived well — very well, indeed — and if I'd hung around my native Martinique like some nitwit, I would have rotted away in unspeakable misery. What would've become of me? At worst, a tramp under the Démosthène bridge, at the mercy of the perverse South American and European sailors; at best, a waitress in a rum shack in the Croix-Mission. But instead, I became Madam St. Clair, Stéphanie St. Clair, Queenie. In other words, by the end of the 1930s, I was the numbers queen of Harlem with no fewer than forty bankers and a hundred runners working for me and always ready to jump to attention. Well, I never bragged about it in public because I know that Negroes are born jealous. On my island, we learned that even before we entered into this world. Along Breadfruit Alley, where I spent my childhood, how many people ran my mother down for nothing at all? Because she'd managed to save a couple francs to buy herself a flowered dress in one of the Syrians' shops. Because a well-heeled man came to recite sweet nothings to her in a fine, florid French that was straight from the dictionary? Because of this because of that. The American Negro is hardly different from his Martinican cousin. Except that everything is bigger here and you don't have to live under the eyes and ears

219

of everyone else. You can decide to disappear for a while, you can make yourself forgotten. But jealousy… forget about trying to send *that* decamping! Sure, hordes of Negroes and Negresses are dying to take over for Madam St. Clair and, indeed, plenty of them have sold their souls to the devil trying to do just that.

That's why not a one of them even so much as lifted a finger when, in December of 1929, a date forever engraved in my memory, the police arrested me one evening as I was leaving the Fulton Theater, where I'd just taken in a concert by the marvelous Duke Ellington and my fellow countryman, the no-less-talented Maurice Chevalier, whom I'd dreamed of meeting. I missed speaking in French and I loved the way he performed, his funny banter, his cheekiness. I did not have a chance to accomplish my dream and, instead, I found myself at the Welfare Island Women's Prison, condemned to eight months behind bars for bribery of police officers and judges. My arrest was a real farce: They accused me of having been in possession of hundreds of betting slips for the illegal lottery as I left the famous cabaret. What an idiotic, unbelievable lie! Idiotic because bets were open from six in the morning until ten o'clock, in the morning I mean, everything stopped in the late afternoon when the New York Stock Exchange numbers—the basis of the system—came out. To be in possession of bet slips in the evening hours didn't hold water. Unbelievable because everyone—including, of course, the police—knew that I had a whole army of numbers runners and bankers at my disposition and that, aside from the brief period when I performed the duties of the latter category, all I did was supervise the numbers game. I was the top of the pyramid! The NYPD's spies, the double agents who infiltrated my organization and whom I regularly put out of commission, the runners and bankers they nabbed every single day, even the bettors… all of them could swear with their right hands on the Bible that they'd never seen Stéphanie St. Clair handing out bet slips.

But still, nothing doing!

The day of my trial, the judges repeated the same accusation—which, in their eyes, was damning—and the whole courtroom erupted into laughter so loud they had to adjourn twice. My lawyer, Elridge McMurphy, as white and experienced as he was, couldn't do anything for me. I'm not sure if I served as the expiatory victim in some settling of scores within the police force or the New York justice system, or if some gentlemanly Whites, incorruptibles like the famous Eliott Ness who hunted Al Capone down in Chicago, wanted to make an example of me. In any case, during the first day of the trial, the judge tried to question my nationality, arguing over the fact that I didn't seem to be who I claimed based on the old, battered passport I'd submitted to the court. "Of course not, bastard!" I felt like shouting. "I got that passport in 1912 and now it's 1931." Well, it's true that I hadn't bothered to renew my passport at the French consulate because it was extremely rare to have to show any form of identification in Harlem and, furthermore, I had no desire whatsoever to travel abroad. Being the queen of New York City's rival lottery was, certainly, an enviable position, but it came with a terrible obligation; I could never absent myself from the neighborhood for more than a couple days. Otherwise, the first scrabbling thug to take note would get it in his mind to replace me, and he'd start bumping my men off willy-nilly. That misfortune struck me once, once only, when I'd thought it'd be a good idea to bring Lewis, my bodyguard—the one who'd briefly replaced Bumpy—to New Orleans. Wandering through the French Quarter had always been one of my dreams, and in fact, that dream became a reality for nine consecutive days. But when I returned to Edgecombe Avenue, panic reigned among my number runners and my bankers. A half-wit calling himself Boss Jimmy had taken it upon himself to depose me and had started eliminating everyone who dared oppose him. Having no understanding of the organization, he proved to be incapable of paying the winners, and a wind of revolt quickly rose against his person. In fact, all I had to do was summon him to my home and make him understand that he was just an uneducated Negro who would never be more than a hatchet-man. I had, out of Christian charity, offered him a place in my organization but, stubborn as a mule, he refused. I had no other choice than to blow his brains out as he was stumbling half-drunk from an illegal brothel on 157th Street.

"So, you must be French then, ma'am?" the judge asked ironically.

"I *am* French, your Honor!"

"Your accent makes that clear, admittedly, but I have one reservation. French from where?"

"From Martinique."

"And where, exactly, is that, if I may ask?"

"In the Caribbean archipelago...."

"Fine! And what is your occupation, please? You were arrested with a whole pile of bet slips for the illegal lottery in your handbag? What do you have to say to that?"

"Nothing, your Honor. Those slips were planted by the police."

My lawyer eloquently emphasized my words and I sensed a momentary nervousness, then panic, among the police officers present in the courtroom.

"And why would they have done such a thing?" the judge enquired in a tone that implied he already knew the answer.

In that instant, I understood that my skin was in the game. Either I'd have to denounce those bastard big brass or I'd spend the rest of my days languishing in some vile prison. Without any qualms whatsoever, I spat out the list of all the policemen and police officers whose palms I'd greased so they'd turn a blind eye to my business or so they'd release one of my men. And that list wasn't short! I had a memory like an elephant, so I was able to detail the sums I'd allocated to each of them over the course of the past year, and the silence that descended upon the courtroom let me know that I'd hit home. I'd been convincing. I wasn't just some foreign Negress with a screw loose ranting on about honest civil servants for no other reason than to make a scene. I was Madam Queen, the queen of the Harlem numbers game, and I had a fair number of the NYPD cops by the balls, even some judges, too, whom I'd paid to hand down lighter sentences than the ones mandated by the law when my men had been caught red-handed or when they'd been arrested for something unrelated to my business.

I'd done it for my dear friend Shortie. If it hadn't been for her colored epidermis, she could have easily rivalled the famous cinema actress Louise Brook, whom we all adored in the wonderfully titled film *The Street of Forgotten Men*. The cinema — it was silent back then, my dear nephew — was undoubtedly one of the few modern inventions I didn't turn my back to. At least twice a month, Shortie and I would go to a private projection room on the second floor of a now-bygone nightclub. A private room to avoid the vulgum pecus who'd arrive midway through a bender and vomit up a regular wave of obscenities in the public projection rooms like the one at the Apollo Theater annex. As soon as the almost unsmiling face of Louise Brooks appeared on the screen, the whispers would stop. The men were hypnotized by her singular beauty, and we women swooned over her boyish hairdo, a kind of helmet with two pointed curls on either side of her face. Shortie and I had different reasons for admiring her style: Shortie saw in it a fashion that had to be adopted at all costs, unless you wanted to pass for a fuddy-duddy; I, on the other hand, felt almost like a sister to that flapper, to that sublime half-woman half-man actress, at least, that's how she seemed. As much as white men provoked a kind of suspiciousness in me, their wives — or at least those of the upper classes — stunned me with their audacity and, in my eyes, Louise Brooks was the quintessence. A free woman! A woman who never lowered her eyes! A woman who confronted life's pitfalls head-on! A woman who didn't wait for fate but tried to forge it according to her own ideas! But it had been such a long time since I'd had any contact with the white race's feminine persuasion (in fact, it had been since the faraway time when I'd lived with the Mulryans and helped Daireen with the household chores). In Harlem, only white men were free to roam. First of all, the policemen, those brutes who'd probably been transferred to the black ghetto after committing some blunder and who, furious at what they considered a downgrading, acted all the more criminal. By dint of arresting Negro hooligans, associating with them, accepting their bribes (and I know a thing or two about that!), they'd end up, for the most part, resembling them—although they, of course, wore uniforms. The other type of white men in Harlem were certainly more pleasant, and it was among their kind that Shortie managed to snag herself a lover, whom she claimed was crazy about her, which was completely believable if you judged it on the mink coat she'd drape over her shoulders as soon as winter arrived and the incredible quantity of gifts the man she called *sweetheart* offered her on a nearly weekly basis. Those men were honest businessmen as well as mafiosos, writers as well as rich (but uneducated) alcoholics who'd inherited their wealth, talented painters as well as failed musicians, true ballet connoisseurs, sex maniacs or simple passersby who saw Harlem as the edge of the universe. They only rarely came in mixed company. Only the moneyed capi of the mob arrived with women on their arms, blondes straight out of some fotonovela who looked unreal in their gossamer dresses, their eyes ringed with black liner and their luscious lips painted something violent. I'd had many a chance to admire them when I worked as a cleaning lady at the Vesuvio Club, back when I was just a dogsbody with the Forty

Thieves. Oh, that piece of shit O'Reilly! I wonder if, in the end, he didn't manage to survive and if he didn't graft on some balls afterward, my dear nephew. Ha ha ha! Well, why not? Medicine has made so much progress that I'm in danger of living to a hundred if it keeps up.

Shortie, my dearly beloved friend, put on a whole Louise Brooks act and started shooting heroin. To be sure, she did so in moderation—more for the look of it than for any pleasure—and it didn't seem to bother her protector in the least. Besides, I suspect it was sweetheart who procured that devil's substance. I never touched it, never touched any other substance like it because crossing zombie human wrecks on the sidewalks of Central Harlem made my stomach turn. Burglarizing, extorting the shopkeepers, dealing Jamaican Ginger here and there, sending nuisances or traitors to meet their maker, I did all that during the first period of my life on this American land, and I don't regret it. If I hadn't, I wouldn't be here with you, dear Frédéric, telling you the story of my life. In the second period, the one you caught wind of in the papers, I threw myself heart and soul into the numbers, and I lived off it for a long time. I lived very well off it, until I decided to disappear. To retreat from Harlem and from that business without telling anyone at all. Out of the blue. As if Madam Stéphanie St. Clair never existed. But heroin, never! Not only did I never touch it, but I refused to make any business of it. I suppose, deep down, Shortie wasn't very happy or proud about what she'd turned into: a white mafioso's black-skinned squeeze. The dope helped her, I suppose, deal with her uncertain and rather dangerous situation because it wasn't out of the question that the gentleman would dump you for a shapelier pair of legs, more exciting curves or for a more docile fling, and then you'd tumble right off your pedestal, falling so far you'd risk really losing it. That happened to one of our friends, Bessie, a kind of tropical liana with endless legs who spoke with a Spanish accent and who, although she refused to admit it, was from Cuba and her real name was Maria or Yolanda or something like that. She made all the big mafiosos' heads turn at the Savoy, the Cotton Club and the Apollo Theater. Unfortunately, Bessie was the private property of a formidable *capo*, Umberto Della Torre, a devilishly handsome wop richer than Croesus. The animal spent crazy sums every night in one or another cabaret, and swarms of whores would try to get their claws into him after he'd asked his chauffeur, usually around nine p.m., to take his girl back to the fold so he could slum it with the Negresses and Mulattos until the wee hours. How did our Bessie manage to charm the man so coveted by every girl? And how on earth did she manage to get him all to herself? That was her own little secret, as she declared to anyone willing to listen, not bragging in the least. So, she lived large for almost two years, until a young lady with a delicate face and hazel eyes turned up. Harlem was constantly welcoming a stream of bastards and survivors from the South. As they said, it was Mecca for the descendants of slaves. That creature (her name escapes me now) wasn't much to look at, just another spring chicken, but she knew what she was doing, that bitch. Ever since she managed to give Umberto Della Torre oral pleasure—at least that was the rumor—the *capo* refused to swear by anyone but her and, without any consideration for Bessie, sent our friend straight to the scrapyard. Bessie couldn't manage to accept a life without flash, so she committed suicide by swallowing an entire bottle of stomach pills.

I was telling you, Frédéric, that Shortie, my dearly beloved friend Shortie, lived in constant fear that her protector, her fornicator, her adopted father, that mafia boss who drowned her in gifts, might one day follow his colleague Della Torre's example. She never opened up to me about it, but I knew her inside out and I must admit that I shared her apprehension. So, she needed her heroin on the regular, her little dose. Fortunately it was little, and so she was rarely high. Doped, if you prefer. But the American government had undertaken to fight against the drug—you could find it on any street corner—probably because it had ended up creeping onto the perfectly manicured lawns of white university campuses. The crème de la crème of the country's youth was at risk, and the authorities had to act. As long as it only ravaged white intellectuals and artists and niggers of all variety, the problem was limited and, therefore, under control, but once it seemed to be spiraling out of control, they had to intervene quickly and decisively. Brigades were created for that purpose, even in Harlem. Not out of concern for the well-being of our neighborhood's inhabitants, but because the police suspected it was the nerve center of the heroin trafficking. They weren't entirely mistaken because you had to find a way to survive in the Valley, another name—far too bucolic—for Central Harlem, where Blacks preyed upon Blacks. They killed each other over nothing, got plastered morning and night, beat their wives and children, pickpocketed or organized stick-ups, refused to help widows or orphans and, of course, shot up.

"Stéphanie, I need your car, my belle. If I took it early this evening, around seven o'clock, would it be any trouble for you?" Every time Shortie sent me that coded message, I knew perfectly well that she wasn't about to go shopping, but that she'd force Andrew, my chauffeur, to take her to the docks along the East River or to some empty lot between warehouses where heroin was sold more or less openly. A discreet man, Andrew tried not to betray my friend to me, and it took me months on end of trying to worm it out of him before I finally understood. At first, I'd been convinced that she was cuckolding her mafia boss with a young Negro lover. Shortie, indeed, lived her life and made the most of her body, as she herself was fond of saying. Before getting her hooks into the man in question, she'd been known to exchange her playthings on a monthly basis. I was tempted to speak with her directly and to make it clear to her that it was too dangerous for me to lend her my vehicle in service of her dubious enterprise, but I couldn't bring myself to do it. Shortie was the first true friend I ever had, and she was the one who introduced me to Annabelle and Mysti. With those three joyful souls, I had the feeling that I was really finding my way in my new American life or, at least, in my Negro version of it. Of being less marginal. I wasn't surprised when, one evening, I got a call from the 153rd Street station ordering me to come down without delay. I'd cursed Andrew, suspecting he'd gotten into some accident, he whom I was always telling to slow down. I was completely wrong. The NYPD had ambushed the East River heroin dealers and had nicked a good two dozen of them along with a couple customers, including my dear Shortie. I had to spend an arm and a leg on her bail, a sum she repaid with interest, begging me never to relate the incident to anyone. If sweetheart came to learn about her mishap, there was no doubt that he would not hesitate to cast her off like an old sock. Except that, a couple weeks later, she had to appear in court and was facing a heavy sentence. Very heavy. I'd also put my lawyer, Elridge McMurphy, at her disposal. He was champion of the bar, and he'd wrested me from the claws of justice on many an occasion. This time, that incorrigible optimist seemed worried. The police wanted to make an example to please the mayor who, in turn, wanted to please the governor of the state of New York, who wanted to please the president of the United States, who'd solemnly sworn war against heroin dealers. My Shortie was in for penitentiary and not for any short vacation, he'd tried to joke. What means did I have to save my friend, I, Madam Queen, the very same woman whose omnipotence (or even grandipotence) was bragged about all across Harlem? In such a case, my intellectual friends—the Du Boises, Hugheses, Cullens and all the rest—would be of no help to me because if they contested the laws of the white world, neither did they approve of the acts they referred to as *Negro delinquency*. Even if they considered the latter to be the result of the oppression we suffered, they saw in it an obstacle in our fight for emancipation.

"Alcohol peddlers, drug dealers, pimps, horserace fixers, gangsters and all that, all those dregs of humanity serve the system of oppression," Countee Cullen had hurled at me one day, before managing to get ahold of himself, realizing that he'd forgotten he was talking to someone who'd created an underground lottery that rivaled the city of New York's own official lottery.

I didn't get too hot under the collar. Deep down, he was right. But all those university graduates with clean hands and upstanding morals, what else did they have to offer us? If we'd had factories, banks, major businesses like the Whites, we certainly wouldn't have found ourselves obliged to break the law. The very existence of the mob proved that was wrong-headed. In short, my heart was in disorder at the idea that I wouldn't see my Shortie anymore when a 137th Street cop, whose palm I greased generously and who'd taken a fancy to me, made me understand with veiled words that Judge Samuelson was partial to bankable coins. He was also the man who'd send Shortie to jail in a couple weeks. Which would destroy her forever because, even as pretty as she was, it was unlikely that sweetheart would wait for her. She'd be replaced in no time flat.

Judge Samuelson lived in a vast patrician home in the center of Manhattan, a home that, alas, skyscrapers were already beginning to encircle. He was a widower and lived with two black employees: a butler and a servant, both of a certain age. Approaching him seemed difficult and speaking to him impossible. Early in the morning, a chauffeur would come fetch him and take him to the courthouse, then he'd bring him home in the evening without making even the shortest stop anywhere. Or, in any case, not in Harlem. How could such an ascetic man be tempted by bribes? What use did he have for them? Time passed me by, and I was still searching for a way to get Shortie out of the mess she'd gotten herself into. I'd managed to exchange a few words with her during the prison's visitation hours. My best friend was down in the dumps. She had somehow managed to convince sweetheart that she'd gone to her dying mother's side in Atlanta, but the day of her trial would soon fly that alibi to pieces. Her almost royal lifestyle was sure to be over and, as she left the courthouse, the very people who used to bow and scrape before her would be waiting, eager to spit in her face. In Harlem, pity was a completely unknown sentiment. An idea suddenly came to me: My neighbor, Du Bois, that great intellectual so highly respected by the white intelligentsia, couldn't he introduce me to Judge Samuelson? He hadn't gotten over his daughter Yolanda's divorce from Countee Cullen, and his morning visits to my apartment were ever more frequent. He needed company, but not intellectual company. He needed someone practical, who had her feet on the ground like me. He wanted to know how his ex-son-in-law had ended up a pederast, if it was a choice or just a natural disposition, what the reason for it was and how he'd managed to justify the marriage. A thousand questions assailed him, and I took it upon myself to provide him with commonsensical answers that had the gift of soothing him.

"I knew your Judge Samuelson at Harvard, where we were students together. He's two or three years older than me, and he can't be far from retirement. We have friendly relations, very friendly indeed," Du Bois declared after I opened up to him.

"I'd like to get in touch with him. Do you think it's possible?"

"Oh la la! He'll never change, that dear Samuelson!" Du Bois said with a smile. "Even when we were young, he was already a spendthrift living beyond his means. And that's without counting his skirt chasing. He married three or four times as I understand it...."

That explained it: The good judge was bowed beneath the

weight of alimony and child support, and his salary wasn't enough. Du Bois called him and arranged a rendezvous for me in a West Harlem restaurant patronized by white bohemians. We wouldn't be noticed there because there was a second-floor room reserved for VIPs. No sooner said than done! When I found myself face to face with the representative of justice, I understood that he—despite his pompous manner—didn't have much of a moral foundation. He accepted the thick envelope I set beside him without flinching and chatted with me about everything and nothing as if we were old friends. The meal was exquisite. No one paid us any mind. Five days later, Shortie was condemned to a year in prison with possibility for parole.

My envelope held fifteen thousand dollars....

Chapter Fifteen

I knew one day or another I'd have them cornered, all those bastards who'd condemned me to that damned Welfare Island prison—a rather inaptly named place—for possession of illegal lottery slips. Oh, all those grand gentlemen were thinking they'd gotten rid of that damn French Negress Stéphanie St. Clair for good, that bitch who insisted on facing off against them instead of keeping a low profile like the other colored gangsters. Well, they'd see what they'd see! In my cell, which was dimly lit day and night, I'd stewed over my revenge down to the most insignificant details, and as soon as I'd returned home (my apartment was shut up for the entire eight months of my incarceration), as soon as that first day came that I saw the sky again and breathed in the open air (I could no longer bear the smell of piss and the asinine chatter of my fellow detainees), I finally felt alive again, my dear nephew. The most trying thing had been those couple days that came every month—my period. Up until my imprisonment, I'd never had any trouble with it, and my flow barely lasted two days. I rarely had cramps or felt weak like the majority of women. While Shortie, Mysti or Annabelle railed against what they considered to be an unfair divine punishment whose regular arrival they dreaded, I, Stéphanie St. Clair, could never quite understand where they were coming from. My numbers business had never been disrupted by my period. But as soon as I was thrown into darkness, things changed completely. I became a regular woman somehow; I didn't feel quite like myself. Horrible pains began to wrack my body, and I bled profusely despite being so near the age of menopause. My sole bright spot was that my fellow detainees suffered even more that I. The prison administration only allowed medical visits in cases of extreme crisis. That stretch of my life made me more forgiving of the feminine sex because I began to understand why they couldn't hold their own vis-à-vis their masculine counterparts. Having a period plunges you into an exasperating state of vulnerability. Or at least that's my opinion.

As soon as I was free, I immediately bought a copy of the *Amsterdam News*, Harlem's most respected newspaper, and found the paper's address. The very next morning, after a restorative night, I went to their office with an article I wanted to publish as a paid ad. The editor-in-chief welcomed me, to my great surprise, as a veritable heroine. I didn't know that the paper had followed my trial closely and with such a wealth of detail that, later, I couldn't quite believe it. Even the color of the various dresses I'd worn! Or one phrase or another I'd uttered, a phrase whose arrogance had provoked a thunderous applause in the all-black audience. Those articles were precious to me because I'd lived through the trial in a kind of trance. I'd been nearly indifferent to my own person and to the circus that was taking place around me. From the first moment of my incarceration, I'd forced myself to forget about all of that and became solely focused on figuring out my next move after my release. It was then that the idea of retiring—an idea that had haunted me over the course of the last years, but always only in fits and bursts—began to take a concrete form. Having saved up enough money to live comfortably for the rest of my days, I began, for the first time, to seriously imagine returning to my native land, the island I'd kept my back turned to for almost thirty years. Even if I no longer had any ties there, the desire to smell certain scents, to hear the now-gruff, now-melodic intonation of Creole, to be lulled by the songs of the washerwomen along the Madame River, even to simply watch the rhythmic steps of the rows of coal sellers carrying their overflowing baskets on their heads, well, I was starting to miss everything. It wasn't exactly nostalgia in the proper sense of the term, but an almost physical longing. A kind of hunger or thirst. Your letter, my dear nephew, revived that feeling.

Nonetheless, as soon as they'd opened the door to my cell,

then the gates of Welfare Island, that longing evaporated as if by sorcery, and I rediscovered not some newfound joie de vivre, but a furious desire to fight, to resist. To cut down those sonsabitches who'd been responsible for my fall. When I reached my building, I took the elevator—for the first time in my life. Even when I felt ill, I'd always preferred to take the stairs up to the tenth floor, leaning on Duke, then on Bumpy, then Lewis and, finally, Bumpy again, my bodyguards and lovers. But on that day, I became wracked with a feverishness that precluded the fear I'd always felt toward that seemingly diabolical invention. The squealing of the metallic doors terrified me all the same, but a fourth-floor dweller got on and greeted me as if nothing was awry. One of those Negro doctors or lawyers living comfortably—and discreetly, I might add—on Sugar Hill, far from the noise and disorder of Central Harlem. I suppose he knew who I was because he gave me a sideways glance and mumbled, "Good afternoon, ma'am!"

I frantically dug through my purse for the keys to my apartment; I couldn't find them at first and cursed the hindrance. You would've thought that some higher power took pleasure in denying me my only wish, the one that had enabled me to survive those long months of prison: to demolish, one after the other, all those who'd dared run down Madam Queen, the Numbers Queen, the queen of Harlem's illegal lottery. I yanked the dining room curtains open, found a piece of paper and a pen and set to writing without rereading a single word. I wrote the following in one go:

CORRUPTION IN THE NEW YORK POLICE DEPARTMENT
Many citizens of this fine city of New York, not to say the majority of them, are swollen with pride because they believe they have the best police in the whole United States or even in the whole world. This is false. Completely false. It is a myth hawked by journalists who have been bought by shameless politicians. The NYPD is corrupt through and through, and our fellow

citizens—no matter to which race they belong—would benefit from understanding this. Corrupt to the bone, to tell the honest truth. I, Stéphanie St. Clair, can testify, for example, to having given sums ranging from three hundred to five hundred dollars to Officer Brian of the 142nd Street station so that he would release a black man who'd been arrested that day. For a white policeman, every Black—as we all know—is automatically suspected of something and, to prevent him from committing a crime, the former has a duty to arrest the latter as a preventative measure. When will we cease to accept such a situation, which benefits neither the police nor the city of New York? For my part, I am ready to testify before a judge about the venality of Officer Brian and about his numerous violations of the code of conduct of the otherwise prestigious police force to which he belongs.
—Stéphanie St. Clair

How surprised I was to receive a phone call the very next morning, a call from the paper's editor-in-chief, informing me that not only would he gladly publish my article, but that he'd also offer me a regular column. I could use my column to write about whatever I wished without any censure to hold me back. Although I was a voracious reader and had always been so, I was less gifted at writing. For years, I'd handed all my correspondence over to my secretary, Charleyne—that is, until the dimwit (I should have seen it coming) got herself knocked up by one of my men, and I had to fire her right then and there. I'd carried on the torch without the least enthusiasm, but little by little, I'd managed to master the arcana of written English.

"The community needs you, Madam Queen," the editor-in-chief added to be sure of convincing me. That was the first time I'd heard that! I hadn't realized that the Harlem Negroes had suffered in the slightest as a result of my absence. Bumpy, who'd been indicted for the thirtieth or fortieth time for drug trafficking—it had become a constant source of strife between us—had managed to hold down my business somehow. The business had already been in a bad way after I'd been forced to deal with Lucky Luciano. Besides, my bodyguard-cum-lover had had to pay dearly for what I'd considered as nothing less than a betrayal, and he was bumped off while lunching in a fine restaurant with the very men he'd imagined would protect him. I didn't have one ounce of confidence in those wops, and I didn't shed a single tear over his corpse. Bumpy died alone, like a dog, in the hospital he'd been driven to, probably hoping I'd swoop in at the last moment to see him off on his journey toward hell. Sentimentalism has never been my strong suit, dear nephew, otherwise I'd never have attained glory. Even the white press had taken it upon itself to recount my exploits, and I savored reading the spiteful articles they'd dedicated to me in the news briefs of the *New York Times*. As I've already told you, I was rarely referred to by name, but any ignoramus could've guessed that it was the apparently mysterious Stéphanie St. Clair in question, that Frenchwoman whose skin was somewhere between ebony and copper and who'd ended up reigning over Harlem's illegal lottery.

I, who'd attended school for no more than five years in total, became the writer of a column entirely my own for the most highly respected black newspaper in the whole United States. The director had no right to change a word of my writing, which was not the case, as I would later learn, for the professional journalists. That unprecedented favor had more to do with my temperament and—above all—my reputation as a person who wouldn't let herself get walked on. My weekly column eventually turned into a biweekly one, then it started coming out three times a week as a result of the readers' pressing demands. Some of my readers would approach me in restaurants or shops to report the affronts to which they'd been subjected, and I made those accounts into my bread and butter, after adding my own touches to them, of course, otherwise Stéphanie St. Clair wouldn't have merited her nickname, Queenie, the little queen of Harlem. I remember that my most successful column—the one that the paper strove to republish quarterly—was called "How to Comport Yourself in Jail." It went something like this:

It must be known that an incarcerated person is still a citizen like all others, that is to say, with all the rights pertaining to that status. This means that, first of all, the guards owe him or her a minimum of respect and may not bark at him or her instead of speaking, as happens all too often. If you become the victim of that which is, in the end, none other than a form of intimidation with intent to tame you like some wild beast, I advise you to keep a cool head and to wait for the guard to calm down. If the guard manages to do so, you must ask in the most neutral tone possible, "I would appreciate if you would address me in a different manner, and I thank you in advance." If, on the other hand, the guard continues to abuse his or her uniform and, thus, authority, you must, above all, avoid responding to him or her in kind because the guard is waiting for you to raise your voice in order to give you a couple stinging blows with a billyclub. White guards are dying to break the Negro, as if doing so would renew the white race's virility. Obey his or her orders but exaggerate them: If the guard asks you to take off your shirt, get completely naked; if the guard demands that you scrub the floor of your cell, do so, then attack the walls! Three out of four times, that will unnerve your torturer, and he or she will cease and desist. On the other hand, there are those who seem jovial, who crack jokes in front of you in hopes of making you smile. Do not, under any circumstance, do so! Assume the most bovine expression possible and drone out a "yes, sir" or a "yes, ma'am" without meeting his or her eyes. This practical advice will considerably improve your time in prison.

It wasn't so much the content of my columns that mattered, but rather, the fact that they were published in Harlem's most important black paper. Although they were banal through and through, they irritated the police and justice simply because they were written by me—as if I were public enemy number two, right after Al Capone. Their harassment of my associates redoubled, this time with the stated intention of forever destroying the illegal lottery. When, having grown rather weary of the whole thing, I wanted to drop the column, the editor-in-chief of the *Amsterdam News* rushed straight to my home and begged me to keep my column.

"Your columns light the way for our people, Madam St. Clair. Especially for those whose rights are regularly trampled upon by the police and the courts. I can assure you of that!"

"So, I'm useful, then, am I? Me? Ha ha ha!"

"I'm not kidding, Madam St. Clair. We'd have to call upon a jurist to write your column, but your personal touch, the concrete examples upon which you base your arguments, that's much more instructive than a simple statement of the rules and regulations. Know that the majority of our letters to the editor are about your column."

"Well, then you ought to pay me!"

"Yes, certainly! I am in complete agreement. Give me a figure and I'll go negotiate it with the boss."

"Ha ha ha! I'm kidding, dear friend. The time I spent in prison seriously slowed down business for me, but I've managed to pick up some steam again. Stéphanie St. Clair doesn't beg charity from anyone!"

I was talking big because my column apparently bothered the fuzz a great deal; I'd been continually denouncing their abuses of power and other violations of the law as soon as it affected us colored people. One evening, I'd received a visit from an enigmatic person, a White in his fifties who was very elegantly dressed. He threatened me directly after having hurled questions at me, all in his rather refined way of speaking.

"I work for the government. An inquiry into your person has been opened. Be assured, this inquiry has nothing to do with your silly little game. Though, if rumors serve, you've turned a pretty penny or two from it. But this.... Now, how shall I put this? It's much more serious than that."

"I'm not sure what you mean."

"Well, let's get right down to brass tacks, then! Madam St. Clair, are you a Bolshevist?"

"A Bol-what?"

"Communist, if you prefer. Please don't beat around the bush. The government is perfectly aware of the fact that white militants have infiltrated Harlem to incite the Blacks against what they call the exploitative capitalist system. Are you one of their followers?"

Stupefied, I didn't know what to say to that man, probably an agent of the FBI. He was the first White I'd spoken to since my trial, when my Irish lawyer, whom I'd convinced to defend me — oh, I completely forgot to tell you this, dear nephew — thanks to my little bit of Gaelic, which made him smile, he'd fought tooth and nail to have my case dismissed. In prison, I had two white cellmates, but they were what's called *white trash*, scum who'd been rejected by their own race. Practically illiterate, one had thrust a kitchen knife into her husband's stomach, the other had poisoned her mother-in-law with arsenic. They punctuated every sentence with resounding cries of *fuck!* and were astonished by my language, which they judged to be affected — of course utterly false, my nephew. Was that why they jumped me during my second week of incarceration? Who knows! Maybe they were upset about cohabitating with a Negress — they did, after all, demonstrate a racial hatred that approached madness.

"Hey, guard! Bring us a bucket of water so we can clean this fucking cell! The stink of that filthy ape makes me want to puke.... What the fuck? Why don't you answer?" the first one would shriek.

"She belches and farts all night long, move us to another cell, goddamit!" the other would whine.

The queen of Harlem had fallen from her throne. Her fine apartment had been sealed, but fortunately the fuzz had been too lazy to thumb through all of the books and old magazines piled up in the W.C., and her booty was still intact. Nonetheless, Annah, her faithful servant, and Andrew, her no less faithful chauffeur, along with her secretary Charleyne had found themselves suddenly out on the street. See, that's what it was like to be a foreign and family-less sovereign! You find yourself abandoned by your court, your soldiers, your debtors, your friends. By your people even! Because Harlem didn't rise up as my slightly cocky nature had led me to believe it would. Quite the contrary: The few bankers I'd allowed to work on their own account suddenly grew wings. The most eager among them—eager to take my place, I mean—was named Murphy. He took it upon himself to convene my associates in his wretched den on 167th Street and ordered them (as I'd learn upon my release) to work for him from that day forth. The cad had to pay dearly for offending Madam Queen like that! But I must admit, there was a time during which my name had practically been erased from Harlem. As if my reign had never existed. That really gave me something to think about—the human condition and my own future, I mean. Who was I really in this black ghetto? It's true I left a decent mark, but now I'd been laid bare and found myself at the mercy of a simple police raid or court ruling. In the end, was my status already ebbing away, and would I be better off, now that my fortune had been made, simply abdicating? All those cogitations occupied my mind (insomnia obliged) during the eight months I spent in prison, and they sure didn't go anywhere after my release. They did fade away for a time because Stéphanie St. Clair had to take her business by the horns again. A lot of people, even though they might have proved to be ingrates, were counting on her—depending on her, even. The queen, having fallen, had to reclaim her scepter and return, by hook or crook, to her throne, but the truth was that her heart wasn't in it anymore.

As for that old song about Bolshevism, well, that was nothing new. Back when I forced myself to read the *New York Times* and the *Wall Street Journal* in their entirety in order to improve my English, I'd stumbled across a sentence in an article published in the latter paper that lodged itself in my mind so much had it shocked me, "Race riots seem to have for their genesis a Bolshevist, a Negro and a gun."

After I'd moved to Edgecombe Avenue, alongside my famous neighbors from the black intelligentsia, I'd discussed communism with W.E.B. Du Bois a few times, in particular during the period when an editorial in his paper, *The Crisis*, had provoked some brouhaha among the white establishment and had cost him a summons from the CIA. The *New York Times* had accused the author of *The Souls of Black Folk* (an admirable book that I'd like to give you a copy of) of being a Bolshevist because he'd dared to write something that, in my eyes, seemed to be a statement of truth, "Today, we raise the terrible weapon of self-defense. When the armed lynchers gather, we, too, must gather armed."

If I seemed like someone who'd just dropped from the clouds, it was a completely sincere reaction, and it convinced the FBI agent that Madam St. Clair had never tangled with those white militants that he'd seen on Harlem's main drags, distributing pamphlets peppered with quotes by Lenin and Stalin, neither up close nor from afar, no, she'd simply passed them by without a second glance. True, she had asked her chauffeur to slow down and get a copy every now and then, but it wasn't out of curiosity. No, in her business it was indispensable—vital, even—to keep informed of everything that was going on in the black ghetto.

Nothing could escape her. Not even the minutest arrival of an obscure Baptist preacher fresh from the Deep South come in hopes of saving the human race with his little Bible recitations along the sidewalks of Harlem.

Well, to get back to my story, that vermin Lucky Luciano had taken advantage of my absence to move his pawns into my territory! The war with the white mafia was heating up. We were counting our dead on both sides, and there were more of them than fingers on our hands. On that account, the wops (more numerous than us, to say the least) had only to wait until I was the last one standing, abandoned by all, holed up in my Edgecombe Avenue apartment. I had—excuse me if I'm repeating myself—been forced to smoke from the peace pipe. I'd held onto a reasonable revenue and, at my advanced age, perhaps that had been the best solution to maintain myself in life. See, Frédéric, I'm only saying this now: Gangsters live in a state of constant uncertainty. They wake up in the morning not knowing if they'll see nightfall. And every day is like that! A stray bullet, a police raid, or more prosaically, a knife in the back during a street scrap could abbreviate your existence at any moment. The important thing was never to show that you were consumed by that fear, otherwise you'd sign your own death warrant, and above all, you had to hide it from your own men. Gangsters can trust no one, not even the person who sleeps beside you at night. In my case, there was no chance of that happening because I couldn't bear the presence of a male pressed against me at night while I slept, which was only a sort of half-sleep anyway. I ended up agreeing to negotiate. Bumpy was gloating, that half-wit! I was furious at him, at myself, at the white gangsters, at the whole universe, but I had no other choice. I was alone with my fate; it wasn't as if I could go ask for help from the NAACP or the civil rights movement, which was in its infancy back then. The latter promised to be very effective, judging from the few actions it

242

had already undertaken. Defending the race, that's one thing, but defending your race's *criminals*, well, that was something else. I didn't hold it against them. I had never tried to hide the fact that my business operated outside of the established rules, and the fact that those rules had been established by Whites prevented me from being assailed by a guilty conscience. I wasn't ashamed of competing with New York City's official lottery. I prided myself on never paying a penny to the IRS, and I had no use for the mayor or even the state governor, even less so for the president of the United States. The racial segregation they'd put in place left us colored people with little choice, and in order to survive, we often had to bend the rules. And then again, the mob didn't seem to have any remorse, and I didn't see why I, with my little business, should have to perform any act of contrition to the authorities or even to society.

"Happy to meet you, signora," Lucky Luciano said upon our first meeting in an empty warehouse along the West Harlem docks.

His voice had no trace of irony, which surprised me. I even thought I made out a shade of unexpected deference. His apartment, where he'd eventually agreed to receive me, was situated in a well-heeled Queens neighborhood where not a single person of color—aside from the cleaning ladies and the chauffeurs—dared set foot. Sinister-looking guys, obviously armed to the teeth, encircled his building, pacing to and fro as other men waited in automobiles whose windows were obscured by curtains. When my Model T stopped in front of the monumental stairway that provided access to his apartment, four mafiosos rushed over, reaching for their guns. My poor Andrew, terrorized, raised his hands in the air and stuttered, "My boss has a rendezvous with yours...."

Seeing me climb out of the car, the hired guns froze in place. A woman! And a Negress at that! But they lowered their guns and escorted me to the lobby, where a butler in an embellished outfit welcomed me with a plethora of low bows. He had an Italian accent thick enough to cut with a knife. Lucky Luciano did too — which surprised me for someone who'd lived in America so much longer than I. He had me take a seat in a luxurious parlor, but he ignored Bumpy altogether. The head of New York's white mafia was stockier and less intimidating than I'd imagined he would be. He had less of an effect on me in person than he had in the newspaper photos, in any case. His left eye — the one whose lid drooped thanks to the bullet that had grazed it — had been part of his allure when he was young, but now it just made him look like a sad clown. He was a rather jovial man, nonetheless.

"Would you like some cognac, Madam St. Clair? Or perhaps some rum? My dear friend Meyer Lansky sends me the good stuff straight from Cuba. He's living there now. You're familiar with the island, I presume. It's rather close to yours, isn't it?"

"I know it by name, yes...."

"Beautiful country! Sun year-round, glorious beaches, sublime girls. Oh, excuse me, you're a woman, my last remark doesn't concern you. Ha ha ha! But be honest, don't you miss the heat? The New York winters haven't been easy on us these past few years, wouldn't you say?"

Fucking wop! I wanted to shout right in his face. And your Sicilian sun, don't you ever miss that? Lucky Luciano seemed to be well-informed about my person and about my business. He gave the impression of not wanting to force anything on me, but rather of hoping to come to an agreement that would benefit us both. But before getting down to business, he wore himself out in circumlocutions, showing me his paintings, one of which he'd bought from my Edgecombe Avenue neighbor, the renowned painter Aaron Douglas; that was quite the surprise. He had me admire his collection of blown glass objects from some village in Italy. The man would not shut up; he was almost endearing. The funniest thing was that our respective bodyguards, undoubtedly tired of standing, never ceased to stare daggers at each other. As if ready to lunge at the slightest provocation.

"Fine, well, let's get to it, my dear lady. I'm sure you're wondering why I requested an audience with you. I have a very clear proposition: You give me the Harlem numbers and, in exchange, my friend Meyer Lansky will integrate you into his ranks in Havana.... There you'll enjoy not only an ideal climate, but also utter peace on the part of the cops, unlike over here. The president over there, General Batista, works with us...."

"And I'd be responsible for what?" I asked in an even tone, feigning interest.

"Well, you'd take care of a slew of things. Horseraces, for example, because Meyer's got a whole stable over there. And the races are year-round, thanks to the fine weather. You'd have a casino, too, one that's a lot like your Cotton Club, but above all, you'd be in charge of a... joy house for high-ranking Cubans and rich American expats. Meyer is convinced that a woman would be better at managing it than he is, especially *une femme de couleur* seeing as the majority of the ladies are Cubans...."

My blood was boiling! I tried to control myself. I tried to remind myself that I was sitting across from the most formidable mafioso in all of New York and even in all of the United States (after Al Capone, of course, who reigned over Chicago), a guy who'd been behind hundreds of killings, a man feared by the police, who made politicians tremble, a *capo* who could bring anyone down to their knees. I exploded anyway.

"A joy house! No, really, are you fucking with me, Luciano? Call it what it is, a whorehouse, and let's be done with it!"

I was so enraged that I was stamping my feet against the parquet without realizing what I was doing, and I had a trace of froth at my lips. My hazel-colored eyes were flashing. In short, I was certainly a frightening sight. It was Bumpy, as soon as we'd left, who painted that terrible picture of my person for me. Lucky Luciano didn't give anything away. He got up from his chair and kneeled right beside me to whisper into my ear, "Bella signora, non hai capito... Non voglio che tu perda la vita.... Let's be reasonable! Harlem is slipping away from you and I'm offering you an escape, no need to lose your life over it."

His voice was falsely beseeching. Heavy with menace, to tell the whole truth. I loved the Italian language, it reminded me of Roberto, my Neapolitan lover back in Marseille, but also of my first forays into the world of gangsters, back when I was a member of the Forty Thieves and we'd have to stand up to the men we never referred to as anything but *those shitty wops*. Sometimes, I'd ended up sympathizing with the Sicilians or the Neapolitans when I was sent out to spy on them for our boss, O'Reilly. Thanks to my memory, I'd managed to pick up a few words, then a few sentences in their language, and I even learned to sing a couple of their songs. The beginning of one of them, in Sicilian, got into my head and without really knowing why, I began to hum:

> *Mi votu e mi rivotu suspirannu,*
> *Passu la notti 'ntera senza sonnu*
> *E li biddizzi toi jeu cuntimplannu*
> *Mi passa di la notti sino a ghiornu….*

Then a sort of miracle happened. Lucky Luciano, the biggest boss of the New York mafia, closed his eyes and, gripping the arm of my chair, began to weep. Soft, transparent tears ran down his cheeks. Drops of dew in the half shadow of the late afternoon in his parlor with its heavy, half-drawn curtains. That moment seemed to last an eternity. His bodyguard, ill at ease, helped him get to his feet.

"I... I'd like to make you a new offer, Madam St. Clair. Stay in Harlem, but let's share the business."

"Accept!" Bumpy rushed over to hiss into my ear. "We don't

have any choice."

I stared straight into Luciano's eyes as I searched through my handbag for my cigarette holder. I lit a Chesterfield and took two nonchalant drags. My man was right: We were dealing with too strong an opponent. As long as it had been the Negro gangs, Queenie had managed to hold onto her throne and reign sovereign over the numbers in full sight of the white police and the white justice. But faced with the mafia, I found myself outnumbered. All that I could hope for was that they'd be generous enough to leave me with the title of marquise or countess. I meditated upon my fate, which I considered humiliating. Wasn't I, Queenie, the little queen of New York's black neighborhood, about to become Lucky Luciano's subordinate? That shameless wop who, as soon as his alcohol dealings were on the verge of failure, had set his sights on my personal territory and, especially, on the numbers, without considering the fact that getting things going had required years upon years of work, of self-sacrifice, of tireless battling against the competition, of resistance to the police's harassment. Yes, indeed, years! And now he'd come along and thought he could take over my organization with the snap of his fingers! Even though, as I've already told you, dear Frédéric, I was bringing in about two hundred thousand dollars of net profit year in and year out, my revenues were nothing compared to those of Al Capone's New York alter ego. Certainly, I'd have less work this way and, logically, fewer worries, but I'd fallen from on high and it was unlikely that I'd manage to remake myself one day because time was passing me by and my years were beginning to weigh on me, even if I'd enjoyed excellent health up to then. Madam Queen, a stowaway in her own kingdom! Shameful....

Brokenhearted, I stammered, "How much?"

"Seventy percent for us, Madam St. Clair. The rest for you."

"Forty for me!"

"No. Take it or leave it."

I took it. I had to take it.

Chapter Sixteen

You're going to tell me, dear nephew, you who looks so much like my departed mother, my dear Frédéric who travelled all the way from Martinique to see me, that I'm exaggerating again. That seventy-seven isn't so old for someone who's fit as a fiddle like me. But I believe it with every fiber of my being: The end of my days is nearing! I like that expression, which, although it's probably been used for—I imagine—centuries upon centuries, hasn't lost anything of its poetry. Though it presents an enormous lacuna, in my case, because I've lived nights as much as days— and perhaps nights even more than days. Harlem didn't really get hopping until the streetlamps came on, when the fauna of the most ill-reputed streets emerged from their lairs: junkies, incurable alcoholics, miserous two-dollar strumpets, quite simply all the poor bastards managing to survive by hustling, along with those bitches with worn-out bodies whose mouths were twisted into a permanent rictus. The real Harlem, I mean, the one that existed between 1910-1930! There was also a notch above, the small-fry mobsters who worked for some boss or another and who were trigger-crazed. With their comically self-satisfied air, they'd strut around in linen suits and fedoras, a cigar clamped between their jaws. Don't forget about my runners, collecting debts from house to house, which they'd bring to my dozen or so bankers—the latter were highly respectable individuals and believed themselves to be hard as nails; they holed themselves away in their homes as soon as night fell to avoid any nasty encounters. But Harlem was, above all, its cabarets—the Lafayette, the Savoy Ballroom, the Apollo Theater and, of course, the Cotton Club—where the white world would come to slum it to the beat of Negro music, nimbly clearing—thanks to their bankable coins—all racial barriers as soon as a voluptuous young Negress caught their eye.

I appreciated, for my part, these two universes: The

dangerous—and to be honest, disgusting—world of the street and the other, the more refined (although not less dangerous) world of those temples of lust that enchanted the giants of jazz. Louis Armstrong! Duke Ellington! The much-too-little-known, alas, Cootie Williams! My word, many others enchanted my stay in that land where the Negro seemed always to be on trial against the whole world. I'm going to admit certain things to you, dear Frédéric, things that are a bit bothersome. I'm an old lady now, and I figure I have the right to no longer keep my true face veiled, to no longer keep certain things hidden in the depth of my being, however bothersome they might be. I'm trusting you neither to bend the truth nor to embellish it. I was no saint in my life, without wanting to say I was a criminal. I supported widows and orphans, as they say, whenever I could. Oh, sure I know—or, rather, I suppose—that since you arrived in this city you must've heard a lot of badmouthing about Madam Queen. A heartless woman, hardnosed, unfeeling, proud of her French origins, occasionally contemptuous and so on. I can't object to any of that, because if I accepted your offer to deliver up my life to you in all its nitty-gritty detail for that book you're wanting to write, it wasn't to make up that life like a painted lady. I've got nothing to hide and I don't want to hide anything of it, you know that. Come on, don't play innocent! I noticed you were horrified when I told you about how I castrated O'Reilly, that Irish nutcase in charge of the Forty Thieves. Maybe you thought I was making up stories. How could a frail creature like Stéphanie St. Clair, your aunt whose memory was never abandoned by our family in Martinique, or so you claim, how could she end up committing such excesses? My dear nephew, New York, and especially Five Points and East Harlem, where I lived from the very start, were—don't laugh!— downright cutthroat when I arrived. Take note of the year, please! 1912, and I wasn't even twenty-six yet. I was fit to be tied! No money, couldn't even speak a word of English and, what's more, a foreign Negress, what could've been running through my mind to think for a single second that I'd not only manage to survive in such a world but assert myself over it? I swear to you, dear Frédéric, that in the beginning I knew damn near nothing at all. I sought out adventure because since I was a child, I'd always dreamed of an elsewhere, but had no concrete plan in mind. I hadn't imagined throwing myself into any particular business and I wasn't convinced—unlike the other immigrants—that by working myself to the bone I'd end up a millionaire.

Allow me to read your lips: What unmentionable shame could there be in your existence, my aunt? Sorry to keep asking the questions and giving the answers, but you're so stingy with your words that I'm starting to wonder if you'll manage to write your book after all. Or, rather, get it written since you claim to be better versed in numbers. I see you scribbling-scribbling-scribbling in your notebooks, you blacken page after page without making a single peep. Oh, I should tell you that I'm proud of you, proud to know that you're a teacher at Schoelcher High School. In my day, no one from the countryside had access to those bourgeois establishments, and certainly not someone from that faraway village of Vauclin like you. *Faraway* wasn't the word we used. No, we'd say: "Over behind the good Lord's back." Ha ha ha! Things have deucedly changed in Martinique since I left, it's been fifty years, a whole lifetime, huh! Don't smile at my old-fashioned way of speaking! It's been a long, long time since I had anyone to speak our language with, and I kept it up only by reading. I devour books. Ha ha ha! Well, what to confess to my nephew who came all the way to my bedside just to write the story of my life? First of all... hmm! First of all, something strange that I've probably already told you—excuse me if I'm repeating myself, but allow me to make myself understood—I never felt black except with White Americans, never with colored people. Hang on, let me be clear! I've never been ashamed of my color and, besides, unlike the Negresses from around here, I've always refused to relax my hair. Oh, the worst, the most hideous were all those jazz musicians and singers who were hellbent on metamorphosing their kinks, as we called them in Martinique, beneath layer after layer of brilliantine, which always started to stink when their orchestras played more than two hours and their scalps started to sweat. No, Stéphanie St. Clair never renounced her race! But faced with American Negroes, I always felt... how can I put this? French. Not Martinican, but French. I know it's bizarre, but no one invents their feelings or sensations. They come up on you, consume you and keep you in their yoke whether you like it or not. And I ought to add that back then, Americans—whether Black or White— harbored a limitless admiration for France. Paris—*Parisss,* like they pronounce it here, which always made my skin crawl—was, in their eyes, the height of refinement, of civilization. My word, being perceived as a colored Frenchwoman proved to be quite useful to me whenever I got myself into a sticky situation, and if I was able to rent this fine apartment we're sitting in right now, it was thanks to that. Edgecombe Avenue was practically the Champs-Elysees of Harlem. Not just anyone could live there! My money, the power I'd consolidated in Central Harlem—we called it the Valley—dear nephew, all that didn't mean anything to the real estate agents. Sugar Hill was certainly a ghetto within a larger ghetto, but it was the center of black elegance, of black distinction, of decorum, of culture—I mean, a bookish place. I rubbed elbows with men like W.E.B. Du Bois, Countee Cullen, Langston Hughes, Aaron Douglas, those great intellectuals, poets and artists. Compared to them, I was just an uneducated thug who only had one single—we're getting back to my point now, dear nephew—attenuating circumstance: The fact that she was French.

I like to imagine that my famous alter ego, Josephine Baker, felt the same thing. When faced with white Frenchmen—as welcoming as they might have proved themselves to be—she must have felt herself most American. Not like a Black American, but an American period. I like thinking that our parallel fates were charted out by a higher being, not some human-faced divinity, but some kind of ethereal entity that reigns over the world and that—atheist that I've always been—I've felt at my side on more than one occasion. How strange it all is, dear nephew! You wouldn't have imagined that a lady gangster could live beyond the present-banal, huh? That she was preoccupied by the meaning of life, no, you must have imagined that she would have been too absorbed with fighting for her life on the one hand and with making her business prosperous on the other. That's not entirely false, except that at certain crucial moments those worldly concerns evaporated and, in a fraction of a second, she had to go over her whole life and make up her mind about certain possibilities. To decide if those decisions would make any sense in regard to her aspirations, by which I mean her happiness in this life. Why yes, dear Frédéric, a gangster sometimes has metaphysical thoughts, even if that term isn't exactly in his or her vocabulary. In any case, those thoughts have long consumed me—for as long as I've managed the numbers, anyway.

Listen, I'll tell you something I've kept secret from my friends, my lovers and my employees, even from my faithful chauffeur, Andrew, the only person I could trust completely: I dream of Martinique every night. Curiously, those dreams faded away during the 1950s when French and French Caribbean people started moving to New York and allowed me to start practicing Molière's language again. For so long, I'd only heard English, Gaelic, Yiddish, Polish and, especially, Italian, and all those languages ended up merging into a single one in my head, which is not to say that I mixed them up. There was, on the one hand, all those languages and, on the other, my own language, the flesh of my flesh, French. Don't look so stunned, Frédéric! We both know perfectly well that it wasn't spoken much on our island at the turn of the century, and that in my neighborhood, down Breadfruit Alley, it was practically unheard of, revered even. Yes, revered! My defunct mother, who spoke it well enough, was very proud to bring it up when someone in our neighborhood dared to use French and committed some mistake. Ha ha ha! But that never stopped her from singing old beguines from Saint-Pierre before Pelée erupted at all hours of the day. There's one that's half-French, half-Creole—it always comes to mind, like a leitmotiv:

> *Maladie d'amour… maladie de jeunesse*
> *Chacha, si ou enmen mwen, ou a maché dèyè mwen*
>
> *(Lovesickness… youthsickness*
> *Chacha, if you love me, you'll walk behind me)*

In fact, I had the immeasurable chance, back then, of attending five years of school and then having been employed as a servant to a cultured Mulatto family. They had so many books, the Verneuils! You told me that Eugène is an important politician in addition to being a teacher. I'm not surprised at all! He was already pretty shifty back when he'd creep nightly into my room to feast on my flesh. You should've seen his angelic face in the mornings when he'd sit down with the rest of the family for breakfast. You would've thought butter didn't melt in his mouth! But, listen, I don't hold it against him. That's just the way things were back then, and you couldn't avoid it. If you've heard talk of me, I suppose that's probably true for him, too. But I doubt he's capable of putting two and two together and connecting the girl he forced himself on back when he was sixteen with the formidable gang boss that Stéphanie St. Clair would become three decades later. Try to remember to ask him when you get back to Martinique! Ha ha ha!

[BETRAYAL

After the marriage of Sufi Abdul Hamid and Stéphanie St. Clair, which was celebrated without the slightest pomp according to the desires of *the first American Muslim*, as he liked to call himself, there was no temporary lull in the war against the Jewish shopkeepers, despite their most fervent hopes. On the contrary, marriage to this woman seemed to breathe new life into Sufi Abdul Hamid and to offer him a second wind! A newly-minted resident of Sugar Hill, he spread his ire to his rich neighbors who were, for the most part, light-skinned individuals. Mulattos, as they said in Martinique. He began to rail against those *light-skinned bastards* quietly betraying the whole race, or so he liked to say. She did not understand what impelled him to claim such a thing because although the neighbors, starting with the great intellectual Du Bois, might have been mixed, they had dedicated themselves tirelessly to defending the cause of the Blacks. The couple's first arguments were over this very topic.

"A good Muslim wife doesn't have the right to defy her husband!" the imam of the Universal Holy Temple of Tranquility would exclaim in exasperation. "Samia, listen closely: This is the last time I'll say it!"

But that Allah zealot had plenty of other worries. His union suddenly had some competition, and that got him into a dreadful state. Until one day, in a fit of exasperation—aside from when he was preaching, Sufi was a calm man—he ended up stabbing a rival. A certain Hammie Snipes, who, after having been a follower of Marcus Garvey and his Great Return of Black Americans to the African continent, had become a communist. He had established a union based on the ideals of the 1917 Russian Revolution (at least, according to him). If there was a single point in common, just one, between Sufi and the white world, it was this: an utter distaste for what the press called Bolshevism. The smallest protest march, the most banal picket line, the most unassuming article critical toward the reigning order would cost you—whether you were black or white, but especially if you were black—the qualification of *communist* or *Bolshevist*. Men like Hammie Snipes were faced with three sizeable adversaries who were, for once, in agreement: The Protestant churches—the Pentecostals in particular—the government of the United States (and the white world in general) and Stéphanie's husband, an advocate of that religion, Islam, who'd slowly but surely begun recruiting his followers from all over Harlem. That didn't stop the police from arresting the Black Mufti nor the justice from incarcerating him for several months. Stéphanie had already known a similar situation, and on more than one occasion with her former bodyguard-cum-lover, Duke (whose eye she ended up gouging out with a fork). So, she was accustomed to the situation. Likewise, with her next man, Bumpy Johnson. Back then, she'd struggled like a madwoman, first of all to bribe the cops into freeing her man, and when they wouldn't give in, she'd contrive a way to deliver fat envelopes to the judge presiding over the case. It had become almost routine, and never failed to annoy her. But this time, she didn't bother to bat an eyelid. She left things to take their course. Sure, she'd visit Sufi in prison, but didn't waste energy attempting to shorten his sentence. A small voice inside her whispered to her that the bastard needed a good lesson and that, upon his release, he'd be less strict with the wife he claimed to love.

She was wrong. On the contrary, Sufi Abdul Hamid, made the most of his stay on Rikers Island by deepening his grasp of Islamic theology and by converting a good number of his fellow detainees. On the day of his release he was fired up, and before so much as exchanging his first freedman's kiss with Stéphanie, alias Samia, he declared, "I'll burn Harlem down! They'll see what I'm made of, those white devils."

And it wasn't just hot air: Sufi became the instigator of Harlem's very first race riot. In 1935, to be exact. That's the expression we use nowadays, ever since the civil rights movement, since Martin

Luther King, Malcolm X and all those black leaders had pushed against the power of the Whites—but, back then, it was more like a misery riot. A hunger riot. To tell the truth, there were people among them who couldn't eat every day or who only had enough to keep from starving to death. That uprising led to the destruction of no fewer than two hundred businesses. Stéphanie was, in the meantime, cloistered away in her apartment. Sugar Hill hadn't been touched, but business in the neighborhood was disrupted for several days on end. The police, reinforced by the National Guard, patrolled round the clock because skirmishes were breaking out on every street corner. A thick smoke, emanating from the burned down buildings, covered Harlem, and Queenie feared it would be the end of all Blackfolk. That they'd all be deported back to the south or transported off to Africa like Marcus Garvey wanted. At least, that was the rumor among the Negro intelligentsia, even in her Edgecombe Avenue building. She was nonetheless rather more serene than those within her environs, and her main preoccupation was to figure out how to reconstitute her network of numbers runners and bankers once the boiling point had reduced to a normal temperature. She was right on the money! Except that the press mentioned two million dollars of damage, and now the Harlemites would have other fish to fry instead of throwing their meager revenues down for some game of chance.

Sufi Abdul Hamid, for his part, was very satisfied with his small person. During the clashes, his exploits (if they could be called such) had brought upon him the admiration of a good number of individuals, and now his mosque, the Universal Holy Temple of Tranquility, was consistently packed to the gills. Far too busy trying to manage the influx of followers, he'd given up on trying to transform Stéphanie-Samia into a model Muslim wife, and they began to make friction in the apartment. A distance was little by little forged between them, without, however, so much as a raised tone or outright clash. But the dear imam had kept his cards to his chest! One of Stéphanie's spies informed her that every afternoon, the man reported to a dilapidated-looking house on 162nd Street and that he remained there until early evening. At first, she thought it was some secret political meeting through which he was seeking to foment who-knows-what plot against the *government of the infidels*, as he called it, but a sixth sense alerted her to the fact that something fishy was going on. Eager to get to the bottom of it, she asked Andrew, her chauffeur, to drive her to the end of said street so she could discreetly approach the house on foot. The door to the building quickly gave in to her energetic shoving. Impossible that it might be a meeting place for dangerous plotters! Total silence reigned over the interior and it seemed that there was not a single living soul in that building. She was walking up the wobbly wooden stairs when she heard a moan. It was coming from one of the rooms on the second floor. At the back. She rushed there. The door resisted longer than the one that had led into the building itself, but it ended up giving way. And there, before her eyes, what a spectacle! Her first true love, the man who'd set her heart a-flutter, who'd awoken in her parts of the soul that she'd never suspected could exist, Sufi Abdul Hamid was inside, straddling a young woman whose face was contorted with pleasure! Stéphanie-Samia knew the creature, but only in passing. She'd noticed her in Muslim garb back when she'd started seeing Sufi Abdul Hamid. Stupefied, the couple separated, but neither of them moved or uttered a single word.

Madam St. Clair took out the little pistol she kept in her handbag and shot twice at *the first American Muslim*. He survived, the bastard! But it cost the queen of the numbers racket the second longest incarceration of her life. Four and a half years without seeing the light of day!]

Let's get back to our story, dear nephew.... And now you're going to laugh, oh, yes you are, I know it already! What I'm about to tell you is both strange and laughable. Here it is: The White

Americans, well, I only saw them as such when they lashed out at me, insulting or aggressing my person. Otherwise, I didn't see their color; that's to say I was indifferent to it. This enraged my lovers and left my friends perplexed. With both, there were few conversations that didn't end up devolving into what the press referred to as *the race question* after a good five minutes. In my eyes, it was an obsession, even if I was aware of the oppression our community suffered. So, as long as a White behaved normally with me, I was as if blind to their color, and the only Whites... how can I say this? The only ones who were permanently white in my eyes were those rotten cops of the New York Police Department, along with those half-senile and completely bald judges who, for the most part, would send you to the slammer for a big old nothing. But now that I'm thinking of it again, here, right in front of you, dear Frédéric, it suddenly hits me. I'd spent twenty-six years in Martinique mixing with Blacks, Chabens, Mulattos, Indians, ah, yes, and Syrians and a couple Chinese people, too. The White Creoles were, for those of us living in Fort-de-France, ethereal creatures—invisible, even. As for the Franco-Whites, unless you worked for the governor or for the admiralty, you could live your whole life without exchanging a single word with them. And then again, we were considerably more numerous than all the island-Whites and Franco-Whites combined, whereas the Negro is in the minority over here. And not only in the minority, but also confronted ceaselessly with the Whites' world, even in Harlem, where, for example, the police are white, the corner stores are run by the Yiddish, the traffickers in the various available paraphernalia are all Italian, just like the numbers game I'd been forced to share with that Lucky Luciano swine. Here in America, Whites are everywhere. We can't forget them like you can in Martinique. In the end, I think that helps explain the Black American, or at least it helps explain why he's so different from the rest of us Black Caribbeans. But, once again, the old lady I've turned into is yammering on about the same old things. I just realized it, unstoppable chatterbox that I am. Excuse me, dear nephew!

Your stay in New York is coming to an end, young man. You've let me soliloquize like a crazy old bat, which I have surely become, but it's been a pleasure to narrate my life to you, to tell you about my tragic and burlesque and happy adventures, even if, out of modesty, I've hidden a few things here and there about the particularly horrible episodes. The press has waxed lyrical about me, but few people in Martinique have any real idea about the obstacles this little Martinican girl has had to overcome in order to reach the throne of that invisible kingdom that is the numbers. The paperscratchers, I mean the journalists, have only highlighted the luminous—phosphorescent, if you prefer—aspects of my life, undoubtedly because evoking my various incarcerations, whether long or short, wouldn't hold anyone's interest. Every *nigger* who dedicated himself to illegal activities ended up in prison sooner or later, either the one on Rikers Island or the one on Welfare Island. Just banalities! Like I told you during our first meeting, I was the queen, but queen I am no longer. I'm just an old lady, wrinkled and hunchbacked, who had the incredible luck of slipping past the gangsters' bullets and the police's nets for fifty years running… well, except on two or three occasions. An old lady who successfully stood up to the worst betrayals of her lovers, especially in the case of Bumpy Johnson and Sufi Abdul Hamid. Well, all that's just to say that I consider myself to be a living miracle. Most of the people I was involved with or worked with have been dead for a long time now, and often they died a violent death. At the turn of the twentieth century, you rarely made it past forty in Harlem. Add ten years or so for women. But me, I'm almost eighty. If that's not a miracle, I don't know what is!

On the brink of a grand journey—I think about it ceaselessly, but without fear—I'm no longer sure who I am. I've inhabited many different characters at different moments in my very long existence. A poor Lowblack in Martinique, the presumptive daughter of some African kinglet in Marseille, a Celtic gangster in Five Points and one of the Forty Thieves, a small-timer with the Sicilian mafia, a number-runner with the Harlem lottery, then a banker and, finally, the Queen of Harlem (and let's not forget wife of *the first American Muslim*). How many lives I've lived, my dear nephew!

I haven't renounced any of them. In fact, I'm proud of them all. If you want to hold on to the most accurate memory of me possible (in my humble opinion, of course), know that I was— and still am—Martinican, French, Irish, Italian, Black American, Harlemite, but above all, dear nephew, above all else, a woman.

An upright woman, as we say in Creole....

December 2013–March 2015

Diálogos Books
DIALOGOSBOOKS.COM

Printed in Great Britain
by Amazon

86587219R00150